D0111512

ALSO BY

STEVE ERICKSON

Days Between Stations
Rubicon Beach
Tours of the Black Clock
Leap Year
Arc d'X
Amnesiascope
American Nomad
The Sea Came in at Midnight
Our Ecstatic Days
Zeroville

THESE DREAMS
OF YOU

Steve Erickson

THESE DREAMS OF YOU

Europa
editions

Europa Editions
214 West 29th Street
New York, N.Y. 10001
www.europaeditions.com
info@europaeditions.com

Library of Congress Cataloging in Publication Data is available
ISBN 978-1-60945-063-2

Erickson, Steve
These Dreams of You

Book design by Emanuele Ragnisco
www.mekkanografici.com
Cover illustration by Margherita Barrera

Prepress by Grafica Punto Print – Rome

Printed in the USA

For Lori, Miles and Silanchi

THESE DREAMS
OF YOU

B ut years later, on a night in early November, when the wind comes in like a swarm, Alexander Nordhoc sits in the rocking chair—that he borrowed but never gave back—where his wife used to breast-feed their son.

It's eight o'clock where he is, in one of the canyons on the edge of Los Angeles. It's ten o'clock in Chicago, and thousands of people sweep across the TV screen and the same park where, forty years ago, police and protesters rioted at the scene of a great national political convention, and Nordhoc's country questioned all its possibilities.

A lexander's four-year-old daughter Sheba, adopted nineteen months before from an orphanage in Ethiopia, sits on his lap. Sheba is the color of the man on the television, in whose form the country now has imagined its most unfathomable possibility. Alexander, who goes by Zan, is the color of everyone else in the family, including his wife Viv and his son Parker, whose twelfth birthday happens to also be on this day.

With the announcement of the man's election, bedlam consumes the living room. "He won!" Parker explodes, leaping from the couch over a low white formica table that's in the shape of a cloud. "He won! he won! he won!" he keeps shouting, and Viv cheers too. "Zan," Parker stops, baffled by his father's stupefaction, "he won." He says, "Aren't you happy?"

On the television is the image of an anonymous young black woman who, in the grass of the park, has fallen to her knees and holds her face in her hands. Do I have the right, Zan wonders, as a middle-aged white man, to hold my face in my hands? and then thinks, No. And holds his face in his hands anyway, silently mortified that he might do something so trite as sob.

It's a country that does things in lurches. Born in radicalism, then reluctant for years, decades, the better part of centuries, to do anything crazy, until it does the craziest thing of all. But it's also a country—inherent in its genes—capable of imagining what cannot be imagined and then, once it's imagined, doing it.

Six years before, another president, a white privileged Texan, swaggered across the deck of an aircraft carrier in a pilot's jacket, a banner unfurled behind him proclaiming the end of a war that, in fact, was only beginning. It was an image that the country embraced almost as much as it believed it. Now, a black Hawaiian with a swahili name? It's science fiction, Zan thinks. Or at least the sort of history that puts novelists out of business.

At the radio station the next day, from where Zan broadcasts four times a week a three-hour music show, he announces following the first set, "The Sam Cooke record—the greatest ever made—was for what happened last night. Forty-five years after the song was recorded . . . but then all the song says is that a change *will* come, not how fast, right?" By the time the song was released as a B-side, the singer was murdered in an L.A. motel under tawdry circumstances. "But is it just me," Zan asks, "or when he goes from that bridge into the final verse, does he redeem not only anything he ever did—including whatever it was that got him shot—but everything I ever did too?"

The national anthem of dreams deferred, sung from the grave by a ghost who doesn't know he's dead. "Everything else," Zan goes on, "was for the kids. The hip-hop manifesto about brushing the dirt off your shoulder, that's for my twelve-year-old son who's gone gangsta lately, though at this point I'm sure he thinks the song is impossibly old-school, being as it's more than half an hour old. And the really old-school one about the lovers at the Berlin Wall—'What's the Berlin Wall, Poppy?'—who get to be heroes just for one day? That's for my four-year-old Ethiopian daughter, who I guess can't get enough of British extraterrestrials in dresses."

Zan has no idea if anyone actually listens to him. The station has about a megawatt to its name. Viv catches the broadcasts on her car radio for the thirty seconds she's in range while driving the canyon boulevard; when she drops off Parker at school, the boy turns the radio down because the possibility some of his homies might hear it is too appalling. He furiously denies that it's his father's voice.

The four-year-old Ethiopian glam-rocker is the only one in the family not thrilled by the election result. Sheba has been the household's sole supporter of the opposing candidate, a man the age of grandfathers and the color of snow, neither of which the small girl has known.

Zan has three theories about Sheba's enthusiasm for this candidate. The first and most comfortable is that in fact he does remind her of Viv's father, who died two years before she was born and whom she sees in all the family photos. The second theory, more vexing if not too unsettling, is that she's just messing with everyone's heads.

The third and most troubling theory is that in her four-year-old soul she's already come to believe the color of snow is preferable to the color of . . . well, pick your racist poison—chocolate? coffee? mud? With what brown does she associate? Since she came to live with the Nordhocs, she's noted more than once that her skin is one color and Zan's, Viv's and Parker's another. How come, the girl asks resentfully, returning from preschool where there are no other black children, you get to have light skin while mine is darker?

Dismayed, Zan isn't sure he's heard right. Was that really the way she put it? "Yours is lighter," she points out again, pulling at his arm and thrusting her thumb in her mouth.

"It is lighter," he says, "yours is darker and it's beautiful.

Some people have light skin and some have dark. Some have light hair and some have dark."

"The man who sings the hero song has red hair."

"Yes."

"Mama has blue hair."

"There you go. Turquoise, actually."

"What's turquoise?"

"A kind of blue. Blue-green."

"Is it really blue or did she make it blue?"

"She made it blue."

"Why?"

"She likes it. It matches her eyes. Some people have light or dark eyes. Some people are tall and some aren't."

I s this the way to answer the question? Is it better than "Because you're black and we're white," if she doesn't yet have a concept of black and white? Or is it an answer that only a naïve white person can give?

On the other hand, Sheba was adopted in the first place out of white naïveté, though less on the part of Viv who lived in Africa as a girl. Viv's father was the city manager of Mogadishu—between Ethiopia and the sea—a freelancer whose career back home in the Midwest was subject to local elections, hired to bring running water and passable roads to a city half a world away. For Viv that was the year (her twelfth, which is to say when she was Parker's age) of other kids' parents abducted in the night never to be seen again, public hangings that were a social occasion, the ocean's edge lined with the innards of gutted camels that attracted sharks when the reefs were breached, and, on a beach against the Indian Sea under an African moon, movies broadcast against a slab of rock. When Viv saw the movie about the monolith surrounded by apes who hurl a bone into the sky that becomes a space station, it actually was on a monolith.

No white sentimentality invents, and no hard-nosed street wisdom disputes, the preternatural awareness of the four-year-old adopted child who shares with other abandoned children a perspective verging on the otherworldly. "Oh, yeah," says another father at Sheba's preschool when Zan identifies her as his, "the little girl who talks like she's twenty." The night that Zan takes Parker to the emergency room with a broken hand and loses his car keys, he's still railing at the experience an hour later behind the wheel when, from her infant's seat in back, Sheba advises, "Poppy, let it go," before plopping her thumb back in her mouth.

Sheba dazzles everyone she meets. Eyes big enough to center whole swirling solar systems, her charismatic entrance into every room brings it to a halt. Not unlike her new brother she's an irrepressible goofball, walking around with small stickers stuck to the end of her nose, spitting water across the dinner table in a stream like the stone water-breathing lion she saw in a fountain—a mimic who spins off her own original permutations. Lovingly seizing on a word like, say, buttocks, enthralled by both its emphatic sound and the unmistakable impact on those who hear it, soon she transforms everything into a variant. When her brother's feet stink, they're footocks.

Eventually the mimicry becomes not only more precocious but blacker, inevitable less because she herself is black than because her white brother—like all kids in the Twenty-First Century, or maybe all kids since the first white boy or girl heard Louis Armstrong blow his horn—is blacker: "Hey there, girlfriend," or "What up, sweet cheeks?" to people who prob-ably shouldn't be greeted in that fashion. When she high-fives, she follows it with the sweep of her hand across her African head and declares, "*Smoooooth.*"

Those few whose reaction to her is openly malevolent are all the more conspicuous for it. In a western Michigan restaurant during summer vacation a woman shoots daggers at them, and it's all Viv can think about for days, rather than the hordes who welcome the girl. "You can't get too defensive about this stuff," Zan says, as the entire Nordhoc family tiptoes across minefields.

The sternest look Zan has gotten is on the afternoon he carried Sheba from the pediatrician's office and, having received her first round of immunization shots, she wailed in betrayal, "DOCTOR SHOCK ME, POPPY!" A black man at a bus stop on the corner closely monitored the father and daughter the entire walk to Zan's car, the two fixed in his gaze, and only as Zan struggled to strap the outraged girl into the backseat did the penny drop: *I'm a middle-aged white guy hustling a screaming little black girl out of a building.*

Sometimes the color confusion has its advantages. When Sheba slams into a grocery checkout line and the person in front whirls around furiously, Zan studies the architectural wonders of the supermarket ceiling as the aggrieved party searches in vain for a wayward black mother to chastise. Then there's the time on Melrose Avenue when a young black guy comes up to Zan and says, "Hey, man, just want you to know you have two beautiful kids," and though it's obviously Sheba who's caught his eye, Zan is touched that he includes Parker in the compliment. Now the only way that Zan knows to conclude the conversation with Sheba about the difference between his skin and hers is to say some squishy white liberal thing like, "You're beautiful," silently adding to no one, You come up with something better. Sheba takes her thumb from her mouth, locks his eyes with hers, and draws a finger across her throat.

O f course when she first starts doing the finger-cross-the-throat thing, it's alarming. Now she does it all the time, little brown buccaneer, to convey irritation at whatever parental lapse has transpired.

Zan thought they were going to get a shy little Dickensian orphan girl. *Please, sir, may I have some more?* with empty porridge bowl lifted pitifully to a merciless world; and when Viv first met her at the Ethiopian orphanage, Sheba seemed exactly that. She barely spoke, only looked at Viv when she thought Viv wasn't looking. Viv would lie with Sheba until the child fell asleep, but when she rose from bed, the girl's hand shot out and clutched the mother's wrist in a death grip.

From California to Ethiopia, Viv brought to the girl pompoms and a toy giraffe and a photo of Zan and Viv in a bag with pictures of cherries on it. The girl cast all of it aside except for a picture of Parker that she kept day and night. She slept with it and woke to it. No one could take it from her.

S o the first time that the shy little orphan girl emits more volume per capita than any single body Zan has heard, it's like a boombox in a confessional. Planting her small feet in the middle of the house, Sheba rears back and roars whims and needs, complaints and demands. She engages Zan, Viv and Parker in discourse about everything under the sun.

Early on, Zan assumes this is Sheba's bountiful curiosity, the expressions of a turbo-wonderment. She sweeps through the house picking up everything within reach and turning things on and off, pushing every button of every machine, appliance and device until all are rendered digitally senseless. This drives Zan to distraction, maybe because it feels a little too representative of the way everything else about their lives is falling apart. "Lighten up," Viv advises, until she finds her new digital camera has been similarly sabotaged, summing up perfectly the way her photography career has flatlined as well.

S oon Zan realizes that, for the four-year-old, the substance of communication is beside the point. "It's like she's afraid," Viv says, "that with the first break in a connection, everything and everyone around her will vanish." Sheba kneads her fingers into Viv's body like a kitten, expanding and contracting its claws. She presses herself into her mother as though to meld herself physically.

Before Sheba came home from Ethiopia, Zan and Viv worried that the shy little orphan girl would be traumatized by the family dog Piranha, a demented mix of jack terrier and chihuahua called a jackahuahua. Named as a puppy by Parker, Piranha so terrorizes the neighborhood—attacking other dogs, chasing neighbors' cars, holding UPS men hostage on their trucks—that an electric fence has been installed around the yard and the dog has been fitted with an electric collar, this in spite of Zan's doubts that Piranha can be restrained by any mere voltage once used to execute Soviet spies. "He's a sociopath," Zan scoffs to Viv, "an electric fence? That dog?" pointing at the animal. Piranha's head jerks up expectantly; he's practically vibrating. "Sniper fire wouldn't stop this dog."

"Aren't all animals sociopaths?" says Viv.

"Maybe I mean psychopath."

"Is there a difference?"

"I think one doesn't know the difference between right and wrong, and the other knows but doesn't care."

"Which is Piranha?"

"Which is Piranha? *His name is Piranha.* Oh, he knows."

"That doesn't make sense," Viv says. "Piranha fish know it's wrong to eat people?"

"He knows," Zan assures her, "and he doesn't care." When Viv left for Africa to go get Sheba, figuring out what to do about Piranha was one of Zan's tasks back home. The canyon's local dog expert, mistress of all breeds and their mutations, told him flatly, "You're going to have to get rid of that dog—he'll terrorize the poor child." From Ethiopia, Viv wrote in an email, *She's so sweet I'm afraid the dog will terrify her.*

Piranha never knew what hit him. Throttled by the small girl within half an hour of her arrival until his eyes bulged, the animal soon was darting shell-shocked from one hiding place of the house to the next. Only when he was hopping up and down the stairs like shrimp on a grill, as if trying to get out of his own fur, did Parker figure out that Sheba had pushed the button on the wall-unit that controlled

Piranha's electric collar. Originally set at four, the monitor now was at nine, the dog zapped silly from one end of the house to the other.

Soon Sheba and Piranha struck an accord. Now Sheba howls out on the deck and the dog howls with her, the two craning their necks and turning their mouths skyward.

Of course Sheba's name isn't really Sheba. "Should we really be calling her that?" says Viv.

"As in queen of," says Zan.

"Yes, I know who the Queen of Sheba was," says Viv, "that's not my point."

"I was only explaining it to Parker," says Zan, though at this moment Parker listens on his headphones to the small fluorescent-green music player barely bigger than a stick of gum that hangs around his neck.

Viv says, "But still." On the birth certificate that came with the adoption, Sheba's name is shown as Zema, which in Amharic means . . . well, Zan and Viv aren't precisely sure what it means. The closest variation means "melody" or "hymn," but from what Zan understands, Ethiopian names only derive meaning from adjoining names, like tarot cards derive meaning from the surrounding cards. Only by putting all of a person's names together do you complete the meaning.

Zan never has been to Ethiopia but somehow this thing with the names seems typical of everything he knows about it. Ethiopia has an extra month of the year and, as best Zan can understand, its own clock, falling half an hour between the time zones of the world.

It isn't so much that Ethiopia invented its own time zone but that its zone is the original time, the temporal referent against which all other zones have contrived themselves. Within weeks of coming to L.A., Sheba has mastered English but, after more than a year, notions of time remain elusive. She has no comprehension of time's terminology. "We'll go to the park tomorrow," Zan says.

"O.K.," says Sheba, and minutes later still waits. "Poppy, let's go!" she says.

"Where?"

"THE PARK!"

"Tomorrow."

"Yes," she nods, and a minute later, "Are we going? WHY AREN'T WE GOING!" Even as she grasps other subtleties, she continues to be confounded by distinctions among weeks, days, hours, minutes. She believes her birthday both precedes and follows whatever day she occupies—not wrong, of course, technically speaking—appropriate for a child of civilization's ground zero, the land where God placed Adam and Eve, the burial place of the oldest human fossil. "We are all Ethiopians," Viv likes to say.

To the family, Sheba's emotional need seems like a dark well that falls to time's center. It sets in motion dynamics compounded by Sheba's singular measure of things. "He's number one!" she protests, pointing at Parker, "I'm number three," and Zan can't be sure if this is errant math, Ethiopia's own system of measurement like its own calibration of time, or whatever manipulation knows to leave out two.

From the beginning Sheba has had an affinity for music. Because this is so much the stuff of racial cliché, Zan barely can tell people about the more earthbound aspects—the girl running for a piano like other kids to a scooter, warbling cheerfully in the yard of the orphanage back in Addis Ababa to the lightning in the sky—let alone that the girl's small body literally hums with song.

Within a week of Sheba's arrival, the family noticed it at the dinner table when everyone heard from her, barely audible, a distant music. "Sheba, we don't sing at the table," Viv gently tried to admonish her, until one day the mother is driving in Hollywood with Sheba in the backseat and picks up Zan's broadcast from the canyon that usually she can't get half a mile from the station. The girl transmits on Sheba frequency. Zan calls her Radio Ethiopia.

Up until around the time of Sheba's adoption, Zan taught popular culture and Twentieth Century litera- ture at a local college. The popular-culture course began with the year 1954, because that was when a white nine- teen-year-old truck driver wandered into a Memphis recording studio—only weeks after the Supreme Court ruled racial seg- regation unconstitutional—and instinctively, unconsciously miscegenated, in the language of the time, white and black music. Caught up in the sweep of a story, by the end of every semester the students invariably shed their old-school/new- school distinctions to afford Zan an ovation. It's the closest he's come to telling an epic; he doubts he's told a story better, cer- tainly not any of his own.

The rest of the teachers in the department were childless and, as certainly was the case with Zan before he had children, there was little comprehension of the infinite variables that children bring, the way that children lay waste to rational odds, how one always has to err on the side of the long shot. Someone who doesn't have children may grasp the volume of time they take up but can't understand the way children won't be compartmentalized, the way children can't be consigned to their own rooms in the city of one's life. Children are the moat that surrounds the city, the canals that run throughout. They get everything wet.

After the faculty meetings were changed to a day and time when Zan had to pick up kids from school, his resulting failure to attend brought down on him admonitions concerning language in his contract. Matters reached critical mass the afternoon that Zan left Parker waiting two hours so the faculty could debate whether a bartender should be hired at thesis readings. Not prone to explosions, Zan exploded anyway and walked out. "Some of us," was the last thing he heard one of the teachers say, "liked the department better before he came."

The suspension of Zan's contract began the Nordhocs' recession fifteen months before the rest of the country's, or before the rest of the country knew theirs had begun too. A series of media and entertainment-industry strikes sidelined Viv's career as a photographer snapping pictures locally for alternative weekly newspapers, sometimes nationally for entertainment magazines, of politicians and singers including not only the new president several years before his election but, some two decades past his prime, the redhaired glam-rocker whose music Sheba loves and Viv loved as well in her youth (distinctly marking her as an oddball among the teenage tribes of the Midwest). "Was his hair red?" Sheba asks, on raptly hearing the account of this photoshoot from her mother.

"Not as red as it used to be," says Viv.

"Was he nice?"

"He was very nice," Viv assures the girl, "one of the nicest, actually. Very charming, gracious."

"He said grace?" The girl is dumbfounded. Often Sheba likes to say grace at dinner—just to get attention, her brother is convinced. God's, at least, if nobody else's.

Viv's photography career has never recovered. The family's income plummeted as Sheba arrived with new realities of $3,000 dental work, for which health insurance reimbursed $700. Viv and Zan have kept themselves afloat on credit cards in order to make the payments on their eccentric house; then the monthly mortgage went from $2,800 to $6,000 as the house's value fell by a third.

It's the perfect shitstorm of bad financial turns. Soon the front page of the newspaper and its running daily accounts of a nation imploding with debt and foreclosures read like the Nordhocs' personal diary. Zan filed with the bank an application to rewrite the home loan, which was turned down because the family was current in its payments; a second application was turned down a week before the bank was taken over by another bank. The Nordhocs fell behind in the payments, offering partial sums that they subsequently learned weren't applied to the balance on the house but rather put in a separate escrow so the bank could continue to charge delinquency fees and push the family toward foreclosure. A third application was turned down as being "incomplete," though over the course of five months and many phone calls no one from the bank ever said the application was amiss; Zan filed a fourth application that was approved—at a monthly payment of $6,500. No one at the bank could or would explain how this figure was arrived at or why the bank offered a payment that was more than what led the Nordhocs to file the application in the first place.

Now Zan and Viv are many months delinquent on the house, which has been scheduled for foreclosure twice only to receive stays of execution at the last moment. Their debt to credit card companies has reached a level Zan doesn't want to know. "We don't know how much we owe?" Viv whispers so the kids won't hear.

"We do know," says Zan. "A lot."

"But shouldn't we figure it out exactly?"

"No."

"No?"

"No."

"Why not?"

"Because," Zan says, "I need to be able to get out of bed in the morning. Because quantifying it with more precision won't make it any less or any easier to deal with. Because sometimes you need a little denial in order to function." In his head Zan figures it's about $135,000. Various credit accounts have been closed or canceled or their limits strategically have been lowered to less than the balance. Wall Street hounds the Nordhocs ceaselessly, phoning hourly; if Zan scrounges up a grand on a $1,200 bill, the lender relentlessly pursues the outstanding $200 dawn till midnight. New bankruptcy laws are a Rube Goldberg contraption, disqualifying the family for owing too much or too little, for earning too little or too much. Zan's conversation with an attorney about the situation is the financial equivalent of being told by a doctor he's terminal.

O ver the course of all the mortgage applications to the bank, Zan has made countless phone calls, copied countless documents, made personal appearances at the lender's local branch to plead the case. He has consulted three government agencies and eight lawyers, several of whom he's paid hundreds of dollars for expertise that proved something less than Zan's. Those not crooked enough to provide useless advice confessed they were too confused to provide any advice at all.

In the ten years since they bought it, Zan and Viv came to love the house more than either might have imagined, particularly after virtually rebuilding it from the ground up. Looking out on a canyon vista, the house is an ark of CDs and books, Viv's photos and butterfly collection and her art that's become a nexus of the two, all ready to float away on the tsunami that their twelve-year-old son expects to see advancing through the canyon from the sea.

Zan admonishes himself that pending displacement is the inevitable fate of those who invest in any place too much. He knows that one day soon the house will reappear on the bank's radar, a new Notice of Sale giving Zan, Viv, Parker and Sheba three weeks before they're homeless. The parents try to keep it from the children but Zan is certain that Parker, not only a smart but intuitive kid, knows something is wrong. "Promise me," the boy says one day in the car, "that we're not going to move," and Zan chokes, "I promise," and ponders the expiration date of lies to children.

Finances weigh down everything. At least twice a day Zan goes online with a knot in his gut to check evaporating bank balances and a loan-processing website that lists which houses have had new foreclosure dates posted.

He believes it's killing him. It coincides with the hackneyed gloom of autumnal years, the astonished pall at the great approaching wind-down; it never occurred to him that life would get harder rather than easier. He travels in a movable depression with headaches that never end, locating themselves around one eye like a vise when he wakes in the morning and goes to bed at the end of the day and wakes again the next morning. Gobbling imitrex nightly for the migraines and diovan daily for blood pressure, he believes that if by some miracle he and Viv should extricate themselves from these circumstances, within months, weeks, maybe days or moments some fatal illness will manifest itself—because at the same time he believes that their money crisis is killing him, he's also convinced that fate is a trickster. At the same time that it's killing him, the constant war for economic survival also is the thing keeping some other doom at bay. Fate waits for the most delicious moment to play its ultimate trick, in some unlikely future when everything finally is all right.

While Zan feels foolish that it's taken him a lifetime to know it, it's reassuring to finally understand that the banks are evil. It lends to the situation a clarity that's confirmed by every contact and transaction. You don't want this house, he tries to explain, pillaged by my children and covered in my wife's butterfly wings, no doors on half the rooms and its driveway so steep it's practically vertical. You're never going to find anyone else who wants to live here. "Loan number?" asks the lender on the other end of the line, in a ritual now familiar enough that Zan has made it a point, on general principle, not to know the number by heart. "Three zero six one three nine five one nine eight," he reads from the application.

"Address?" the woman says.

"1861 Relik Road. That's R-e-l—"

"Are you receiving mail at that address?"

"Yes."

"Are you living at the residence?"

"Yes."

"You are not renting the dwelling or—"

"We live here. It's our home."

"You have an outstanding balance on the property of one million, one hundred forty-seven thousand five hundred sixty-two dollars and eight cents. Are you prepared to make a payment in that amount today?"

"No," Zan sighs.

The lending agent says, "How then may I assist you today, asshole?"

Z an looks at the phone in his hand. "Excuse me?" he says.

"How may I assist you today?" she says.

"That isn't what you said."

There's silence on the other end of the line. "I'm sorry?"

"That isn't what you said."

"That is what I said."

"You said something else," Zan insists.

"That is what I said, sir. How may I assist you today?"

Zan chews over the moment and clears his throat. "I'm calling to find out the status of our most recent application for a modification of our home loan. This is the fifth we've submitted." He thinks. "Or maybe the sixth."

"Let me review that," she answers, and there's a pause. Then, "The application is still being processed, motherfucker."

Now Zan doesn't feel the need to examine his telephone. "What?"

"The application is still being processed."

"That isn't what you said. You said something else."

"I'm sorry?"

"You said something else. What did you call me?"

Another pause. "Sir, I'm not sure what you think I said, but the application is still being processed and a modification officer will be getting back to you. Cocksucker." Lying in bed at night, Zan concludes that maybe the new president isn't going to save their house. He gets up and turns on the light because otherwise he becomes insufferable even to himself, in his sense of persecution and guilt over how his children now find themselves in this predicament. He wonders about the terms of his life insurance policy and how it might take care of his family if he could somehow will himself into an aneurysm; he reflects on the perversity of karma and how it could be that the family's luck could go so bad on the occasion of adopting an African orphan. Aren't you supposed to get points for that on the karmic scoreboard? He muses (if that possibly can be the word) on how his time is nearly over and yet his moment, whenever or whatever that ever was supposed to be, still hasn't come. He thinks about his father-in-law who died six years ago and his last words: "*That* went fast."

Once the preconceptions of meek Dickensian orphanhood have been laid to rest, Zan realizes that Sheba is the single most defiant child he's known. If need be, she'll abdicate the role of child altogether in order to assume authority; she self-administers time-outs when the parents don't.

"I'M HUNGRY, YOUNG MAN!" she bellows at her father when she wants something to eat. She calls Viv "young lady" and Parker "baby," which incites the boy into answering, "You're the baby, you're the baby!" Eventually Sheba expands defiance's repertoire, the tenor of insult becoming more nuanced until finally, some months later in London when she, Parker and Zan wait to board a double-decker bus, she snarls to the father, "Out of my way, *old* man." Drawing her finger across her throat at him, she stuffs her thumb back in her mouth like Churchill corking his face with a cigar. "I'm a professional!" is her latest rallying cry and coup de grâce, learned from her brother or television and employed to end any contentious conversation. "Eat your carrots, Sheba," says Viv.

"Leave me alone!" says Sheba. "I'm a professional!"

"Clean up your room."

"I don't need you telling me, I'm a professional!" When she becomes a teenager, Zan grimly resolves, I'm faking my death. A particularly boisterous and pyrotechnic plane crash off the coast of Tahiti, or a naked walk into a ravenous sea.

Earlier in his life, Zan decided it's the scandinavian in him that accounts for the pathological orderliness he since has surrendered. This realization preceded another that he lives with four agents of chaos, if you count the dog; but his attempted reconciliation with chaos notwithstanding, the violation of the house by rats represents something so primal he can't abide it despite the house itself having become a locus of uncertainty. He dreams of rats the night that Viv tells him she's counted four. He dreams of them coming out of the holes that his son has punched in the walls in small explosions of new adolescent violence; one night Viv wakes to something running down her arm. Zan will let a tsunami take the house before the bank does, but not the rats, not yet.

Some years ago Zan had the house sealed, so he isn't sure where the breach has occurred. It's possible, he believes, that the rats came right through the front door, which sometimes has stood open for hours when Chaos Agent Number Four, otherwise known to Zan as the Fucking Dog, pushes his way in. Whatever the explanation, now the vermin can be heard scampering across the kitchen floor at night and scurrying through vents. For $500 that they don't have, Zan hires an exterminator, an aging latino giant named Jorge who lumbers through the house and crawls beneath it laying traps.

Every week Jorge returns to the house and retrieves the traps with the snapped carcasses of rodents, about which he talks with a tenderness born of an executioner's familiarity.

To Zan he describes the animals' habits and patterns intimately, lowering his voice—so the children won't hear—on the grislier details such as the rats cannibalizing each other. Several weeks and half a dozen dead rats later, the family still can hear them, with Piranha particularly agitated, periodically ransacking the house at the rodents' sound and scent. "He doesn't have trouble cornering FedEx drivers," Zan notes. "But a rat he can't catch."

"A FedEx driver is bigger than a rat," Parker defends his dog. "The FedEx driver isn't hiding in the vent."

Zan broadcasts his radio show from a station located behind the local Mexican eatery called the Añejo. This is up the road from an old abandoned railway car that was turned into a bridge and crosses a creek that rises with the winter and vanishes in the hot summer. For a man given to silences, he's loquacious on his broadcast. "You say more on the radio in five minutes," Viv points out, "than you do in a week off it."

"That's because," Zan explains, "on the radio no one interrupts you. It's the closest to writing that talking gets." Still he concedes that a life on the airwaves isn't something most people would have foreseen for him. "This is Radio Zed," he intones, "as in the numerical designation of the decade we live in, broadcasting to all corners of the canyon and, who knows, maybe beyond. We opened today's show with Augustus Pablo's 'Chant to King Selassie,' followed by 'Tezeta'—which means 'memory'—by the Duke Ellington of Ethiojazz, Mulatu Astatke, then Delroy Wilson's 'This Life Makes Me Wonder.' Polly Jean Harvey's 'The Wind' was in honor of the coming Santa Anas that strike terror in all our canyon hearts during fire season, and the song by Van Morrison about Ray Charles, who 'was shot down but got up to do his best,' was followed by the Genius himself with 'Busted,' in honor of our bank statement. We ended with 'Always Crashing in the Same Car,' back from the days when my daughter's favorite rock star was hanging in Berlin. As usual, that one's for Sheba," says Zan, "but also in honor of the time Parker and I hit an oil slick on the way to school and spun out on the boulevard half a mile from here—which is to say almost within the sound of my voice."

Even as her older brother listens to glowering black rappers on their way up the river, Sheba remains besotted by the limey spaceman in the dress and make-up from thirty years ago. She sings his songs all the time; and mostly because he's the annoying new obsession of his new sister, Parker cannot abide the man. Songs about electric-blue rooms and sons of the silent age drive him batty *because they don't make any sense*: "Seriously?" he wails in the car at the CD. "Turn it off!"

The small studio from which Zan broadcasts was discovered in what everyone believed was the Añejo's storage space. There was a microphone, sound system, disc player. The bar's owner, Roberto, explained, "Canyon had a station once, to the extent anyone could get a frequency in these hills," but that lonely frequency has been as unoccupied as the canyon's repossessed homes. "I have this idea," Zan said to Roberto one day, "I'll play music a few hours a night, do a little show—it will be a way to advertise the bar."

"Do a little show?" Roberto said. "Don't you have to have a personality for that kind of thing?"

"I have a personality," Zan said evenly, "don't you worry about my personality. What about a license?"

"A license?" laughed Roberto. "For what?"

"To broadcast?"

"*It's the canyon.* License? We don't need no stinking license." A few CDs lay scattered on the floor. "But what about the music?"

"Don't you worry about the music, either," said Zan.

On the way to an art workshop for kids that she teaches for extra income, Viv drops off Parker and Sheba at the Añejo as Zan's shift ends, and in the car driving home Zan pulls off the road at the old railroad bridge down the road. The canyon abounds with competing legends all ending with the same conclusion, that the bridge is haunted, the only matter of contention being by whom, the ghosts of displaced Indians or the victims of devil rites or crazed hippie killers. This is the bucolic canyon from which, forty years ago, Charles Manson fled because it was too weird for him.

Parker has been jonesing to see the railroad bridge since he noticed it one day from the car on the way to the ocean. But because it's dusk, when the canyon light fails so fast and the heat so quickly turns cold, the boy doesn't want to linger, as he and his sister and father stand in the middle surveying the decayed wood and listening to the sound of the creek beneath them. Up one corner of the bridgehouse runs a ladder to the rafters. From the apex of the frame, Zan and the kids have a view of the canyon and whatever should roll in from the ocean.

P arker says, "Let's leave." He's a fearless kid who will brave things Zan never did as a boy—some death-defying stunt on a skateboard, some preposterously lethal warp-speed roller coaster—but dark closed places push his courage to its breaking point. "Zan," he says.

"I want to stay," says Sheba.

"You only want to stay because I want to go," Parker says.

"I want to stay!" she says again, though it's not at all clear what it is she wants to stay for other than to momentarily seize control of a life that always feels outside her control. "I WANT TO STAY, I WANT TO STAY, I WANT TO STAY," and the railroad car becomes a megaphone, the four-year-old's voice careening from bend to dell and hilltop.

As the babble of the creek rises from the dark through the boxcar windows, a twelve-year-old imagination bubbles. Peering from the bridgehouse's rafter toward the ocean, Parker says, "When it comes, will the tsunami reach this far?"

The four were driving down Pacific Coast Highway, mostly in silence but for the harmonics coming from Sheba's body, when they passed new signs demarcating "tsunami safety zones."

"Stop singing," Parker was crying in exasperation to his sister.

"I'm not," said Sheba.

"She can't help it," said Zan, "it's not coming from her."

"It *is* coming from her," said Parker.

"I've never noticed those," Viv said about the signs.

"It's coming from her but not actually. *Through* her."

"How big," said Parker, "is a tsunami compared to a regular wave anyway?"

"No," Zan agreed about the signs, "they're new," then to Parker, "Big."

The signs apparently meant to indicate what level of ground people must flee to in order to be safe. "Would one hit our house?" said Parker.

"No," said his father.

"We don't have to worry about tsunamis," said Viv, and though she didn't mean it that way, the implication was there already were enough things to worry about. Zan wondered if

Viv was thinking the same thing, which was, If the bank takes the house, bring on that damned tsunami—but more likely Viv was just trying to strike from her children's running list of horribles one more horror. "The ocean might come up into the canyon a bit," said Zan, and Viv shot him a look: *Oh, great. Tell them the tsunami's going to come into the canyon.* "Just a bit," Zan hastily stressed. "Where the canyon begins."

"Über cool," said Parker. He's at the age where it's hard for Zan to tell the cool from the holocaustic; lately Parker and his friends call something "sick" when they mean it's great. What does that say about the era? wonders Zan. How and when did something outstanding become "tight" and what connotations could it have to his twelve-year-old? When I was young, Zan remembers, things were "wicked." Wicked was good and soon we were doing things that we thought were good that for centuries people thought were wicked. In our slang lies the future.

N ot long ago, Parker asked to trade his larger room in the house for a smaller one with no bathroom attached—which is to say a room that no one else in the family ever has reason to enter. The boy now is at an age when he happily barters twice the space for a door he can shut to the rest of the world. Lying in bed in the dark, Viv uttered to Zan four words that portended doom as surely as *We are at war* or *All hope is lost*: "He's becoming a teenager," and the father shuddered.

Parker with his otherworldly beauty that always bewildered his parents, soon to kamikaze into acne and wet dreams as well as a newfound status—that Zan never could have imagined when he was Parker's age—as the class heartthrob. Possessed of a new vanity so surreal and implacable that the boy views the speed bumps on the canyon boulevard as put there solely for the purpose of disrupting his immaculately positioned hair. Parker the stoic with his monk's smile, allowing of course for the melodrama of a budding artist who already makes his own movies on Zan's laptop as well as writing and drawing *Shrimpy Comix*, about a mutant, or maybe just odd, crustacean. Of course all this is interspersed with adolescent tantrums, but also the occasional moment when Viv catches their son reading to his sister *Shrimpy* #3, hot off the press, as the girl curls in the crook of the boy's arm listening.

In the car on Pacific Coast Highway, Parker said, "If they have a huge earthquake in Tokyo, would the wave roll all the way across the ocean here?" He's never been to Tokyo but is fascinated by the idea of it, an animé city.

T ogether Zan and Viv reached the same conclusion, which was there was no getting around a conversation about tsunamis. "No," said Zan. "If they had one in Hawaii, maybe." Viv shot him another look.

"I don't understand how it works," said Parker.

"The ground under the sea moves and the water is . . . displaced." He looked at Viv: *right?*

Viv shrugged. "First the water goes all the way out."

"If you ever go to the beach," said Zan, "and there's a lot more beach than you've ever seen, don't go play on it."

"Get far away," Sheba interjected for the first time from her booster seat in the back. Viv had the usual look on her face that said, Is this useful information or child abuse? Parenthood is another word for fear management. In the backseat Sheba stared out the window, already seeing the wave in the distance.

When they got back to the house, Zan stopped at the top of their insanely steep driveway and dropped Viv off at the mailbox. He drove down the drive and got out of the car, anxiously gazing back up at Viv; he loved the days they got only junk mail, except for the once a year when there was a royalty check from some foreign country full of perplexing people who read Zan's books from years before. Everyone had been in the house for five minutes when Viv said, just as Zan was thinking it, "Where's Sheba?"

Zan rushed back out onto the deck of the house and peered over the rail at the car parked below, from where Sheba was extracting herself. The little girl glared back up at her father. "YOU LEFT ME IN THE CAR!"

"I'm sorry," Zan sputtered, horrified, "I thought you were with Parker."

"Thank you VERY much for RUINING MY DAY, *parents!*" she declaimed, and months later the girl still hasn't forgotten. Wherever they are or whatever they're doing, out of nowhere, in the middle of any conversation or some rare silence, she mutters, "You left me in the car," and who knows what scenario she considered in those moments strapped in her booster seat, having been left at an orphanage by her grandmother when she was two years old, having been left by her mother at the grandmother's door when she was four months old: Did she wonder, *Is this where I wait for someone else to come take me?* and as she waited, did she watch for that hawaiian tsunami to come roaring down the driveway?

Not until Viv got to Ethiopia to bring Sheba home did she learn the truth about the girl's first two years. The second morning in Addis Ababa, she went to meet a woman who had been identified by the adoption agency as a kind of caretaker; the woman was in her mid-sixties but seemed older. She had blue cataract eyes and was dressed in traditional clothes, and accompanied by her grown daughter. When the women began to cry, Viv learned that the older woman was Sheba's paternal grandmother and the younger was Sheba's aunt, the sister of Sheba's father.

The grandmother spoke Amharic but the aunt spoke English. The aunt explained to Viv that—notwithstanding the adoption agency's account, which always was vague—Sheba was raised by the grandmother. Supporting her family by making moonshine tej, the local honeywine, after her land was seized in the Eighties by the communist Derg that followed the fall of Haile Selassie, the old woman eventually was no longer able physically or financially to care for Sheba, who at the age of four months was left on the doorstep by the girl's mother, an unwed Muslim.

When Viv first met Sheba, the girl vacillated between a psychic desolation almost impossible to fully accommodate and the insubordination that meant survival for someone so young needing so much. Then, just when Viv thought she was turning a corner with the girl, Sheba wanted nothing to do with her, an abstinence that lasted for days. *What have I done*, Viv wrote to Zan, *what have I gotten us into*. But the girl always followed her new mother with her eyes, and in the middle of the night, as the sax line of a song drifted through the open window of the hotel room, Viv felt a small finger constantly moving along the outline of her face to make certain she was there. Sheba grabbed Viv's face in her hands and pulled it close as if to share the same breath.

Sheba's father disputed his paternity. A former veteran of the Ethiopian Air Force and one of the countless wars that the country fought with the countries around it—or maybe it always was the same war—he insisted that wounds he suffered in battle made it impossible for him to be Sheba's father.

"The old war-wound excuse!" Zan said in disbelief when he heard it. The father had no job to support the child. That he was Christian when the mother was Muslim only made the circumstances more difficult. But the grandmother acknowledged the baby girl's DNA even as the father wouldn't, and only after two years when she became more infirmed did she take Sheba to the local orphanage, where for two weeks the little girl waited vainly in the yard for her grandmother to return.

Relatively quickly, Sheba was assigned by the adoption agency to Viv and Zan, who had filed their papers some months before. Now the couple is amused by people who believe prospective parents saunter through orphanages choosing a child like someone picks a kitten at the animal shelter. The adoption process, involving medical tests, hours of online schooling, an impossible paper chase of countless forms and documents, and the scheduling of African court dates, was followed by Viv's twenty-four-hour hejira to Addis Ababa by way of Chicago, London, Frankfurt and Cairo to get the girl.

I chose you, were the grandmother's parting words before Viv left Ethiopia to return with Sheba to Los Angeles, *I chose you through God to be her mother* and only in the final moments did the girl's father bring himself to admit that Sheba was his daughter, as though anyone looking at the two would have any doubt.

Given Viv, it's not hard to believe she's been chosen. Out of several billion women Sheba's grandmother somehow plucked the truest heart, Viv who once wanted to bring to the house all the old homeless men of the canyon for a Christmas shower, Viv who will give away to the destitute whatever little money the family has left if Zan doesn't stop her. Viv who would be field marshal of the world's needing and needed as surely as she field-marshals the family priorities, when the family isn't chafing at her command. "I'm a flawed human being," she moans plaintively to Zan.

Fifteen years ago, before either of the children, a photographic series on church stained-glass windows led Viv to her great artistic endeavor. These were steel-framed recreations of the windows in the wings of butterflies that had died after their full butterfly-lives of several weeks; as Viv would have it, the juxtaposition of wing and steel is a metaphor for life, but Zan knows it's a metaphor for the woman, the fragile and gritty joined in all five-feet-two of her. The pieces attracted attention as evidenced by their exhibition in a number of galleries and acceptance into the permanent collections of two Southland museums, but most prominently by their plagiarism: Over the past several years Viv has found herself at the center of one of the art world's most notorious *scandales*, when both the idea and medium of the butterfly stained-glass windows were stolen by the world's most successful artist—a man as well known for cavalierly "appropriating" other people's ideas as for making tens of millions of dollars dipping elephants in plastic. While numerous people have pointed out the grounds for legal action, it sums up the Nordhocs' lives emotionally as well as financially that they have nearly as little psychological wherewithal as they do financial resources to sue the bastard.

Rather Viv has poured her heart into Sheba's adoption, which is less glamorous than television images of movie stars jetting in to scoop up African children. Months after the girl comes to live with them, Zan and Viv realize that the adoption they supposed might universally be regarded as a good thing is viewed as a gaudy display of trendiness. "We're Brangelina!" Viv exclaims in dismay after watching a TV news story about an actress facing a public-relations backlash on the occasion of her third (or fourth) (or fifth) adoption.

"Well," allows Zan, "the Brangelina of canyon dwellers about to be foreclosed on, anyway." Viv remains in contact with Sheba's family back in Addis, every month sending money to Sheba's grandmother; almost two years after the adoption, Viv continues to ask about Sheba's birth-mother. The more that the grandmother and aunt and agency respond, "No one knows," "It's not good to ask," "It will make trouble," the more determined Viv becomes.

She has visions of the mother driven from her home, becoming a prostitute or stoned to death. As someone who already was a mother before Sheba, Viv knows that if the woman is still alive then she'll wonder what happened to her child and someday Sheba will wonder who the woman was who gave birth to her. Warnings and admonitions aside, Viv hires a young journalist she met in Addis to find the girl's mother. "I hope I'm doing the right thing," she frets to Zan, "I hope I'm not making trouble. Why does everyone keep telling me to leave it alone?"

About most things Zan believes that Fate—the same fate that he knows is saving for him the Ultimate Trick—unfolds as it does for better or worse. There are things never to be known;

not every question in life is to be answered or even necessarily should be. Some secrets have their integrity. He's also aware that, until Sheba's arrival, his role in the adoption often has been that of a bystander.

Yet Zan wonders about Sheba's mother as well. If she's alive, then somewhere on the planet is a woman with a hole in her heart. He thinks of her lying in bed or on a mat at night wondering, before she finally sleeps, who her daughter is or where she could be. He knows that when Sheba is older, this will become a burning question, and he imagines the recriminations for not having pursued the answer.

Already Sheba resents the claims that Parker makes on Viv's belly that she can't. She covets his time in Viv's womb and it becomes a weapon in the alpha-struggles between siblings that Sheba can't win physically. "How did THIS PERSON," she demands, pointing at Parker, "come out of YOUR TUMMY?" outraged that her brother should have had such sanctuary and that Viv could have given it. The day will come when Sheba ponders the unknown womb from where she was delivered.

The phone calls from debt-collection agencies grow more frequent. Every now and then someone can be seen through the kitchen window prowling around the property line, furtive and stealthy, sent by the bank to determine if anyone still lives in the house. Again Zan writes to the home lender formally requesting a review of the last mortgage application. The house's fate is suspended in some national economic ether; with not a bit of the romance that the word implies, the Nordhocs are outlaws, squatters in their own home.

Zan keeps the kids out of school to watch on television the inauguration of the new president. There's nothing like missing school to make Parker civic-minded. Zan resolves not to be so boring as to hector his children that this, after all, is history. On the television, the president raises one hand and places the other on the Bible. Zan blurts, "This is history."

Zan receives an invitation from the University of London to lecture on the Novel as a Literary Form Facing Obsolescence in the Twenty-First Century. While Zan finds giving or hearing such a lecture too odious to contemplate, the £3,500 that the university offers lends itself to contemplation. At the radio station he reads the letter again.

Dear Alexander Nordhoc, it says, *we really really do think you're a writer.* Actually the invitation doesn't say that. When Viv and the kids come by, Zan shows it to her. "I'd do it," he tells her, "if they invited me to talk about music."

"What do you mean you would do it *if?*" says Viv. "It's a trip to London."

"They don't understand," Zan explains, shaking the letter at her, "that I haven't taught in two years, or been a novelist in fourteen . . . "

"You're always a novelist, you've written four novels. That makes you a novelist."

"The last was fourteen years ago."

"The last was *written* fourteen years ago. But it may have been read by someone, you know," she shrugs, "fourteen days ago."

"It's from James," Zan points at the invitation.

Viv sighs, "I noticed."

Who knows what that sigh means? Wistful, regretful, oh-please-let's-not weary? "You sighed," he says. "Uh," says Viv.

"Yeah," he says.

She shrugs.

"Wistful? Regretful."

"More," she says, "oh-please-let's-not weary."

"I was getting to that one," says Zan. "James" is J. Willkie Brown, as his byline reads, chosen presumably because he doesn't want to be mistaken for the Godfather of Soul or, if he even were to consider the more vulgar "Jim," star football players who used to beat up their women, in more innocent times before star football players murdered them—as if either point of confusion is likely, given that J. Willkie Brown is a Brit of distinctly Anglo complexion.

He also is a former lover of Viv's, from a brief affair that happened during Zan's first and only real separation from her, sixteen months before Parker was born. That was the Nineties when Brown still was a British expat in L.A. about to abandon music journalism once and for all, given that he hadn't understood anything about music since 1987 and therefore it couldn't possibly be worth writing about anymore.

Since both Zan and Viv have agreed that their separation was more Zan's fault, he's bothered less by jealousy over the affair than what a wrong turn it represents for Viv, the other man having gone on to great fame and success and presumably not being $135,000 in debt and foreclosed on. Following his music reportage in the Seventies and Eighties, Brown increasingly spent the last quarter century writing about politics from a more and more radical perspective while also cultivating a persona at once elegant and swashbuckling, embedding himself with insurgents and revolutionaries from Berlin to Istanbul to Karachi. His celebrity is such that the University of London has created the J. Willkie Brown Chair, occupied at the moment by J. Willkie himself.

Zan's single triumph over Brown is that, in time-honored journalistic tradition, the world-famous journalist always longed to write a novel. While Zan knows how dubious this is, he's not telling; it's the only thing about Zan that there is for Brown to envy, and that now Brown invites him to lecture about the state of the novel is irresistible, even if Zan can't help smelling a trap. "I smell a trap," he says to Viv.

"What are you talking about?" she says.

"The novel as a literary form facing obsolescence?" James' way of telling me how washed up I am, Zan thinks to himself.

"It's a trip to London," says Viv, "it's thirty-five hundred pounds. What's a pound worth?"

"A buck and a half?"

"So it's better than thirty-five hundred dollars."

"I have to pay my own expenses."

"So you get a cheap flight and a cheap hotel and come back with a couple thousand dollars maybe." She says, "He's famous. It could lead to other things," then adds quickly, "I mean, of course, you're kind of famous too—"

"It's O.K.," he cuts her off.

"You are," she insists. "In your own way."

Zan wakes in the early hours with the usual terror and sits up in bed. He looks at Viv sleeping; the thought, he realizes, is infantile, but for the moment he entertains it anyway, that Viv wrote to J. Willkie Brown asking if there was something to be done in terms of throwing Zan this bone of an invitation to London. Infantile because the thought is so much about pride and ego when in fact it would have made utter if humiliating sense for Viv to have done just such a thing.

He considers sneaking downstairs to peruse Viv's email, but he's never done that and finally can't convince himself there's a reason to now. He collapses back into his pillow and returns to his restless sleep, listening to the rats in the vents.

Sometimes when no one else is awake, Zan returns to a new novel that no one knows he's writing. The novel is about a middle-aged L.A. writer who, feeling discouraged and despondent—this isn't remotely autobiographical—escapes to Berlin a few years after the fall of the Wall. The middle-aged writer befriends (or so he believes) a young German skinhead who's besotted with the New World, except it's a New World of white supremacists and cracked midwest Nazi messiahs.

Within the first nine or ten thousand words of Zan's novel, this and that happens, most of which Zan knows he'll wind up cutting. The story really begins when the young German skinhead follows the protagonist one night and, near the entrance of the U-Bahn, with a gang of other skinheads who call themselves the Pale Flame, viciously beats the writer and leaves him for dead in the street.

Or maybe actually he *is* dead. This novel being not remotely autobiographical, it's hard for Zan to be certain. In any case, before the writer passes out, he has a kind of reverie of his memory floating away, like a balloon that Viv got for Sheba while shopping, which the girl let go just for the sensation of watching it vanish in the sky.

As the dying man lies in the street, a black teenage girl emerges from the shadows where she's hidden while the incident took place. She recognizes the members of the Pale Flame as men who would do to her something worse than what's being done to the man, which is to say worse than murder. It may be hard for Zan's reader to imagine something worse than murder, but Zan believes there's such a thing, and the girl believes it too.

Zan knows that a novel keeps secrets from its author, and the first secret this novel keeps from him is that, like his own daughter, the teenage girl in the story is a transmitter, broadcasting from parts unknown. Like Sheba, her body perspires in song. Once the skinheads have left, the girl approaches the man in the street; clearly he's dead but she feels obligated to make sure. By his side she kneels, clutching to her all of her papers and books, when she hears herself rise in volume—and then when he stirs, she's so startled that she flees, dropping by his side an old battered paperback she's had since she was a child, before she could read.

Why is she black? Zan wonders, annoyed with himself for asking. Can I make her a black girl? When he sees her in his head, she's black, so that should be the end of it, *but do I have the* right *to make her black?* She's not a major character at all, rather someone who sets in motion a plot, so is it exploitative to make her black when there's no point to it?

Or is it wrong to think there has to be a point to it? Characters are black only because they need to be? But what do I know about being black? Isn't any white person who writes about race asking for trouble? Of course I don't know anything about being a teenage girl, either. For that matter I don't know anything about being anyone else, other than who I am.

Also secret from Zan is a drawing on the opening blank page of the old battered paperback that the girl has dropped. Nor does the unnamed man left for dead in the street know of the drawing, because by the time he wakes, it isn't there, having been ripped mysteriously from the book in the hours between.

It's a drawing of a woman who happens to be the teenage girl's mother. The sketch is crude and quick but not untalented, done with colored pencils, the woman in shades of brown except for her distinctive, misplaced gray eyes. None of this can mean anything to the man lying in the street; but though Zan knows nothing of the drawing either, it means a great deal to him, because he met the subject of the sketch once, in an encounter so brief and frenzied that it lasted only seconds but saved his life.

Zan grew up in the white L.A. suburbs. His parents were midwesterners who came, as his father acknowledged one night during the evening news while black people were being hosed down and attacked by dogs on television, from a past where white and black didn't meet. Whatever their attitudes about race, Zan's parents tried to protect him from those attitudes; the n-word wasn't used in the house. Nonetheless not a single thing about the black experience penetrated Zan's own until he was the age that his own son is now.

That was when he came home one afternoon from school and on his parents' stereo played a record of country songs sung by a blind black man. This wasn't the sort of music that Zan had heard before, and though for decades afterward purists would declaim the aesthetic offense of a soul genius committing his voice to such white songs and white strings and white arrangements, to the twelve-year-old Zan the music's surrounding whiteness made the blackness of the voice all the more shocking.

Decades later Zan understands that, as epiphanies about race go, this is pretty pathetic. Still, it rearranged the furniture in Zan's head, knocked out one or two of the walls. Zan would know for the rest of his life that this was the most subversive record ever made, the white trojan horse that smuggled a blind black man into the gates of Zan's white city. Every afternoon, returning home from school, Zan snuck the record down to his own room and listened to it over and over, the volume low because it felt like something he should get in trouble for, like reading a forbidden book.

The only child of a socially and politically conservative family, lower middle class when he was smaller, on the edges of upper middle class by the time he finished high school, Zan was a fifteen-year-old rightwinger before the erosion of his adolescent certainties by the television images of Negroes at the mercy of flying police sticks. That erosion was the end of one nascent political identity, such as it ever was, and the beginning of another, such as it ever would be, and by the time Zan was a college student, he found his political psyche outflanked on all sides. Students graced their dormitory walls with posters of the leader of a revolution in China, one of the great killers of the Twentieth Century; and for all the ways that Zan's parents came to suspect their son was kidnapped in the night by leftwing professors who implanted a Marxist chip in his brain, in fact Zan felt less a part of anything and more an odd man out of everything. One afternoon between classes, in the tumultuous aftermath of four students murdered by the National Guard at another school in another part of the country, Zan stopped in the middle of the campus quadrangle to note a line of armored police to one side and protesting students to the other, with him squarely in the middle alone, which so summed up his ambivalence that it would seem to have been staged. Whatever else was true, however, and for all ambivalence's varieties that cluttered philosophical clarity, one thing was incontestable to Zan and it was that his political conservatism failed the nation's great moral test of the decade, which was how to redeem the transgression of slavery that betrayed his country's original promise.

Within Zan's first week as a college student, he published a piece in the university newspaper about the prospective presidential candidacy of a senator who, like Zan, once was a rightwinger and now was . . . what? besides the brother of a martyred president, and embraced by blacks as no white politician had been since the president who ended slavery a century before.

In his student writing group that met off campus, Zan remained odd man out from the beginning. When the joint was passed he was the only one who declined, which raised eyebrows a week later when the class arrived to find it narrowly had missed a police bust. Zan immediately was suspected as the rat, "then we read your writing," one of Zan's fellow students explained later, "and realized you're the trippiest one of all." Zan's teacher was a New Englander named Logan Hale, a novelist in his mid-fifties of some renown; as a young man Hale had been Leon Trotsky's bodyguard in Mexico in the Thirties, resigning when he became convinced that Trotsky's inevitable murder in fact was, for all intents and purposes, suicide—contrition by Trotsky for the Stalinism that he not only hadn't stopped but, in his own mind, set in motion.

An anti-Stalinist, Trotsky-estranged Marxist, Hale was a dedicated outsider wary of being any movement's flunky, and though Zan didn't share the professor's politics, the iconoclasm was irresistible. Zan saw in the mentor another odd man out; it's possible Hale saw in a protégé the same thing.

Another story about Hale, less reliable than the one concerning Trotsky, was that he was Billie Holiday's lover in the mid-Forties when he worked on his first book, a ghostwritten autobiography of a white sax player and clarinetist of middling stature who dealt drugs, mostly marijuana, to other musicians including Holiday. Hale never disputed or discussed this rumor about him and Holiday, maybe out of sheer gentlemanliness, if it was true, or because he knew a great piece of public relations, if it wasn't.

One afternoon the presidential candidate Zan had written about for the university newspaper made a campaign stop at the campus. Zan never had seen close up someone who might become president. The day was ravishing: fluttery and saturated with itself in the way that days were back then; but Zan had no sense until later how unusual the afternoon was.

There was a frenzy about the campaign for this candidate that Zan wouldn't see again until forty years later, in the campaign of the man whose election and appearance in Chicago Zan watched that November night with Sheba sitting on his lap. It was a frenzy not simply of hope but yearning so desperate as to be hysteria, and that afternoon in the campus quad it seemed to him the crowd might devour the candidate, a slight man whose frailness conveyed less strength than an impossible, even irrational courage, inspiring in the crowd a savagery that was tender but savage nonetheless. The candidate and crowd shared an appetite for sacrifice and would make a ritual of it.

Zan got close to where the man stood. Was it on a platform? or in the back of an open car not unlike that in which the man's brother had been shot? In any case, what Zan never forgot was the pain burning in the man's gaze and the ecstasy—like he was Joan of Arc—of a crowd so increasingly unhinged that it wouldn't have surprised Zan, wouldn't have surprised anyone, had anyone told him or everyone else at that moment that within the month the man would be as dead as his brother.

Though in fact the maelstrom created by this candidacy had grown from the brother's death a few years before, it was its own thing now, concurrent with the way this man became his own candidate. It was hard to know whether he would have become a great or disastrous president but it seemed inevitable to Zan that he would have been one or the other, poised as such men are at a tipping point. By the time the crowd tore the coat from the candidate's back and plucked the cufflinks from his wrists, it so had lost control that craziness found a gravity and vortex, catching Zan in the undertow around his ankles.

He felt his feet lifted off the ground and the rest of him pulled under. Enveloped by panic, flailing wildly and reaching for anything he could grab, Zan called for help but the noise and movement were too much for anyone to hear or reach him.

Then, as he was swallowed by the crowd to be trampled or crushed underfoot, a hand, young and female and black, reached to him from the sky and he took it.

Now in the novel that Zan writes about the writer dying in the streets of Berlin, the black teenage witness to the beating kneels clutching her belongings, hears the music coming out of herself and, as she bends to touch the man's body, is so startled when he stirs that she jumps back.

Dropping by the man's side her old battered paperback, she flees into the mouth of the U-Bahn and only when the train arrives that will safely take her away from what's just happened does she realize the book is missing. Because it's a book that she's had since she was a child, she seriously considers going back; but of course she can't go back. The skinheads might return, the police might come, or the dying man in the street might rouse himself to consciousness and strike out at her in a rush of adrenaline.

N o, she concludes, she can't go back. The book is one of life's markers now, one of experience's receipts destined to disappear one day, and now on this night it has, in this way. So she steps onto the train and is swept to the sanctuary of Berlin's tunnels, before the last five minutes overwhelm her like a wave.

S he's black, Zan decides once and for all, pushing the laptop away. Fuck whether I have the right to make her so. My imagination gives me the right. Hearing a Ray Charles record when I was Parker's age may not mean I *know* anything but it means that I can imagine something I wouldn't have imagined otherwise. It's a little like what Descartes said about God, that the fact men can imagine a god proves there must be one.

Viv receives an email from the Ethiopian journalist she hired. *Hello Viv*, it reads, *this is to inform you that I have at once uncovered a most tantalizing lead and also confronted an unexpected obstacle in our search for Zema's mother. Since we believe she was Muslim it narrows my investigation to suggest one of two different women, the first with family heritage in Oromia to the south and the other with no family in Ethiopia and who in fact may have grown up not in this country but somewhere in Eastern Europe and then immigrated. Of course few people who I meet are very willing to talk and the closer I come to answers then the more silent that people become but I persist and press on and hope to have more news soon.*

For months the new president is the only thing that makes Zan happy, the only thing that interrupts the billowing gloom of his life. At the moment it doesn't matter if this is delusion. By now Zan knows better than to place hope in any one thing or person; it may be that the fact of this particular presidency rather than its occupant is what cheers him, because it signals the existence of the politically miraculous. Zan also has identified the connection between the candidate of forty years ago whom he saw in the campus quad, whose presence ripped the fabric of the collective rationale to reveal behind it a national delirium, and this current man with so many parts of the country making up his form.

There has followed the new president's election a mini-Era of Good Feelings, remarkable for the overwhelming sense of national crisis with which the feeling coexists. Zan finds the hysteria for the new president at once inspiring and unsettling, since it's as unsustainable by the public as it is by the man himself.

Not everyone shares such sentiment. Skepticism crosses political and philosophical lines. *I heartily dislike him*, writes a good friend, an anarcho-syndicalist who lives in the Texas Panhandle. *I never did and never can trust him. A prima donna with that damned smile I can't look at and all his round-the-world photo ops who nonetheless is unwilling to make people afraid of him—the worst of both worlds. He'll never be worth a shit.*

Viv receives another email that is both exciting and disconcerting. *Hello Viv*, it reads, *I am writing to alert you in regards to the search for Zema's mother that the trail of the woman in Oromia has led to nothing but that I believe I draw closer to the other woman who is indicated to originally be from Czechoslovakia or Poland or Germany—perhaps you might contact the aunt and grandmother to see if at least they will confirm this?—and now may be here in Addis closer than we ever suspected, within a mere few kilometers of Zema's orphanage. I hope to deliver good news soon.*

In front of her laptop, staring at the email astounded, Viv says, "Czechoslovakia or Poland or Germany? Good lord. Sheba might not even be Ethiopian?"

"We are all Ethiopians!" Zan declares grandly and his wife glares at him. "Well, Sheba's half Ethiopian anyway," he points out.

"How can she not be Ethiopian?"

"The father is Ethiopian," Zan persists. "In Muslim cultures, that counts."

"The father isn't Muslim," she says. "Ethiopia isn't a Muslim culture."

"There are lots of Muslims in Ethiopia."

"Twice as many Christians."

"O.K."

"Well."

"Sheba is half Muslim. In the Muslim culture, the father counts and he's Ethiopian."

"But he's not the half that's Muslim," she says.

"So he would count only if he *were* Muslim?" though Zan admits to himself that this discussion, his half in particular, doesn't make sense to him anymore. "Why don't you write to Sheba's grandmother, like he suggests?"

Viv writes the email and sits before the laptop waiting as though an answer will appear immediately. *I chose you to be her mother*, is the answer when it comes from the grandmother, as translated by Sheba's aunt, *through God*, almost exactly as she said to Viv two years ago.

The night before Viv receives the message that changes everything, Piranha disappears, having braved and broken through his high-voltage corral once and for all. Viv stands on the deck of the house calling, but only when Sheba howls her half of their duet does the dog howl back in the distance. It's a howl that defies interpretation. Maybe it means *goodbye*, maybe it means *so long, suckers*, maybe it means *help I'm being pursued by coyotes*, maybe it means *you try wearing one of these fucking electric collars and see how you like it*. In any case, he's gone.

Returning home from the radio station the next afternoon, Zan finds Viv fetally curled up on the couch in the family room. She buries her head in the cushion.

He sits next to her, puts his hand on her thigh. She doesn't move; on the white cloud-shaped formica table that Parker always leaps over, her laptop is open. "Hey," says Zan.

He looks at the laptop and an open email: *Hello Viv. I write to you with troubling news and that is the woman who I believe might be Zema's mother appears to have disappeared under suspicious circumstances related to my questions about her. It is not clear if she has run afoul of the law and is in jail or something more ominous has taken place. It also is possible that she has fled the city or even the country. In any case if indeed there ever was someone at the end of the trail, now she has vanished. For reasons and by means too complicated to explain here, it would seem to have come to the attention of the authorities that you have been sending money to Zema's grandmother and family which has raised suspicions of child-trafficking and the possibility that Zema was sold to you by the mother, though it is difficult to be certain how seriously they take this. It all is most unfortunate I know but is becoming a common concern as adoptions are on the rise. The police*

*are not answering any questions but ask many and it is all most
confusing I am afraid. For the moment nothing has happened to
Zema's family but an investigation seems under way and no one
is saying anything and strongly I would suggest that whatever
contact you have cease for a while and that any inquiries as to
Zema's mother stop as well. It also is possible that the woman
in question is not Zema's mother at all, this has not been estab-
lished. I now must be careful with my investigations and perhaps go "undercover" awhile but should I learn more information I will attempt to send it along in as discreet a fashion as I
can. I am sorry for this news.*

Viv says something and he leans over to her, his ear in her
turquoise hair. "Everyone told me to leave it alone," he
hears her mutter, "everyone told me and I wouldn't.

Zan is furious at the email and all its vague implications.
"You don't know what's happened," he argues. "We don't
know that this mystery person, whoever she is, is Sheba's
mother. I mean, we can't tell that there even *is* such a person."

Viv doesn't answer.

"All we know," says Zan, "is that some woman he thought
he was looking for and that he never found might have . . . left
the country, or . . . "

" . . . or been thrown in jail, or worse," she finally turns to
him. Her face is red.

"The odds are she isn't even Sheba's mother," but as soon
as he's said it, he knows what she'll say.

"So? I still got an innocent woman thrown in jail. Or
worse." Every time she says "or worse," it becomes worse.

"You don't know that. We don't know *anything*."

She searches his eyes and whispers, "Zan, they think we *bought* Sheba."

I t's hard to know how long she's been thinking it when she says, "I have to go." Later he feels sure she's been considering it awhile, maybe before the email.

"Go?" he says, at first genuinely confused. They're upstairs sitting on their bed. She's been distraught all day, more than any time since her art was stolen two years ago, succumbing to an unshakeable silence, and only does her voice find its usual spiritedness when she says, "To Addis Ababa."

W hen she was in her late twenties, Viv returned to Africa for the first time since she lived there as a girl, to climb Mount Kilimanjaro on the border between Tanzania and Kenya. Immediately following this successful ascent—a framed certificate on the wall attests to the achievement—she sat for some hours at Kilimanjaro's nearest airport drinking with a number of other overly exuberant western adventurers who at some point realized they had drunk their way through the week's one and only flight to Europe.

T his discovery was followed by a mad drive through the night to the next airport, across hundreds of kilometers of revolution-beset african desert in an outlandish episode that involved no gas and "borrowed" cars and armed soldiers and herds of zebra crashing into them. The story always has summed up for Zan what he loves and admires about Viv, and the ways in which they're different. On the one hand, Zan's soul will pass through many lives before one of them steps foot on Mount Kilimanjaro. On the other hand, there's not the remotest possibility that Zan ever would have missed that flight.

It's possible, Zan believes, that this now almost legendary chapter in Viv's life imbued her with a . . . *unique* sense of life's odds and risks. Interestingly, motherhood threw life into the gear of fear, in which Viv worries about things that Zan takes in stride, maybe too much so.

In any case Zan has come to understand well enough his dynamic with Viv that he knows to fully express what he feels about her returning to Ethiopia would be counter-productive. Rather he takes a deep breath and attempts to modulate his agitation. "Baby," he says, "it's not a good idea."

For a moment she sinks back into the afternoon's abyss.

"If nothing has happened, if this woman doesn't even *exist* let alone is in jail, then it's a waste of time. If something has happened and the police are arresting people, it's all the more reason you shouldn't go."

"We could all travel with you to London," she urges, and now it's clear this indeed has been going around in her head awhile, "for your lecture, or residency, or whatever it is . . . the kids can stay with you and I can go onto Addis and you'll wait for me in London." She says, "I know it's a lot to ask but we talked about it anyway."

"Talked about what?"

"Going to London with you."

More harshly than he intends, he says, "We never talked about that," then, "sometimes you think about telling me something and once you've thought it, then you think you've done it."

"Sometimes," she answers, "maybe you just don't remember me telling you," and bursts into tears.

S he cries in bed while Zan holds her, until both hear the creak of the bedroom floor. They look up to see Sheba in her Avengers underpants, thumb in mouth, watching, frightened. "Mama?" she says, "Poppy?" and Zan and Viv know the girl believes every drama is a signal that life is about to leave her behind or hand her off to someone else.

"It's O.K.," Viv says, "Mama's O.K.," and opens her arms and the child falls into them. No one speaks for a while and after a minute Zan says, "We'll do what you want."

O ver the coming days Viv rides a roller coast of highs and lows. Every new twenty-four-hour cycle brings a new email resolving nothing, and adamantly she won't be dissuaded by circumstance or Zan that she is directly responsible for what's transpired and setting in motion a chain of events, even as it's unclear what that chain is or what's the consequence of the motion that is its result. With this, Zan realizes that, whatever the risk, Viv's trip to Ethiopia is inevitable. No one will be able to live with Viv otherwise, least of all Viv herself.

L ying in bed in the dark, she says, "What if the bank takes the house while we're gone?" It's the night before they leave for London. Zan is encouraged by the question not because he believes Viv will abandon her plan to go—at this point he's no longer sure she should—but because, in what quickly has become the all-consuming Ethiopian drama, she hasn't forgotten other realities.

"Well?" she says.

"I guess whether we're here when they take it isn't going to matter."

"When?"

"If."

"You said when."

T he flight for London departs at seven the next evening. Leaving for the airport that afternoon, Zan and Viv gaze around at the house before locking the door behind them. As they wait at their gate for the flight, Zan watches a news cable channel on the television. Parker listens to the fluores-cent-green music player around his neck and Sheba climbs over all the furniture in the terminal.

W atching her, Viv says to Zan, "In London you'll need to find a salon for her. Some place where they can do her hair."

"All right," Zan says absently, watching the news.

"Are you listening?"

"Yes. Sheba's hair." Ever since the girl came to live with

them, Viv has been confounded by Sheba's hair. Once in a shopping mall, a black woman approached Viv and pointed out that the hair was different and couldn't be neglected and demanded constant attention.

"You never should have started calling her Sheba," says Viv.

After this has sunk in a moment, Zan turns his attention from the television. "What?"

"You shouldn't have called her Sheba. It sounds like a B-movie," she protests. "*Queen of the Jungle*."

Zan says, "That's Sheena." Coming almost two years after the fact, this is an unforeseen point of contention. "What should we call her?"

"Not so loud." Viv glances the girl's way. "Her real name, maybe?"

"Do we know that 'Zema' is her real name?"

"Well, we know it's no less real than Sheba," says Viv.

"We have no idea what it means. 'Zema.' It sounds like a power drink."

"It means 'hymn'."

"That's *kind of* what it means."

"It's close enough."

"People have been as vague about her name as they have about everything else," including, he wants to point out but doesn't, her mother. "It means different things depending on how the stars are aligned that day, or the given meteorology. A fog happens to roll in, and for all we know suddenly it means 'Death to the Great Satan' or something."

"Sheba sounds silly."

"Won't it seriously mess with her sense of self if now we go back to calling her something else?"

"Her sense of self is going to be O.K.," Viv answers firmly. "Yeah, if we don't start calling her Death to the Great Satan."

Zan would like to note that Viv has been calling the girl Sheba too but decides it's best to accept the full brunt of the accusation. "It's a cool name," he says. "She can be a rocker with that name."

"Or a stripper," Viv retorts. For a while they don't say anything. Zan gets up and crosses the lobby to the television. On the cable news, a black man argues against the new president's foreign policy; he looks unhappy, sour, and Zan isn't sure he would have recognized him—certainly given the political viewpoint he now expresses—if he weren't identified at the bottom of the screen where it reads RONALD J. FLOWERS and, beneath that, "Los Angeles Director, Civic Organizers Network." Zan listens for a while and returns to his seat next to Viv. "Ever tell you my Ronnie Jack Flowers story?" he says.

"Yes. It's why you don't write novels anymore—I've heard it." She says, "Sorry. That came out crabbier than I intended."

After a moment Zan says, "You can't hold yourself responsible for everything." He means to offer it as, in part, a rapprochement.

"That story's about you," she answers, "not me."

The mother, father, son and daughter checker coach, only two of the assigned seats together, which means that Zan and Viv take turns with Sheba while Parker has his own seat across the aisle. On Zan's shift, scruples waver and soon he has the four-year-old swilling Benadryl; as the plane

flies into darkness, Sheba sleeps on her father's lap with Parker
slumped two rows ahead.

Viv says to Zan, "While you're in London, you need to have
the Talk with Parker." Trying not to look as glum about it as he
feels, Zan nods. "He's twelve," Viv insists, and Zan says, "All
right," realizing it sounds snappish. "I know he's twelve."

"He's going to start wondering," says Viv.

"He's beyond wondering. He's already figured stuff out."

"He doesn't know anything."

"He knows all of it."

"Did you? At twelve?"

"I don't remember how much I knew or exactly what, but
I had gotten the gist of it."

"The *gist*?"

"Yes, the gist."

"Shhh," she says, looking at everyone around them sleeping.

H e repeats emphatically, "The gist."

"Did you have the Talk with your father?" says Viv.

"My father was appalled by the whole subject. He
gave me a book that I barely looked at. Everything I know
about sex I learned from James Bond movies."

She rolls her eyes. "Yes, that explains a few things." After a
while she falls asleep and Zan turns on his laptop and reads the
news on the airplane WiFi that he had to pay for. Soon a
woman in the seat next to him strikes up a conversation that
Zan immediately realizes is intended to be political.

Zan never has picked a political argument with a stranger before. Actually he doesn't pick political arguments with anyone; he's so averse to confrontation that when people talk politics, he's as likely to sink into even greater silences. It's hard to tell what age the woman is. She could be an older-looking thirty-eight or a younger-looking fifty-one. She looks older than Viv, who looks ten years younger than she is.

The woman is wearing a new ring that she's shown off to the flight attendants. Zan decides she's just gotten engaged— maybe, to put it cruelly, in the nick of time. He isn't sure what leads the woman to draw conclusions about Zan's political views, which are less predictable than the woman assumes; maybe it's something she's seen Zan reading on his laptop. Later he'll wonder—though this might be unfair—if she saw Zan with his black daughter. In any case she immediately means to straighten him out on some things. After some back and forth that Zan wants no part of, she blurts, "The big difference between us is that I believe in personal responsibility and you don't."

He says in disbelief, "I don't?" He looks back to his wife's seat to see if she's catching any of this, but Viv sleeps. Zan doesn't understand Viv's sleeping habits, how the slightest thing at home keeps her awake but she can sleep upright on a plane in a seat smaller than a coffin. "No," the woman says emphatically, and Zan, visions of foreclosure in his head, wonders if she's right. But she doesn't know me, he thinks, doesn't know my life; in fact—and there it is right on the edge of his brain—if she's just getting engaged then in all likelihood she doesn't have kids, and he hears himself snarling at her, "Do you even have kids? and if you don't, then you have no clue what responsibility is." Finally having gotten some guy to give her a ring, her chance of having children now, at either thirty-eight or fifty-one, is as far from her as the ground below them is now; and she looks stricken, her sense of power suddenly shattered, and bursts into tears . . .

Except she doesn't, "because," Zan later relates to Viv, "I didn't say that. It was there on the edge of my brain and there it stayed, because as much as I would have liked to let her have it, with her I'm-all-about-personal-responsibility-and-you-aren't, as much as she asked for it, as much as she deserved it—"

"—you couldn't bring yourself to," says Viv.

He knows it's the way a woman can be most profoundly hurt, "and maybe that's my fucking problem," he mutters, more to himself, maybe it's the problem with all of *us* (whoever we are) when it comes to dealing with *them* (whoever . . .), a softness, no killer instinct, mush for fortitude. "She didn't have any problem telling me I have no sense of responsibility."

"I know," Viv says, and takes his hand.

The flight is half an hour late into London, eating into Viv's connection time that's precious to begin with. In the midst of the mindboggling bazaar of Heathrow's duty-free shops, Viv has only the time to say, "I'll email," then, "I'll call," then she and Zan seem to realize they've no idea when they'll next see each other and have spent most of what time there was bickering.

Viv grabs the kids goodbye then kisses Zan, and "O.K." is all he can say. Shaking off the Benadryl stupor, Sheba begins to wail and Viv is slightly stricken. "It will be O.K.," Zan says to Viv as he scoops up Sheba, nodding in a way that means, Go. Both will remember how quickly all this happened.

In her usual manner, Sheba begins making her presence known to London as soon as she, Zan and Parker are in the car that's been arranged to take them from the airport. "I WANT MAMA!" she screams, and the driver jumps in his seat, eyes filling the rearview mirror. "How long is Viv going to be gone?" asks Parker.

Zan says, "A few days," and turns his gaze outside in a way meant to preclude further explanation. It's been more than twenty-five years since Zan last was in London, and as has become true with so many things, it doesn't seem so long ago at all, and even as it doesn't seem so long ago, it seems another lifetime, before Sheba, before Parker, before Viv. At the time he just had finished what would become his first published novel and still was more than a year from selling it and nearly three years from publication. Turning in the backseat of the car and craning his neck to take in this and that, he realizes he's seeing less what he's looking at than whatever memory it marks in some mental almanac that's already begun to crumble.

The driver of the car clears his throat and ventures into something that Zan guesses he's been considering since Heathrow. "Well done, then," he says, "you Yanks."

"Sorry?" says Zan.

"Well done," the driver nods in the rearview mirror, a tentative smile, "the new top man. You did it!"

Zan looks at Parker, and Parker looks back at his father and shrugs. It's a few seconds before Zan understands; everyone wants to talk politics these days. I should introduce this guy to the woman who harangued me on the plane, he thinks. See how "well done" she thinks it is. "Oh," Zan says, "yeah, it's . . . kind of unbelievable, really."

"Think he'll turn it all around, then?" says the driver.

"Everyone hopes so. Almost everyone, anyway." Zan realizes that, seeing Sheba, the driver assumes he knows how Zan voted: Is this cause for indignation? An assumption made solely on the basis of Sheba's color? On the other hand, well, the assumption happens to be correct, if not the reasoning. "She was for the other guy," Zan jokes to the rearview mirror, pointing at Sheba in his lap.

The driver laughs, maybe with some relief that he hasn't given offense. After a pause he says, "Funny place, the States. Given the bloke you had before, I mean."

"Yeah," says Zan, "funny place."

Politics, such as it is, doesn't come up again until the car nears the hotel in Bloomsbury, where Zan and his children have been put up by the university. The driver has taken the long way to show off the city, turning south to come into London by way of Hammersmith, then cutting through St. John's Wood to Regent's Park where he slows and points to a distant, grand red-brick mansion with white columns. "Winfield House," the driver says.

Zan says, "I don't think that's our hotel."

The driver chortles. "Your ambassador lives there. Or used to," he adds, suddenly a bit unsure.

"Really," Zan says with all the enthusiasm that politeness can muster. He looks at his kids to get a more accurate reading of just how boring this is; Parker's expression confirms that it's somewhere around Def-Con Two. Sheba has fallen asleep again. The inventor of Benadryl, Zan thinks, should get the Nobel Peace Prize. "I heard your President Kennedy lived there, didn't he?" says the driver. "That's what someone told me."

Zan realizes the driver might be correct. "I believe so. As a boy."

The driver does a double-take. "He was ambassador as a boy?"

"No, of course not. He wasn't ambassador, his father was ambassador."

The driver gazes at the red mansion. "They say the new man is like him, then?"

"Who?"

"President Kennedy?"

"Uh," Zan shrugs, "maybe." He says, "The campaign was more like his brother's."

"Was he the one shot?" Parker says.

"Both of them were shot."

"The heck?"

Zan is shocked by the tactlessness of the conversation, but it's history that's been tactless. "The father was ambassador," he says, looking at the house, "before World War II. One of his sons became president. He was shot. A few years later his brother ran for president and he was shot too. Some people think the new president's campaign was more like the brother's."

"Would the brother have become president," says Parker as the driver starts up the car, "if he hadn't been shot?"

"Hard to know. Some people think so." Zan says, "I'm not so sure."

The driver pulls out into traffic. "Funny place, the States."

In the small Bloomsbury hotel, Zan and his children have a room on the third floor. The woman at the front desk says, "Are you Alexander Nordhoc, the author?" An international warrant must be out for my arrest, he thinks. WORLD'S MOST OBSCURE AUTHOR FLEES DEBT COLLECTORS reads the headline in his mind, INTERPOL ON THE HUNT. On their first day the father and children wander the neighborhood, submitting to fish and chips at a corner stand; twice Zan yanks Sheba from the path of oncoming taxis. "We're not in the canyon," he admonishes the kids, "this is a big city, a real city. Not like L.A."

That night in exhaustion Zan and Parker try to sleep, only to pay the price for all the peace Benadryl bought on the flight over. Sheba is fully awake and on California time. The next day Zan drags them onto a double-decker bus, the four-year-old snarling, "Out of my way, *old man*," and then a boat that sails up the Thames, finally crossing Millennium Bridge to ride one of the glass pods of the Eye, the revolving wheel on the river's other side. That night in the hotel, Zan's laptop finally hitches a ride on some unsuspecting wireless network nearby to find an email from Viv. Reading it to the kids, he tries to feign cheer.

Hey u 3 I made it, am safe in Addis. Flights went smoothly & I feel O.K., no jet lag yet. Already miss you guys, P&Sh are u seeing London or just watching TV in the hotel? u must be thrilled I'm not there to bug you. hey I know u miss me you scamps. Internet service is 30. per day & since I only really email you maybe I'll skip tomorrow. Miss u a whole lot &look at your picture and kiss it and of daddy too. xoxoxomom

On the third day Zan takes the kids to the Tower of London. What kid doesn't love the Tower of London, he wonders, with its lopped queenly heads once bounding down the stone steps? Nonetheless neither Parker nor Sheba wants to go into that part of the tower, which makes the excursion seem beside the point, so Zan takes them to what supposedly was the bunker from which Churchill addressed London during the Blitz and plotted the salvation of civilization. The three Nordhocs enter a large lift that lowers them underground, and before the door slides open and the father and children step into the bunker, Parker's dread of dark closed places takes over.

In an attempt to replicate the war experience, the bunker has been appointed with mannequins sleeping on surrounding cots. Parker takes one look at the fake people and it's the final straw: "I want to leave," he says firmly, fighting to remain calm. "I want to leave too," Sheba says, her own fear overwhelming the usual obstinacy that would insist on doing whatever her brother doesn't want to.

Zan has to admit it's creepy. "O.K., we're leaving," he assures them, but Parker doesn't want to go back on the lift so the father dashes from door to door until rashly he flings open the emergency exit—only to find himself on the street, out on the sidewalk, traffic rushing past him. He realizes that the "lift" is a ruse. They haven't been underground at all. "I don't know," he says to the silent kids on the Tube back to the hotel, "if that's really where Winston Churchill was during the Blitz."

At two in the London morning, still fully in the thrall of jetlag after the kids have begun to readjust, Zan tries to compose his lecture on the Novel as a Literary Form Facing Obsolescence in the Twenty-First Century. Instead he peeks at the fitful story he began back in the canyon; his main character, the washed-up, middle-aged L.A. writer left for dead in the Berlin street by both skinhead murderers and their witness—the black teenage girl who dropped her book by his body—stirs and opens his eyes.

The writer rolls over in the road with a groan and only notices the dropped book because he's lying on top of it. He grabs it from under him and pulls it away; cognizant enough to realize he should get out of the street, he crawls toward the U-Bahn entrance where the girl ran half an hour before. In the entrance, he collapses and once again passes out.

When Zan's character wakes in the morning, a couple stands over him and says something in German. The writer stares at a gentleman, in a bowler hat with an umbrella on his arm, and the woman beside him, dressed fashionably if rather in the style of Old Europe.

The German gentleman offers his hand to pull him up. Repeating something, he looks at the woman, tips his hat to the man on the ground and passes on. It's not until the writer is on his feet that he registers the book he's held all night.

He stumbles into the morning light, and the fog of pain gives way to clarity. Disoriented, he tries to think where he was last night before the attack, but as he gazes around, nothing of the cityscape is familiar even as something about the terrain is. He realizes he should be looking at the topographical scar that is Potsdamer Platz, occupying where the Wall was a few years before; but now not even an echo of the Wall can be glimpsed, there among all the antique cars that fill the road and the passersby who dress quaintly. Not until he resorts to the tradition of the unwittingly time-traveled and picks up a discarded newspaper does he realize that, somehow, he's found himself in March 1919, four months after Germany's defeat in what's still called the Great War and will be known as World War I only once history trespasses the vicinity of another, greater war.

Everyone who walks by stares at him, as much for how out of time he appears as for the dried blood on his face. He puts in his coat pocket the paperback dropped by the teenager. He's still a day or two from the revelation that this battered book, which he knows well, which all of the Twentieth Century knows, its literature having begun with this book, in fact will not be published until 1922.

At a pub off Leicester Square, Zan isn't certain whether he's allowed to take Parker and Sheba in, except that the establishment serves food and it's listed in the guide book. "Are you sure?" Parker asks in the road outside, wary, looking the pub over.

"The book doesn't say you can't go in," Zan answers.

"What's an ad-lip?" says Sheba, trying to conjure such a mutation in her head.

"Lib," says Parker. To his father, "What's so special about it anyway?"

"It was famous in the Sixties," says Zan. He opens the door of what used to be called the Ad Lib and Sheba marches in assertively though Parker hangs back. No one tells them to leave. They get a table. "A lot of famous musicians came here. Actually the club was upstairs. It's closed now."

"So now," Parker points out, "there's nothing special about it at all." Zan tries not to bore his children too much about the Sixties. His son will have none of it, and while Sheba might be more interested, and though certainly it's not impossible, Zan can't say for a fact that in his earlier career the androgynous spaceman whose music she loves ever actually was on the premises. "Stop singing," Parker mutters to his sister, whose transmission frequency this afternoon is particularly high.

"I'm not," she says.

Notwithstanding the ministrations of $3,000 dentists, Zan and Viv have given up trying to break Sheba of her thumb-sucking. Amid everything else, they've decided it's a problem that will have to resolve itself; in the meantime they've not so much learned the rule of Sheba's thumb but that there is one—such as in the way she now takes her thumb from her mouth in order to fix on what she sees outside the pub window.

Sheba has been looting her way across London all morning, from the shops of Piccadilly to Covent Garden—all of it boring for the kids because Zan can't afford to buy anything—but now a calm overtakes her so sudden and extraordinary that the father feels accosted by it. When she slightly turns in her seat, Zan turns to look as well, following the girl's line of sight; with a start, his attention is as seized as Sheba's. "What is it?" says Parker.

What appears to be a young African woman stands across the street watching Sheba back.

On her second day in Addis Ababa, after the long flight from Heathrow, Viv still isn't clear about her course of action. She's rejected any idea of going to the authorities. If the sensory bombardment of a new place hasn't so much dispelled her depression and sense of crisis as distracted from it, as well there's a new apprehension that she herself has trouble gauging in terms of what's real and what's paranoia.

The words of the last email from the investigative journalist whom she hired to find Sheba's mother— . . . *suspicions of child-trafficking . . . possibility that Zema was sold to you...difficult to be certain how seriously they take this* . . . —have gone through her head since she read them. Passing through customs at the airport, she braced herself. Checking into the hotel, again she waited for some polite invitation to a backroom from which she would never emerge. Once in her own small hotel room, she expected a knock at the door; opening her bags, she stared long and hard at the contents trying to remember exactly how she packed everything, if there's a sign of anything out of place. She goes back and forth in her mind whether it's best to keep out of sight or to keep in plain sight, and when she's in plain sight, like the lounge or bar, she pays attention to whose sight she's in, who lingers as long as she does, who leaves when she leaves.

The balcony of her room overlooks to one direction the other more upscale hotel in the distance. Its figure-eight drive circles two lush roundabouts before spilling out into a city impaled on a monumental broadcasting tower, time's antenna; around a pool in the other direction, cabana umbrellas erupt like pale blue mushrooms. They're nearly a color—a shade not quite green enough—to match Viv's hair. Contrary to western impressions of Africa as hot, Addis is misty and cool. A mile and a half up, it's closer to the sky than almost any city on earth, called by some of the locals Eucalyptopolis for the trees. Big thunderstorms roll in nightly, the clouds' percussion to the chanting that Viv hears from the mosques.

Walking through the Tukul Bar, Viv is surrounded by a hubbub of languages. Transactions are made on all sides of her, some more dubious but no less explicit than others. Her first night, an arms dealer tries to pick her up; like genies, hosts and waiters appear and retrieve wishes and disappear.

Assuming she can't locate the journalist, she decides to track down Sheba's father, aunt and grandmother. She has no idea what to make of their silence to her last message, but the implications seem more myriad than obvious.

Viv's driver takes her up Avenue Menelik II with its tree-lined promenades, past the Jubilee Palace toward the merkato, retracing the direction to the orphanage where she first came to get the girl almost two years earlier. The orphanage is a single building with three rooms, the largest including makeshift beds and cribs shared by two dozen children who range from babies to young adolescents. Each child has a single set of clothes, most have no shoes. The toddlers who haven't learned to use the bathroom wear plastic garbage bags as diapers.

There are a few isolated toys and a television that gets no reception but is connected to a DVD player. A new DVD different from the same four or five that the children watch over and over is an event at the orphanage, with all the children gathered around to watch. The food is a kind of stew that the children eat with injera, the slightly sour Ethiopian bread with a sponge-like texture that Zan never has gotten used to back in Los Angeles. On Viv's first trip to Addis, one night she took all the children out for burgers and Cokes; some got sick. Viv also brought with her antibiotics that she persuaded a number of doctors in L.A. to prescribe before she left.

There's a dirt yard where the children play during the day within a surrounding fence and gate that's manned by a guard, a quiet young man that the children love. When Sheba lived in the orphanage, in the middle of the night she crawled from her bed where two other children slept, left the building, ran on her little legs across the muddy yard through the night rain to the small outpost where the guard stayed, and slept at the orphanage gate. She would curl up on the guard's chest and sleep through the night.

When Sheba left the orphanage, the guard couldn't bring himself to say goodbye, and at first Viv felt it rude to press the matter. Twenty meters beyond the gate, however, the new mother stopped the car and led the girl by the hand to the gatehouse where the guard clutched her to him, tears in his eyes, and whispered goodbye.

On her arrival at her new home in the canyon, when Zan took the girl in his arms for the first time and lifted her from the backseat of the car, he couldn't know that, pressed against his chest, she was reminded of the guard at the orphanage. Though in Viv's absence Zan prepared the girl's room, painting it pink and yellow, those first nights she would leave the only bed she's ever had for her own to cross the house like crossing a yard of black rain, stealing to her new parents to curl in their arms like she did at the orphanage gate. Now on Viv's return to the orphanage, the young guard that was too embarrassed by his despondency at Sheba's departure remembers Viv the moment he sees her and his quiet face breaks into a smile as they embrace.

Everyone at the orphanage is happy to see Viv but no one offers answers to her questions. No one to whom she speaks will claim or confess to remembering where Sheba's father, aunt and grandmother live. The woman who runs the orphanage makes a phone call; though Viv can't be certain, since the conversation is in Amharic, she supposes it's to the administrator of the adoption agency. On hanging up, the woman tells Viv, not unsympathetically, "It all just makes trouble."

"I'm afraid the mother may already be in trouble," Viv answers. "I'm only trying to help her."

"But do you understand," the woman says, "that should you find her, she may not know of the adoption, and that while of course the adoption is legal and final, still . . . " and the rest trails off.

"Still?"

"She might want back her child."

Ever since Sheba came to be part of their family, now and then her combativeness crumbles long enough for Zan to catch her in a private moment. In such moments there is about her the palpable conviction that she'll never possess the same love of her parents that they have for her brother. That she's been passed from one party to the next out of love— from a single mother who couldn't care for her to a paternal grandmother too old, to the orphanage and then Viv and Zan—is too exquisite a thing for the child to understand, or maybe anyone; but there's no escaping how Sheba is short-changed, and it breaks Zan's heart.

The African woman standing across the road from the pub at Leicester Square wears a mix of traditional and western clothes, jeans with a shawl for her head. "Sheba?" Zan says to the girl, and though she doesn't respond, the woman looks at him as though she heard him, breaks from the girl's stare and picks up the shopping bag at her feet and walks on. Sheba doesn't move or speak but follows with her eyes the woman's retreat into the city bustle.

In the pub, one of Zan's two remaining credit cards is declined. Later that night, with the little girl snoring next to him in the double bed while Parker sleeps in a perpendicular single bed, the father goes online to check the limit on the card and finds the bank has lowered it to below what he already owes. This leaves one card left with credit. Zan monitors as well, each time with that familiar knot in his stomach that he brought with him eight thousand miles across the Atlantic, the website that posts foreclosure dates.

Zan can't risk lying in the dark thinking, because hopelessness will overcome him. To distract himself, he composes in his mind playlists for the radio show, as if Sheba could transmit them to the canyon an ocean and a continent away. After mentally compiling countless unrelieved hours of Joy Division, Nine Inch Nails, Rammstein, Celtic Frost, Cradle of Filth, Carnage, Dismember, Revolting Cocks, Dark Tranquility, Morbid Angel and Kevorkian Death Cycle, Zan dreams of rats streaming out of every crevice of the house in death-metal mode the moment the family locked the door behind them on the way to the airport. A mosh pit of revelrous rats stampedes across his imagination.

In Addis Ababa, Viv sits in the car outside the orphanage walls lost in thought, discouraged and wondering what to do next, when the young guard from the gate taps on the window. As he exchanges words with the driver, the guard peers back over his shoulder toward the walls and orphanage beyond; he motions to the driver with his hands, indicating the road ahead.

The driver turns to Viv in the backseat and says, "I can take you to the girl's family." Viv looks at the guard and says softly, "Thank you," pressing five hundred birr toward him through the window that, after a longing glance, he refuses. She gestures, insisting, but he shakes his head emphatically. The driver explains, "He wants to say he loves the little girl," and Viv nods, raising her hand to the guard in a final goodbye.

The house where Sheba spent most of the first two years of her life is two rooms, the larger one a square nine meters, the smaller one with a single cracked window, one large bed, two chairs, a tiny table and, most prominently among the belongings, an injera maker.

Sheba's father is in his thirties, maybe nearing forty in that way that's impossible to determine among Ethiopians, more than six feet tall and limping slightly from his time as a paratrooper in some Somali War or another. *Solemn tho forthcoming* Viv describes him in the last email that Zan will receive from her, *seemed at first a little awkward & I think in this male-oriented culture he feels inadequate he couldnt care for his daughter. His mother (Sh's grandmother) had 10 children, 2 died, her husband died & she had difficult time raising & feeding them,* and though Sheba's family weep to see her again, Viv can tell they're wary. There have been questions from the police about the money, and the family doesn't seem especially surprised by Viv's return. When she raises the subject of Sheba's mother, trying to explain that now she's less concerned about contacting her than helping her if she's in trouble, a heated exchange takes place between Sheba's aunt and grandmother, during which Sheba's father is even more circumspect than usual.

It's obvious to Viv that the aunt and grandmother are upset, maybe even angry. Later, as translated to Viv by the driver, the father describes Sheba's mother as beautiful and "fat"—Viv realizes after some back and forth that what the father and driver mean is voluptuous. The father and mother were together less than a year, maybe more briefly than that, when she became pregnant, and as Viv asks more questions it becomes less clear that any of them, including perhaps the father, ever met the mother's family.

The grandmother declares, through the translation by Sheba's aunt, You are her mother now, we chose you. You will make the best decision. Only at the last moment does she impart to Viv something new, which on the tape of Viv's recorder is almost impossible to hear over the rain: instructions where the driver should take her, with no indication who or what will be found there.

Zan barely can bring himself to return J. Willkie Brown's phone calls or overcome what petty satisfaction lies in making the other man call first. When they meet at a bookstore near Montague and Great Russell Street, sipping cold coffee drinks—the new London seems to have more coffee than tea now—on the afternoon of the family's fifth day in the city, Zan spends most of the first few minutes fretting over whether the young woman behind the counter neglected to decaffeinate Sheba's mocha. Maybe decaffeinated coffee, he worries, is one of those notions that Europeans find oxymoronic to the point of senseless.

It seems to Zan that Brown visibly labors not to go out of his skull at the children's very presence. Always thin with a loping gait, he's lost even more weight since Zan last saw him years ago, in a way that appears distinctly unhealthy; his once long hair is now cut short and he's as disheveled as writers are expected to be, or as disheveled as Brown expects that writers are expected to be, anyway. Appraising the kids with an affected patience, he has a voice and manner of speaking that's less bombastic than slightly and quietly superior.

Sheba gives not the slightest evidence of decaffeination. "I trust this is all right, then," Brown finally says uncomfortably, looking at the place around them; the two men shift where they sit. "Fine," says Zan. "I was going to suggest a pub we were at yesterday called the Ad Lib—or it used to be called that. I don't know what it is now."

B oth of them perpetually uneasy, Brown nods, musing, "Swinging London. Sixties landmark," he remarks to Parker sitting in the next chair. "The upstairs part, actually."

Parker tries to be polite about it. "My dad said."

"Dawn of Man as far as they're concerned," says Zan.

"How is Viv?" asks Brown. Good for you, thinks Zan: *Let's get to the elephant in the room.* "She's fine," he answers. "Parker, you think you can keep an eye on her?" Sheba is starting to gyrate; soon she'll be toppling glass cases of rare Eighteenth Century manuscripts.

"Why me?" Parker protests.

"Still at it with the photography, the art . . . " says Brown.

"Sorry?" says Zan.

"Viv. The art. . . . "

"Yes."

"Heard about the great scandal, of course. Arsehole."

Z an says, "What?" For a moment he thinks J. Willkie Brown is slipping insults into the conversation, like the bank officials on the telephone.

"He's an arsehole," says Brown, "everyone knows he's a plagiarist. You should sue him."

"Oh," Zan answers, "yes. We would if he could afford to."

"Surely there's a solicitor who would take it on, contingent on the outcome? Of course it's a hard thing to prove, plagiarism. Nothing's original, I suppose."

"No, nothing's original," Zan says, "but this comes damned close. Stained-glass windows recreated in butterfly wings? There's not a single documented example of anyone doing that before Viv."

"Well there you are."

B rown says, "Off to Africa, then, is she?" watching Sheba and appearing to become even more nervous than her father.

"It's complicated. I . . . " Zan glances at the girl, " . . . should explain another time."

"Right," says Brown. "But I trust she'll be back before the lecture next week." Discernible in his eyes are images of Sheba amok on the university grounds.

"I hope so, for all kinds of reasons. Mainly I'm worried about her."

"Viv always was resilient," Brown shrugs.

He's trying to be reassuring but Zan doesn't need any reminder of how well Brown knows Viv or whatever way it is he thinks he knows her. "She gets lost," Zan says, "she has no sense of direction."

"Mount Kilimanjaro and all that, as I remember."

"Mount Kilimanjaro is *up*," Zan points out, "that direction she's mastered. Most people would have taken the Mount Kilimanjaro experience as a warning, given that she missed the only flight out that week. Viv took it as a lifetime Get Out of Insane Situations Free card. Except when she's being a mom and worrying the kids are going to drink the Drano. Listen, James," Zan announces somberly, "here it is in a nutshell: I'm the family's sanest person. Do you understand? Can you wrap your head around the implications of that? Can you envision the . . . the . . . state of general derangement this portends? *I'm the most stable member of the family.* That's like Ahab being the captain of a Carnival Cruise line. Sheer dementedness increases in direct proportion to the decrease in physical size, until you wind up with the world's worst dog, who finally breached an electric fence for the sheer thrill of it, like someone tasering himself."

Brown says, "I'm certain you'll hear from her soon," which is curious, since Zan hasn't actually said anything about *not* hearing from her. Brown clasps his hands together and rubs them, torturing the empty space between his palms. "Hotel is satisfactory, I trust."

"Sure," says Zan.

"Working on anything these days?"

"Uh . . . "

Brown can't be certain what this means, since Zan isn't either, but replies, "A novel, I presume?"

"Yes."

"Brilliant. It's been a while, hasn't it? Since the last."

"Yes," says Zan, "and you?" changing the subject: *Let's talk about what you really want to talk about.* "Still the journalism, of course."

"Yes," Brown says, "a proper piece about the impact that torture at Guantanamo has had on the Muslim world. The waterboarding, sexual humiliation. All that."

Zan struggles to suppress a nationalist impulse, though not as much as the impulse to puncture what he regards as the other's pomposity. "The president signed an order," he says.

"Oh well, then, right," Brown answers, "it's all sorted."

"I think an order against waterboarding is a good thing, James."

"Yes, though he won't let us see any photos, will he? The sexual humiliation, none of that."

More fed up than he expected, Zan looks at the kids. "That's not torture," he says, surprising himself.

"No?" says Brown.

"Tawdry, stupid, puerile, counter-productive. Pick one or all of them, but not torture."

"Really?" not actually said as a question.

What is it about the fucking British? Zan seethes, mostly at himself for being baited into this. Politely hostile. Gracefully aggressive. Zan says, "Torture is fear of death—like waterboarding, thinking you're going to drown. Infliction of pain. Drilling someone's teeth like that movie where Laurence Olivier is a Nazi"—he goes for the British actor, of course—"pulling out fingernails, hanging by eyelids on meat hooks. Being tied to a chair and made to watch a naked woman? You pay money for that in Vegas."

"I see," says Brown. What happened to the trusty silence into which Zan reliably falls when confronted by the indignation of others? It's like the woman on the plane berating him for irresponsibility; suddenly he's surrounded by people whose politics take on the tone of personal accusation. Or is it just a sign of Zan's newly less-than-robust objectivity about things concerning the new president, a deeply dangerous protectiveness? In his own way, has he gone off the rails about his country no less than everyone else?

Zan rises from his seat. "Abdul," he continues, "probably goes back to jail afterward and all the jihadists have a good laugh about it. Parker, are you watching her?" he barks at his son, gazing about a bit madly for his daughter only to realize she's at his feet, staring up at him. Neither child says anything, watching their father intently; Zan is aware he's slipping into a rant. "Gets back to his cell and it's, you know, 'Feature this, guys, they *tortured* me with the naked woman today!' A routine, like Br'er Rabbit and the briar patch. 'Oh no, whatever you do, not the naked woman! I might tell you anything if you make me watch the naked woman!'" He looks at the kids and it's clear that, while slightly scandalized, they find this the most interesting thing their father has said in years.

Brown peers up at him from where he sits. "Of course," he ventures calmly, "given the attitudes some of these men are raised with about such things, it *is* torture, isn't it."

"Sincerely," Zan says, "maybe that says more about some fucked-up attitudes about women and sex than it does about what can objectively be called torture." He's abashed at his lapse. "Sorry," he snaps at the kids, "you know you're not supposed to say that word."

"Sex?" says Parker.

"The other one."

"Fucked-up," volunteers Sheba.

"We've heard you say that before," Parker observes.

"You say it all the fucked-up time," Sheba agrees.

"Thank you, children," says Zan, "for that authoritative consensus. Sheba, don't say it again." He sighs. "The waterboarding was horrific," he quietly gathers their things, "a disgrace to everything we're supposed to stand for. Let's leave it at that. Listen," he says, uncertain if he's disappointed in himself or has discovered something new, "I've got to get them back . . . "

"We'll carry on next week," says the other man, "catch the train out to the college together, if that's agreeable."

"How far is it?"

"Twenty minutes from Waterloo. Longer if we miss the express."

"James," Zan says, "if Viv isn't back by then, I may need to line up a nanny of some sort. Sorry, I know this isn't what you signed up for. It's not what I had in mind either."

Images of Sheba's havoc receding in his eyes, Brown emanates unmistakable relief. "I'll look into it," he says.

Zan writes to Viv as breezy an email as he can muster, though he doesn't do breezy in even the breeziest of circumstances. He writes about the city, kids, what they've been doing, concluding, *Assume you're not returning to London w/in nxt 48 hrs so looking into childcare prospects for when residency begins next week.*

When there's no answer, Zan sends another email, then phones Viv on her cell, though he knows she has no connection where she is. He phones the Ghion Hotel in Addis Ababa. The weekend passes; Zan, Parker and Sheba spend Saturday afternoon at Leicester Square eating a surprisingly excellent pizza and poking around an old-fashioned Covent Garden toy shop where the manager—a young guy from Vermont who wants to be a fantasy writer and has been in England long enough to pick up an accent—plays with the kids a game involving small toy creatures locked in epic battles. Sheba keeps knocking over the creatures she isn't supposed to, to her brother's growing rage.

Parker is so enthralled with the game that Zan can't resist paying £80 for it that they can't afford. Back in the room, the boy puts on hold the pending fourth issue of *Shrimpy Comix* to spend the night gluing little creatures and painting them; for Sheba, Zan buys a smaller preassembled set that she complains is smaller than Parker's and preassembled. The only thing the father can find on the hotel television is news.

When he goes online and learns the house has been scheduled for foreclosure in three weeks, only then does he realize how numb to everything he's become.

Foolishly, Zan convinced himself the bank forgot them. Now he imagines them all stranded in London, with nowhere to return. In the background on the television, the BBC reports that back home a bizarre new phenomenon has taken hold by which some segments of the public suggest the president is an impostor. They contend he was born in a secret african veldt and, as a newborn, smuggled into the country under the cover of a false birth certificate and false birth announcement in a hawaiian newspaper so that forty-seven years later he could seize the presidency. Some propose that this is God's warning of the end of time.

For a while Zan half listens to a woman in South Dakota who's interviewed about the pending Rapture and end of the world. What finally gets his full attention is her glee, which isn't so much about going to heaven as it is about everyone who will be left behind; finally this woman will be superior to all the smart-alecks on television and those in their high stations who thought they were superior to her. The End Time constitutes its own kind of revolutionary politics. The woman counts down the hours until she'll get to see the looks on the faces of the secular elite as she ascends and they're below with the flames licking their feet. Among the crosses and pictures of Jesus is an image of the president as something not unlike a creature that Parker glues and paints at this moment; underneath the image is the word ANTICHRIST. "Is he a spaceman?" Sheba cries enthusiastically.

Of course Zan and Viv have told their son and daughter nothing about their financial problems and, as with the Talk, Zan suspects they don't need to. He's insisted to Parker that things are all right and feels certain the boy isn't having it, has picked up on too many signs. Zan is meditating on a house lost to the bank and rats, being in a foreign country with two kids and credit cards that don't work and a missing wife and no babysitter that he can't afford anyway, when there comes a knock on the hotel room door, unheard at first over the clap of thunder outside. "Sheba," he warns uselessly for the hundredth time in both their lives, "don't answer without knowing who it is," as she bolts for the door, for the hundredth time ignoring him. "Who is it?" Zan says, but when the girl stands in the open doorway transfixed and unanswering, he knows.

On the afternoon forty years ago when he was a university freshman and went to see the small frail man running for president, Zan got close to where he stood just as the moment exploded, the event spilling beyond the bounds of control. The thing that was bigger than everyone, candidate and crowd alike, took over, and the frenzy that this man incited in the crowd lifted Zan off his feet, catching him in the undertow. When it threatened to pull him down where he would be crushed, trampled or both, a young female black hand reached to Zan from the sky and he took it.

An aide to the candidate, she discarded her clipboard, grabbed his arm with her other hand and pulled him from the crowd. He saw the young woman's face only half a minute, maybe less, long enough to register her eyes so gray as to be a glint short of silver, before the candidate's bodyguards removed him and deposited him back at the crowd's edge.

The woman wasn't much older than Zan, four or five years, and wore dreadlocks that weren't particularly typical yet in the late Sixties. She smiled at him but her gray eyes didn't smile with her mouth; in her eyes were fear and the anticipation of the unspeakable thing that was on everyone's mind. As she pulled him to safety, she leaned over and whispered in his ear a single word.

The following summer, Zan had a job delivering pizzas in his father's car. This was when the valley at night just north of Hollywood was still a crater of caves, except the caves weren't in hills but in the night-air and you could drive in one and emerge somewhere else. One evening an order was called in from one of the dorms at the same local college where Zan would teach more than thirty years later. As Zan parked the car, someone sang on the radio *and Ray Charles was shot down, but got up to do his best* and Zan pulled the portable pizza oven from the front seat and strolled into the dorm to find himself the only white boy in sight.

While the front desk called up to the room, Zan waited in the lobby, a dozen black faces studying him intently. One very stoned kid staggered up and peered into Zan's eyes like they were an astronomer's telescope trained on cosmic emptiness; he asked something that Zan didn't understand and, before Zan could answer, drew back his arm like a slingshot and let go, bringing his hand across Zan's face.

Zan reeled. The guy hit him again and then again. Later Zan would wonder if it was to his credit or something less admirable that he never had to suppress an instinct to strike back; in any event he was rational enough to know it wasn't a good option. He felt more humiliation than pain or anger, which was the point, of course. As calmly as possible he leaned over, picked up the oven from the floor and walked from the lobby, back out the front door of the dorm with whatever dignity he could manage, which in this case meant not breaking into an all-out sprint.

He almost reached his car when he heard the footsteps behind him. Years later, the middle-aged L.A. writer in Zan's new novel will hear in the Berlin street footsteps much like these, preceding his doom. At last Zan was angry enough to turn and find himself confronted by a group larger than the one in Berlin but smaller than the one in the dorm lobby.

About half a dozen of the dorm's residents, all black, had with them in some kind of vague captivity the guy who hit Zan. "Tell him," one of them commanded. Weaving where he stood, too stoned to make sense, the assailant mumbled, "Sorry."

"He's sorry," the other student translated to Zan.

"O.K.," said Zan.

"Don't call the police."

"O.K."

"Promise not to call the police."

"I'm not calling the police. I *am*," Zan pointed at the dorm in the distance, "going back inside and selling this person her pizza."

Back at the pizza joint, the indignant Cuban owner reached for the phone to call the police. "Don't," said the eighteen-year-old.

"Bullshit," said the owner.

"I told them we wouldn't."

"Why?"

"The San Fernando Valley Riots, over a pizza? I'm O.K." Reluctantly the Cuban put the phone back in the cradle. No further deliveries, however, were made to the dormitory. Two decades later there would be a famous movie by a black film-maker about a pizza place at the center of a riot in Brooklyn one hot summer night. When Zan sees it, he'll wonder if he thwarted history just long enough for someone else to make it up.

For a long time after the pizza incident, Zan told no one about it. He certainly didn't tell his parents. Finally he wrote about it, showing what he wrote only to Logan Hale, who remarked on the young man's detachment. "You were *mugged*," Hale exhorted him, "you have a right to be enraged," but the rage never came. For the most part Zan forgot about it, only for the memory to surface again years later still shorn of fury, as far as he can tell.

The day after she visits Sheba's family, the driver takes Viv deeper into the city than she's been. The Entoto Hills loom to the north. Taxis blue and white like the umbrellas around the hotel pool fill the roads, and a plume of smoke rises from the Meskel Square where Viv sees a burning pyramid. They've been driving half an hour when they park the car in a neighborhood at the city's center. The driver leads Viv by foot down a series of winding, narrow stone steps into a labyrinth of tunnels and bridges, lined by high walls covered with moss, to the deepest root of the eucalyptopolis.

A sirocco blows in from the moon. Viv hears the mournful songs of the nearby mosques. As the woman with the turquoise hair follows the driver, watched by Ethiopians in the distance, the walls of the passages resonate with distant chants and the thunder of a gathering storm.

To the south, Viv glimpses an ancient underground church carved from rock, bubbling up out of an earth radiant with three thousand millennia, the oldest place that human-time remembers, barely. Around her, she feels the monsoon of the storm above and the Nile-saturated ground below yearn for each other; the woman and driver pass inviolate stone corners still smelling of the mustard gas with which Mussolini's army massacred a million Ethiopians seventy years ago. The passage is crisscrossed by alleys where people in white gauze float in and out of the shadows.

The trip is so clandestine and mysterious that it can't help seeming as though Sheba's mother should be waiting at the end of wherever it leads; but finally Viv stops the driver. "No," she says, "this isn't right," and looks over her shoulder behind her, with no idea where she's come from.

S tanding in the doorway of the Bloomsbury hotel room, the young African woman wears across her shoulders the same scarf that covered her head when they first saw her yesterday outside the pub. Otherwise, the jeans make her look like any contemporary western woman. "Hello," says Zan.

"Hello," the young woman nods, "I'm Molly," pulling the scarf from her shoulders and rolling it and slipping it into the bag she carries under one arm. "I understand you are looking for a caretaker for the children."

Startled, Zan says, "Come in." Sheba has said nothing, the young woman locked in her focus, but now blurts, "Have you ever had any little girls in your tummy?"

"I think she wants to know," says Zan, "if you have children of your own. A daughter she can be friends with, maybe," but he's not sure that's what Sheba really means. "Sheba, go play with Parker," he says.

Still gluing and painting his creatures they bought in Covent Garden, Parker says, "She can't play what I'm playing." Sheba starts to cry; Zan closes his eyes. It occurs to him maybe Viv is right and the young African woman might be offended by the name Sheba. Would they call an adopted Mexican child Montezuma? "Parker," Zan says as calmly as he can, "help me out. Do something your sister can too, or find something on TV."

Molly kneels to Sheba's level and says to the girl, "Let me talk with your father a moment, all right? Then perhaps you and I will play." She rises and turns to Zan as the girl backs away still watching the woman. "I apologize for the intrusion of coming to the room. I tried to ring you earlier from where I'm staying but no one answered, and I don't have a mobile."

Like many of the small hotels in the area, this one has no telephones in the room, so Zan can't be sure whether Molly means that she called the front desk downstairs or tried his cell, which hasn't rung at all and which she wouldn't have the number for anyway. While Parker was in the room gluing and painting, there was half an hour when Zan took Sheba to the little market around the corner, darting in and out of the rain, then down the street for a sandwich and the English butter cookies with which both of them have become mildly obsessed. At a newsstand, Zan bought a copy of a British music magazine with Sheba's favorite artist on the cover, a retrospective. There was a call earlier on Zan's cell from J. Willkie Brown that Zan didn't answer and hasn't returned.

A small table huddles in the corner of the room and Zan and the young woman sit down at it. On the table is a small pot for hot water and a small selection of teas. "Operative word, obviously," Zan waves at the room, "is small."

"Of course," she smiles.

"Sheba and I sleep in the big bed," he says, "and Parker has the small one. She hasn't gotten to the point yet where she wants to sleep alone."

"But she will," Molly says.

"I keep reminding my wife that Parker was the same when he was younger. Never wanted to fall asleep alone. Then one night when he was nine or ten," Zan snaps his fingers, "not only does he want to sleep alone, he barely wants his parents in the same house." Zan is more rattled than he realizes by the news of the foreclosure. "Have you been in London long? I'm sorry," he stops himself, "I shouldn't assume—"

"No," she says, "you're quite correct, I am not from London." She cocks her head in thought. "I've been here . . . a short time."

"Your English is excellent," says Zan. "I hope that's all right to say."

Her accent is indeterminate—a bit British, a bit the singsong precision of an English by way of Africa, maybe a bit something harder, from some other corner of the world. "Thank you," she says. "My mother spoke

English so that's what I spoke before I moved to Addis Ababa ten years ago."

"Are you Ethiopian?" Zan says. He's not sure how disquieted he is by this.

"Half," she says. "My mother was born there but came to London as a small girl and grew up here."

"And your father?"

"He may have been British but . . . it is not as clear."

"Sorry to pry."

"It's all right."

"You grew up in England then. I didn't think 'Molly' sounded African."

"Actually I was born and raised in Germany. In Berlin."

Over these few minutes the room has gradually, at first imperceptibly, filled with sound, as though frequencies are crossing, catching half a dozen musics from anywhere and everywhere. Zan still isn't clear on the woman's genealogy but says, "What are you doing here?" which doesn't come out the way he intends. "I mean, in London."

"So far I have been taking care of children," indicating Parker and Zan, "sometimes I clean houses . . . " She shrugs. "I do what I need to and what I can."

"Seriously, jerkwad?" Parker says to his sister. "I just spent like twelve hours gluing that! You don't even know how to play this game."

"Poppy!" Sheba wails.

Zan says, "Parker, I asked you to—"

"There's nothing I want to do or watch or play with her," Parker answers.

Zan indicates to Molly the hotel television. "It only gets half a dozen channels and nothing the kids care about."

"I am certain it must be difficult for them in a strange country," she says.

"I think they're liking it," though he doesn't really think so at all.

"Not the dark place with the dummies or the place where the heads are cut off," says Sheba.

"Very civilized children, then," she jokes. "I have never been to your country," she adds, "but my mother lived there, in the late Sixties and much of the Seventies, after leaving England."

"Really?" says Zan. "Where?"

"Around and about. Mostly in Los Angeles."

"That's where we're from."

"Yes," she smiles, "I know."

"Where's your mother now?"

"She is no longer alive."

"I'm sorry."

"It happened long ago. I would like," she says, "to go to your country someday. Especially now. Now it must be a very exciting place."

The weather outside has cleared and Zan suggests a walk. The four circle the small park across the street from the hotel, which is part of a crescent of small hotels. "It's hard getting them out of the room," Zan explains to Molly; they all sit on a bench, Parker and Sheba fighting over a Game Boy. Zan says, "Let's do this. I'm taking the children with me to the university tomorrow. James is going with us. Why don't you come as well? See how it goes."

"She's going through your purse," Parker says to Molly about Sheba. Molly ignores it. "James?" she says to Zan.

"Sorry," Zan scoffs, "Mister J. Willkie Brown, as he prefers the world to know him. Of course I'll pay you for the time. What's your rate?"

"What do you think is fair?" she says.

He tries to calculate currency exchange. "Ten pounds an hour?" It's more than he can afford—these days anything is more than he can afford—but he doesn't want to be the foreigner exploiting a black woman in her country, or more her country than his, anyway.

Parker says to Molly, "She'll break that camera." Sheba looks at her brother and draws a finger across her throat. "Sheba," Zan says to the girl, who's pulled a small camera from Molly's purse, "that's not yours."

"I don't mind," says Molly.

"Thank you, that's nice of you," Zan says, "but she can't think it's O.K. to go through other people's things."

"She broke Viv's camera," says Parker.

"SHUT UP, PARKER!" Sheba says.

"Mom was pissed off," says the boy. He adds, "That's a really old-school camera." This is the first time Zan has heard his son say "pissed." Also, if he had nothing else to think about, he would monitor the occasions when Viv is "Mom" and when Zan is "Dad"—an excavation of Parker's references and forms of address. Sheba attacks the button on the camera. "Stop it," Zan says and takes the camera, handing it to Molly. "It's an old-school camera," Sheba says, mimicking her brother.

"I have had it since I was a little girl," says Molly, "about your age." Parker is trying to fathom cameras existing that far back in time. "It's a ghost camera," Molly smiles, bending down to Sheba. "Oooh."

"That's not scary," the four-year-old informs the woman. "What's a ghost camera?"

"It means," says the woman, leaning into her explanation to make it sound as mysterious as possible, "that sometimes you take a picture but a minute later when you pull out the film, it has disappeared."

"I think," Parker says, "that's another name for a camera that doesn't work."

Z an shoots his son a look. "I'll phone you tonight," he says to the woman, "and we'll make tomorrow's arrangements."

"I'm afraid I don't have a mobile," says Molly.

"Of course. You said."

"I assume you take the train from Waterloo Station."

"I think that's right."

"Shall I come by the hotel or meet you at Waterloo then?"

"You suck," Parker says to Sheba.

"I hate you!" Sheba answers before turning her attention back to Molly. Zan says wearily to the woman, "At eleven at Waterloo," instead of what he was about to say, which was, I'm sure the kids are going to love you.

A s Molly disappears down the road from Cartwright Gardens, Sheba watches her as intently as she did from the pub window. Zan waits to see if the woman looks back and convinces himself that at one point she's paused, for the slightest of moments, summoning the will to stare straight ahead.

She's pretty, more round than heavy, and has some of the extraterrestrial features of Ethiopians. She doesn't look anything like Sheba who, Zan remembers, takes after her handsome father. Perhaps the very strange thought that will grow stranger and bigger in his head never would have occurred to him if he and the children hadn't seen her outside the pub, returning the girl's watch with her own, or if she hadn't told him where she was born. "Good lord," he can hear Viv exclaiming in front of the laptop a few weeks ago, staring at her email. "Czechoslovakia or Poland or Germany?"

All of his life Zan has made an aesthetic out of coincidence. In part it's the very unlikeliness of this young woman, who's not quite here and not quite there, not quite this and not quite that, that makes what Zan thinks and feels not only possible to him but nearly inescapable. It would be so utterly in keeping with the late tenor of their lives, with the way the stars have aligned so mischievously since Sheba's arrival, with the feeling that these last two years the universe has been putting them to a test, setting Viv off on some misbegotten journey to find an answer that in fact finds them. But more than anything, what keeps yanking Zan back from both sleep and reason that night, as his mind struggles to find both, is the music that Molly made when she came in the room. As when Sheba arrived in the canyon, the woman was filled with songs, snatches of them, few belonging to her—as if any music belongs to anyone—with the room turned into a receiver, tuned between stations, Sheba at one end of the dial and Molly at the other.

The lead character in Zan's novel still doesn't have a name. Almost in petulance but hardly to be mysterious, Zan marks the character with an X, as though he's a spot on a map. If Zan were writing with a quill, he imagines slashing the parchment.

Having been pummeled and beaten nearly eighty years into the past to the spring of 1919, X manages to get himself a tiny cabin on a cross-Atlantic ocean liner sailing from Le Havre to New York. His only company is the battered paperback copy, mysteriously dropped by his body, of a novel that won't be published for another three years.

There are amenities of the future that X misses—music, most of all—but otherwise he feels little sense of loss. Halfway in his voyage, at the longitude of thirty-three and a third, he wanders the decks of the ship, mulling how whatever chance he ever had of becoming a great novelist in the Nineties now is gone, when the epiphany hits him.

He stares at the paperback and rushes back to his cabin where, at a small table before the porthole, he begins to copy the words in his own hand (oh yes, definitely his own hand). When the ship's captain lends him a typewriter, X calculates that if he copies even just five pages a day, he'll finish by the fall, more than two years before the book is published.

It doesn't take long for X to realize, of course, that once he finishes this book, the entire future of Twentieth Century literature—from massive tomes about tubercular patients in German mountaintop sanatoria before World War I to gripping epics of the Spanish Civil War, with Gary Cooperish saboteurs boinking seductive latina guerrillas—is at his fingertips, waiting to be rewritten. He lies in his bunk at night staring at the dark ceiling, listening to the waves outside the portal crash against the ship: *I will be the greatest genius of all time.*

"The Novel," Zan begins his address to the University of London seminar, "as a Literary Form Facing Obsolescence in the Twenty-First Century. Or, the Evolution of History to Pure Fiction, which at least is where we'll begin. The novel is born in a series of rewrites," and behind him is a blowup of the image from the television report of the new president with the word ANTICHRIST underneath. The university must already want back its £3,500, Zan wonders soberly; he looks out at sixty or seventy students not including Parker, for whom spending time with his sister has become so unacceptable that he prefers listening to his father's drone. Somewhere outside the hall, Zan hears a shriek that he knows is Sheba, somewhere else in the building with the new nanny. Parker looks toward the sound too, then at Zan, where son and father catch each other's eye and the boy smiles.

A series of rewrites, says Zan, "of a single story written nearly a century if not more after the life of the man who inspired the narrative, and titled according to authors who almost certainly didn't write them. In other words they're noms de plume—'Matthew,' 'Mark,' 'Luke,' 'John,' to put them in their later order."

The thing is, Zan explains, the original narrative wasn't Matthew's but Mark's. "Mark's was the first version written," says Zan, "certainly the most straightforward," referring only obliquely when at all to what later became basic tenets about the protagonist's divinity. The climax of the story, the protagonist becoming undead—"forerunner of the current zombie phenomenon in fiction," points out Zan—is underwhelming compared to later versions. The executed man's mother goes to the tomb, finds the stone rolled aside from the entrance, her son's body gone. A stranger is there in his place. "He's, uh, just *gone*," the stranger says, ending the story on a note as modern as it is enigmatic.

The historian Mark doesn't speculate much, reports facts as best as he can determine them. Along comes Matthew, who rewrites Mark's version, speculating perhaps wildly.

The history becomes historical novel. Facts are orchestrated to suggest a conclusion as to what the facts mean. This version of the story attracts a following—not the last time a science-fiction writer starts a cult—and Mark's history is demoted to supplemental text. Matthew's more lyrical version is elevated to a place implying something authoritative. Of course this doesn't stop other competing revisions, not to mention time-honored squabbles over originality and who's derivative of whom.

"Luke" rewrites Matthew. Then "John" rewrites all of them. "With John's version," Zan says, "we witness the advent of the experimental novel," more impressionistic, less concerned with narrative, a new kind of novel in which history recedes and defers to a "truth" bigger than mere facts can capture. The protagonist virtually disappears. When he does appear, he's a more dramatic figure; he doesn't simper with compassion, sorrow, *mercy*, "he doesn't wallow," says Zan, "among lowlifes and deviants with innocuous promises of love, charity. He's a *hero* not a mere protagonist, with new fire and fury. He's newly distinguished by the animating power of hate and judgment."

The audience in the hall stares back at Zan dazed, but only one or two have left. Parker slumps in his seat, arms folded across the chest, in a perfected pose of boredom; but Zan can see the boy watching his father, surreptitiously.

Afterward some of the students from the audience invite Zan to a local pub on the edge of the university. Zan and Parker find Sheba and her new nanny in the college cafeteria where, in the corner, the girl's attention has been successfully engaged by a stack of children's books. Molly doesn't look so good to Zan—exhausted or ill: We've burned her out in less than twenty-four hours, he thinks; except that Sheba may be the quietest her father has seen her short of unconsciousness.

The university isn't ye olde English campus of Zan's fantasies, with rolling knolls and cobblestone walls veined with ivy. It has an industrial look about it, though the walk to the pub is more like it, through a forest of hazy trees like crucified green clouds. Almost demurely Sheba follows with one hand clutching Molly's.

The small crowd chitchats, some with Zan, who barely can think after the lecture. At the pub he craves a shot of tequila but settles for vodka, not wanting to embarrass anyone with presumptuously exotic requests. "Right, then," says J. Willkie Brown, setting the vodka on the table between them in one of the pub's back rooms. Zan isn't inclined to ask Brown his opinion of the lecture; he would be genuinely unconcerned if he weren't being paid £3,500. Brown says, "What's next?"

Z an says, "Well, we wait for Viv to come back from Addis Ababa." To his surprise, he has to suppress an impulse to tell Brown about the foreclosure.

"Yes, of course," says Brown, "any news on that front?"

Zan chews his lower lip. "No."

"Hmm," Brown just nods. Off in the area of the bar, Zan can see Molly getting Parker a Coke and Sheba a Sprite; the boy is trying not to get talked to by some of the students while Sheba reverts to form, climbing on things. "A bit of a hand-ful, aren't they?" He tries his best to sound good-humored about it.

"This is nothing," Zan says. "Peace in our time, to quote a British prime minister. It's like the nanny has cast a spell on Sheba."

"I see. So what's it all about?"

"The nanny?"

"Viv in Africa."

Zan looks at Sheba, out of earshot. "Her mother," he answers, nodding at the girl. "I mean her birth-mother."

"I thought she was an orphan."

"Well, James, orphans have mothers. They're just not moth-ers who are in the picture anymore."

Brown says, "But this one is in the picture now, I take it?" "It's not that she's in the picture," says Zan, "it's the way she's *not* in the picture."

Brown shakes his head and shrugs.

"We've been trying to find out about the mother for a while." Zan glances back at the girl. "Someday she'll want to know. She'll be angry if we never tried to find out. She'll be angry at us anyway about one thing or another, about all kinds of things, but this one she'll have a right to be angry about. A couple of months ago Viv got a journalist in Addis on the trail, he asked some questions, and now there are these . . . well, they're not even *reports*, they're too undefined to be reports, they're rumors . . . or what have you . . . that this journalist Viv hired was getting close to some discovery about the mother and, in asking all kinds of questions, something happened to her. She's in jail. She's in hiding. She's fled the country. She's dead." He looks at Molly. "Listen, what do you know about—?"

"Another drink?" asks Brown.

Zan realizes he's downed the one hand he has. "O.K.," he says, pulling some money from his pocket, "let me—"

"Don't be bloody silly." The Englishman gets up to get another drink. Zan continues watching Molly and Sheba, calls over the waitress and orders fish and chips for the kids. When Brown returns, Zan says, "The kids like your fish and chips."

"Hmm," says Brown.

"Thanks for the drink," says Zan.

Fortified, not that Brown necessarily needs it but he supposes Zan does, the Englishman says, "The flaw with your lecture, of course . . . " He pauses to see how this beginning registers; Zan raises an eyebrow and Brown continues, " . . . the flaw is that it presumes there's a history at all, doesn't it? I mean the whole original business, Jesus and God and all that. Hardly the stuff of history, is it?"

"How do we know?" says Zan.

"But you don't mean you believe in God?" says Brown.

Zan makes a show of pondering this as though he never has before. "Fifty-one days out of a hundred."

"What kind of faith is that?"

"The best I can manage. Whether anyone calls it *faith* or not, I don't much care."

"But why bother to believe at all?"

"Because it's not a matter of whether I can be bothered, it's a matter of what I do. Believe, I mean."

"Are you certain?" Brown says. "I mean, people who believe do so because they rather want or need to, don't they?"

"Well, a lot do. Maybe most. But no more so than those who don't believe."

"How's that?"

"Not believing because you need not to, no less so than the person who does."

B rown shakes his head. "Not following."

"Sure you are." Everyone picks arguments with me these days! thinks Zan.

"I don't believe because there's no intelligent reason to."

"Horseshit."

"You've become rather more forceful than when I used to know you, Alexander. Rather more talkative."

"So everyone tells me lately. Maybe I always think I'm on the radio."

"Or the vodka perhaps."

"Probably."

"But that doesn't mean that what you say makes more sense, does it?"

"Listen, if you're being purely rational about it, then agnosticism is the only stance that has any logic to it. The atheist is just another kind of zealot. You're zealous in your non-belief but the zealotry is no different from the zealotry of faith."

"But how can you believe in God?"

"Fifty-one days out of a hundred . . . "

"Explain to me *one* day out of a hundred."

"Who cares?"

"Meaning you can't answer, can you?"

"Meaning do you care."

"I'm positively riveted."

"Because it makes more sense to me," says Zan.

"God makes more sense?"

Zan explains, or tries to, and Brown does him the courtesy of appearing to be absorbed if in no way persuaded. "Right, then," he says, with a small gesture of his hand, "so why not a hundred days out of a hundred?"

"I'm scandinavian," Zan explains. "We don't do joy."

On his third vodka Zan muses out loud, "Ronnie Jack Flowers."

Brown makes that little gesture with his hand again. "Don't know him."

"*I* knew him," Zan says, "twenty, twenty-five years—"

"Are you all right?" Brown interjects.

"Why? Don't I seem all right?"

"Oh, certainly."

"Do I seem drunk?"

"Not necessarily. But then I'm not sure I would know, would I? With you, I mean."

"Twenty, twenty-five years ago . . . "

"Ronnie Joe . . . "

"Ronnie Jack. Black, hard-left politically. Radical politics in the Sixties, militant . . . "

"Panthers, then."

"I don't know. Maybe. But armed resistance, anyway, up against the wall, all that. I think I *am* a bit drunk." Zan holds his head a moment. Because he's prone to migraines, it's normal that with the first sip of liquor his head begins throbbing. "But when I knew him, like everyone in the Eighties, he had left the Sixties behind."

It was a common story in the Eighties, of course—former Sixties radicals in the mainstream, doing well. Ronnie Jack loved the best clothes, the best cars, the best stereo equipment, good food, beautiful women—the Stalinist from *Esquire*, still talking left "and I mean left," says Zan, "I don't mean New Left, I mean Marxist-Leninist left," which seemed quaint even with the Cold War still going on. Ronnie Jack took the goodwill trips to the Soviet Union and considered the people there to "have it pretty good," in his words; and if, as Zan did once or twice, the contradiction was noted between Ronnie's politics and the high life he lived, Ronnie would answer, I just think *everyone* should have the best clothes and best cars and best stereo equipment and beautiful women.

Zan and Ronnie Jack worked in the same building, where the former wrote for a travel magazine and the latter was in the public relations department of an insurance firm. They met through Jenna, a Stalinist that Zan was dating and with whom Ronnie Jack—more the ladies' man than Zan ever was—had gotten nowhere. "Wait," Brown says now, "you were dating a Stalinist?"

What can Zan say? She was a hot Stalinist. Brown hair, brown eyes, the smile and body of an italian starlet. "But didn't the fact," says Brown, "that she was a Stalinist . . . ?"

"Oh, of course," scoffs Zan. "But you know, I convinced myself it was somehow no different than one of us being a Republican and the other a Democrat, and particularly since I was neither, I thought we just wouldn't talk politics. What I didn't know is that if you're a Stalinist, there's *nothing* that isn't political." Jenna literally was a card-carrying member of the Party even if Zan never saw the card; and he was so fraught to sleep with her that he went to a couple of meetings, where everyone was ancient, the median age well over seventy—so it became obvious what the Party saw in Jenna, which was the same thing Zan saw: a sexy young woman in her mid-twenties, putting a beautiful and glamorous face on the movement.

After that, it became difficult for Zan to take seriously certain national paranoias. The idea that these codgers were going to take over the country, that the country had to be on its guard against them every moment, was laughable, not only because they were feeble in body but because among them there wasn't a single independent thought. If, for instance, in the course of one of Jenna's monologues about fascism it was pointed out that Stalin and Hitler had a pact, Jenna denied it ever happened, insisting it was a creation of an elitist media—something Zan hears back home now, where no compass is consulted in common, where the designation of north is considered by some a state plot, where facts and information are the coordinates of suspect maps, where people who actually *know* things are the enemies of "common sense." Soon sex with Jenna wasn't worth it anymore, not least because sexual licentiousness was yet another myth about a doctrinaire Left that in fact regarded eroticism as decadence, a mass social opiate like religion. She was the single most repressed woman he ever knew.

What survived Zan's affair with Jenna, at least for a while, was a friendship with her comrade if not lover Ronnie Jack. Perhaps the fact that neither man was sleeping with Jenna provided a bond. Then Zan got fired from the travel magazine for "insubordination" and being a "disruptive influence," the last time until lately that he was considered by anyone as volatile, and which he took as a sign to finish what still could be called his most recent novel—"most recent!" Zan laughs to Brown. "That makes it sound, well, fucking *recent*, doesn't it?" In the novel was a very small character, a few paragraphs in a single chapter, based on Ronnie. Zan changed a detail or two but not, as it turned out, enough, because when the book was published, someone in the insurance company where Ronnie worked read it and concluded that the black man working in his department was the Stalinist with a militant past in the Sixties—and Ronnie lost his job.

Zan pleads to Brown, "What are the odds? This was twenty years after all the Panther stuff, if that's what it was, and this novel was read by, you know, a hundred and thirteen people on the planet, eighty-seven of them in Japan or some place—and one just happens to work in the same insurance company as Ronnie Jack Flowers? It was enough to make me believe in all their conspiracies after all. And what I didn't understand in my white naïveté is that west of Connecticut there literally was a single black executive in the insurance business. If I just had left out the word 'insurance,' nothing would have happened. One detail too many. Mostly, though, I thought, Who cares? And of course that was the most naïve thing of all. Who cares anymore what anyone did in the Sixties? Isn't half the workforce former radicals now paying into pension funds?"

Brown says, "Another vodka, then?"

"No," says Zan.

"This story is somehow directed at me, I take it?"

"I'm not sure anymore," Zan says sincerely, "but then I'm not finished. Let me finish and we'll decide."

"Lovely," Brown shifts in his chair.

"There's two points, really, one I was trying to make to Viv, whose culpability in the matter of whatever happened to the woman who may or may not be Zema's mother—"

"Whose?"

"—Sheba's mother is far less than mine in the whole Ronnie Jack Flowers affair, and that point is, Viv is responsible for doing what she can to make things right, but she can't hold herself responsible for how things turn out, because we live in a world where sometimes the right thing is just not going to turn out. The other point has to do with Ronnie himself, who I saw being interviewed on a 'news' cable channel, if you can call this particular channel such a thing, while we were waiting in the airport to come to London and for Viv to go on to Ethiopia."

Brown says, "He's become a prominent figure, then."

"Now," Zan explains, "he's vice-chairman or co-director for something called Civic Organizers Network, and his politics are as far to the right as they once were to the left. And here's the thing—Ronnie hasn't changed at all, as far as I can tell. Because the specific content of his views is beside the point. The point is the totalitarian pathology, the pathology of zealotry or, if you want to put it in more secular terms, ideology. Because what the zealot or ideologue really believes in is the zealous nature itself, the devout embrace of hard distinctions—the crusade against gray. It's a story as old as the original novel, historical or not—the Damascan convert. The completely adamant non-believer who becomes the believer, and the thing that hasn't altered an iota is his adamancy."

"Not to mention that perhaps this chap's politics were always as opportunistic as you suspected."

"That's not for me to say, and it takes me off the hook for nothing."

"I think perhaps this story," says Brown, "is less about my zealotry, as you've characterized it—that part, I assume, *is* directed at me—and more about why you haven't written a novel since."

"Touché," says Zan, lifting to him the empty vodka glass. "I would drink to you if my glass weren't empty."

"I offered you another, didn't I?" Brown points out. "And I assume this new novel you're writing now," he continues, gesturing in the direction of Zan's daughter digging into her fish and chips, "is about a white man raising a black daughter at the same time a black bloke is president of his country?"

Zan is shocked. "Of course not."

"Why not?"

"Because there are things about race that no white person can understand. Because no white author has the moral authority, not to mention insight or wisdom, to write such a book. Don't be daft, as you Brits would say."

They get to the station in time for the night's last express back to London. On the platform the two men shake hands; Brown watches the nanny pull Sheba onto the train, Parker leading the way. "So it's working out, then," Brown says.

"I think so," Zan answers. "In the back of her four-year-old little brain is always the question whether we'll be one more family who sends her away. So everything's a test, of course, to see if she can push us to do it."

"Oh," says Brown, "yes, quite. I meant the nanny, what's her name."

"Molly."

"Molly, right. Odd name for an African bird, isn't it? I

assume that's what she is, African. I meant you worked it out with the child-care."

"It's strange," Zan says, the train starting to move, "because we actually saw her, the afternoon before she came to the room, in a . . . peculiar way . . . at the pub where . . . wait," he says, stepping onto the train, "what?"

"How's that?" says Brown, walking alongside, trying to keep pace.

"*I* worked it out? Didn't *you* work it out?"

"Uh," the other man says, the train speeding up and leaving him behind, "you know I intended to, but . . . "

"But I thought *you* arranged it," Zan calls from the train.

"Have a good rest of your stay," Brown calls back, waving. "Regards to Viv, if you hear from her."

D id he say if? Over the building roar of the train, Zan strains to hear the word's echo: Or maybe he said when. Was it when, or if? A few minutes later in their seats, Molly says, "No, it was Mrs. Nordhoc who arranged it. Sorry. I thought you understood." On the seat beside her sits a small portable radio; a blip of music comes from its speaker. When the nanny holds the radio up to Sheba's head, the signal comes through more clearly. In fascination Parker stares not at the effect his sister has on the transistor but the obsolete device itself. "That radio looks as old as your camera," he murmurs before sinking back in his seat to the slight sway of the train.

Zan says to the nanny, "Viv arranged it?" Sheba is about to fall asleep, her eyes drooping. "Don't let her fall asleep," says Parker to Molly.

"Parker," Zan says to the boy's tone, but then to the woman, "I'm afraid he's right. She'll nap half an hour and be up the rest of the night. They've still got some jetlag anyway." Molly rustles Sheba a few blinks back into consciousness, turning up the radio in the seat beside her; she moves the knob from station to station until she finds the song. Sheba's head perks up. "Oh my god, seriously?" Parker groans from half-sleep; Sheba looks at Molly and smiles. *We can be heroes just for one day.* "I like this song!" says Sheba.

"I know," Molly smiles back.

You know? thinks Zan. "You heard from Viv?"

"Well," the nanny seems to sort through her sentences over the song, "not directly. Through a friend. A friend of a friend in Addis." She sings softly along with Sheba and stares out the window of the train.

"But when?" says Zan.

"A few days ago, I think it was?" She says, "No, of course it must have been longer than that. A week or more?"

"A friend of a friend? Can I contact this person?"

"It's difficult," Molly nods, "very poor mobile service, you know, and email . . . " and turns back to the window.

"I ask because I haven't heard anything from her in days."

"I am certain that she is all right," Molly answers, "as long as she remains in Addis Ababa."

It may be that Zan has made an aesthetic out of coincidence, but he would find Molly's appearance more reassuring if it somehow were more explicable. He would feel more reassured if Zan had mentioned in the email to Viv the need for a nanny *before* the afternoon they saw Molly outside the pub. In that case Zan can imagine scenarios, slightly far-flung though all of them are, by which a young London woman—alerted to the situation of a white foreigner in town with two kids, one a young black girl—would happen to pass by the pub and take notice. But in any case, wouldn't Viv have written something? Maybe, as Molly indicated, Viv said something to someone in Ethiopia, who then said, Oh I know a woman in London, and then Viv forgot in the midst of everything going on. As Zan too often reminds her, sometimes she thinks of telling him something and then later remembers doing it though she hasn't.

Zan would find Molly's mysteriousness, and all the mysteries that her mysteriousness engenders, more purely irritating if it weren't for the sense he has—which has grown as surely as the transmissions from Molly's and Sheba's bodies together—that the woman is haunted. Or she is more than haunted, she's branded by a secret, and all that lies between her and her secret is everything about her that's so indefinite. There's no way for him to know if Molly has come to Sheba to try and live down this secret or to try and draw closer to a resolution; but this is the one thing about her that Zan knows is no accident, even among all his other conjectures, the most prominent of which is whether, for all concerned, hers is a secret to either be unlocked, or locked away for good.

A   t the hotel, he carries his daughter up to the room and lays her down in the larger bed. For a while Parker plunders cyberspace on his father's laptop. Sheba sleeps what her brother calls the zombie sleep, eyes not fully shut, lids only half lowered; the distant music that the girl transmits rises off her sleeping body like steam off a summer sidewalk. Brushing Sheba's hair from her eyes, Zan is reminded that he promised Viv to find a salon for her in London, and that reminds him to check his email where, after the long day, he feels certain there will be a message. When there isn't, it's all the more of a shock.

Zan turns from the laptop and looks at his daughter where she sleeps, noting how the girl was different today with Molly, less manic, tethered to something or someone she's never been before. Two hours later, unaware that he's fallen asleep, Zan wakes to the sound of weeping.

S heba isn't in the bed next to him. The sound of crying comes from the bathroom where the door is closed.

In the dark Zan rises from the bed, looks over at Parker, goes to the bathroom where the door is locked. "Sheba," he calls through the door.

"Go away," comes a little voice.

"Sheba."

"Leave me alone."

"What's wrong?"

"Leave me alone."

"What is it?"

"Leave me alone."

"Sheba, open the door."

For half a moment he wonders if he should leave her but he says, "Sheba. Did you have a bad dream?" She just cries. "Sheba?"

"No."

"Did you have a bad dream?"

"No."

"You have to let me in."

He hears her unlock the door.

She's sitting on the bathroom floor. Because he's still only half conscious and his brain is full of vodka, Viv, Molly, J. Willkie Brown and Ronnie Jack Flowers, he belatedly registers that this is something new, the four-year-old sitting on the bathroom floor crying, and that this is not crying for attention, this is crying in private, the way grown-ups do when they want no one to know. She looks up at him. "You don't love me as much as Parker," she says simply.

"Sheba," he says.

"You can't." It's not even an accusation. It's worse, what the girl considers a realization.

"That's not true," Zan says.

"You *can't*," she repeats, as though begging him just to confirm it.

"It's not true," he says firmly, and bends down to pick her up.

For a moment he has her, pulling her to him, when she explodes and pushes him away. "It *is* true! It *is* true! Congratulations, Parker!" she calls into the dark of the next room, "bravo! They love you more! What the hell is wrong with you people? Why did you bring me from Thyopia," as she calls it, the only thing she says now that remotely sounds like a four-year-old, "if you can't love me as much as Parker? I want to be back in Thyopia where I was born and not here with some old family that's just mean to me and rude. I would rather live in Thyopia for the rest of my life. Why didn't you adopt a white daughter? This isn't my real family, I was never in Mama's fucked-up tummy! What the hell do you want from me? I hate you all! You don't pay any fucked-up attention to me anyway! I know why Mama went back—to make them trade another kid for me! Some fucked-up white kid! What do you want with me anyway? I'll put the *hurt* on you, young man!" she warns him. "You can't tell me what to do! *I'm a professional! You left me in the car!* You can't tell me . . . you can't . . . " and then, exhausted, "I'm sorry," she begins to sob, "Poppy, I'm sorry," pleading, "I'm only four, I'm not twelve like Parker, I act braver than I am . . . I don't . . . " and she speaks as though from somewhere out of time, from some vantage point out of age, seeing herself in a way that Zan never knew a four-year-old could see herself, talking about herself as Zan might or another grown up. "I'm sorry," sobbing, "Poppy . . . "

Z an sweeps her into his arms more determinedly than any time since he first swept her out of the backseat of the car bringing her home from the airport, and says, "Shhh, shhh, listen to me," he clutches her to his chest and she squeezes his neck, "listen to me. Are you listening?"

A muffled reply comes from his shoulder.

"I love you. You're my little girl. I love you and Parker the same. Mama loves you and Parker the same. You're a member of this family and always will be. It will never, ever, ever change."

"Promise?" muffled from his shoulder.

"I promise. It will never ever change no matter what you do or say, you're part of this family forever, whether you want to be or not," he declares.

"What about my Thyopia poppy?" she peeps from his chest.

"He's your poppy too. But so am I."

"Two poppys."

"Yes."

"I'm sorry," she begins to cry again.

"No, shhh. Nothing to be sorry for."

Sitting up, Parker watches them from his bed. "Sheesh," he says.

"YOU SHUT UP, PARKER!" Sheba bellows over Zan's shoulder.

"Parker, go to sleep," says Zan.

Parker plops his head back down on the pillow. "Who can sleep?"

Almost instantly Sheba is out, snoring in the other bed. Parker doesn't groan in protest because he has a vested interest in his sister sleeping, and then from the bed he rises to retrieve his father's laptop. "What are you doing?" says Zan.

"I want to film her sleeping," the boy says. "She says she never snores. She's got the zombie eyes, which creep me out but would be über-tight to have a movie of."

"Go back to bed," Zan says. For a few minutes the father and son sit watching the girl and listening; Zan looks at Parker. Hesitantly, sensing an opportunity in the quiet of the night, Zan begins, "Uh, Parker, listen . . . "

"The heck, Zan," the boy says, "we're not going to have the Talk, are we?" and retreats back to beneath his pillow.

They wait for Viv. It seems clear to Zan that something is wrong. From his cell phone, he never reaches anyone in Ethiopia, as if the country at the beginning of time is inside its own time; and whatever information Molly ever had about Viv only becomes more vague like the rest of Molly, who becomes more enervated and remote.

The morning after her midnight explosion, calmly Sheba tries to explain to her father. "I have to let out the fear. The fear comes in," she inhales, "it must go out."

Zan would fire Molly except that, besides the fact he needs a nanny, he can't bring himself to sever the only person who's claimed recent contact with Viv, however speciously. Moreover there's Sheba's growing attraction to her—a manifestation, maybe, of all the coming conflicts over identity. As the little black girl becomes more racially conscious in her white family, is it a function of a larger dislocation having to do with orphanhood, or in fact is there no dislocation larger than the racial, including orphanhood?

Zan feels a prisoner of mysteries he can't name let alone solve, and implications of secrets so secret he barely knows they're secrets. Calls to the bank about the mortgage, difficult enough back home, are impossible, particularly within constant earshot of the children; money dwindles. The £3,500 wired to his bank account by the university has been consumed by the cost of three extra round-trip tickets to London and Viv's flight onto Addis Ababa. At the moment there isn't enough available credit on the single remaining card to cover the hotel bill. Zan envisions a three-in-the-morning escape, involving suitcases hurled from the window to the street below, and shushed children as they creep downstairs past the front desk.

He takes the kids and Molly to Hampton Court outside London where the Thames turns south and west. It's twenty minutes beyond the university on the same train out of Waterloo that they took to and from Zan's lecture; on the way the nanny's transistor plays yet another song by the girl's favorite singer: *Jasmine, I saw you peeping*, and Parker rises from his seat and moves to the other end of the train.

Disembarking at Hampton Court, the four have lunch at a pub down the road. Parker listens to headphones plugged into the little green music player hanging around his neck; Sheba plays with Molly's old camera. The group follows a small red bridge that leads to the palace. On this day the rare fine weather they've had in London finally succumbs to the norm, the palace's bright sunlight-hued red and verdant rolling grounds clashing with the dark billows of gray rolling cross the sky.

Fully as Zan expected, the children's fascination with the palace is minimal. Tales of wayward clergy and various kingly wives drugged or beheaded, or dying in childbirth, whose ghosts still reside only make Parker and Sheba uneasy or give rise to questions that Zan can't answer. If he's being honest, Zan's interest in the palace isn't so keen either, or maybe he's just distracted; in any case the father, son, daughter and nanny move beyond the house onto the grounds where the court's famous three-hundred-year-old maze rises against the blue and black sky in passages of brilliant foliage. Also fully as Zan expected, Parker and Sheba find the maze more interesting. The skies continue to threaten. "It's starting to rain," Zan says, as though the kids possibly would find this relevant; the boy and girl dash into the maze with the nanny behind. "Don't get lost," the father advises absurdly.

Nobody really gets lost in there, Zan is assuring himself at the maze's mouth when, twenty minutes later, first Parker re-appears and then Molly, without Sheba.
Molly looks at Parker, Parker looks back at her. Molly looks at Zan, shaken. "I thought she was with you!" she says to the boy.
"She was with you," says Parker.
"You lost her on purpose!" says Molly.
"Hey," says Zan.
"I did not!" the boy cries. "She was with you!"

From far off near the middle of the maze, they all hear the rise of a small and distant voice singing. *Jasmine, I saw you peeping.* Zan is furious but there's no time for that;

as calmly as he can, he says to Parker and Molly, "All right, let's go back in and get her. Keep one hand on the same wall of the maze as you go in—that way you can follow it back out and not get lost." He can hear it now, for years to come: *You left me in the maze!* As he follows the other two, Sheba's song continues to drift back to them through the hedge.

T he three dart back and forth within the maze when there comes "HEY, WHERE IS EVERYBODY ANY- WAY!" rattling the foliage like she's just around every corner. Then, much less certain, "Hey?"

"Sheba!" calls Zan.

"Molly!" the girl calls back.

"Sheba!" Zan says.

"Molly!" Sheba's voice sounds on the move but in the maze Zan can't be sure, since he's on the move too. "Sheba," says Zan, "just stay in one place! We'll come to you!"

"Molly!" She's beginning to cry now.

"Just stay in one place, Sheba!" Zan adds, "It's Poppy."

"Molly!" the girl keeps answering, crying now. It seems to Zan that the hedges grow higher and closer together. "Zema!" he hears Molly call.

Z an stops. He hasn't heard Molly call the girl this before; he tries to think if he ever used that name in front of her. "Sheba," he calls again, "please answer! Please answer Poppy!"

"Molly!" the girl cries. "Molly, Molly, Molly!"

He turns a final corner to find Sheba mid-passage just as, at the passage's other end, the nanny turns her corner as well—and Sheba runs to her. Did the girl see the father before she saw Molly? Was a choice actually made, or would she have run to him had he turned his corner a split second sooner? Sheba runs into Molly's arms and, catching the girl, the woman looks up at Zan; she's terrified. "I'm sorry!" she blurts. "I . . . she just saw me first! She's scared! I didn't mean to lose her, I thought she was with the boy and I shouldn't have said that to Parker, please don't . . . " and behind him, Zan hears Parker's footsteps as the boy stumbles onto the scene.

Please don't . . . ? Is it merely the prospect of losing a job that has so riveted her? or something more. "She's all right," Zan says hollowly, "that's all that matters," and the girl says to Molly, "Chillax, sweet cheeks." Watching the two of them, Zan backs away and turns to the passage out, trusting they'll follow.

On the train from Hampton back to London, Molly sits staring out the window stricken, some private prophecy having been fulfilled, and almost unconsciously grabs the girl close to her so hard that Sheba, who usually presses herself into others as if to meld her body to theirs, pulls away.

Five days after his lecture at the university, Zan meets J. Willkie Brown at the pub off Leicester Square. "Well," Brown says, arriving after Zan, "the kids?"

"With Molly," Zan says. "Thanks for coming."

"Right. African lady with the English name."

"James . . . "

"Anything from the bar?"

"No, thank you."

"I'll have a pint," Brown says, signaling to the bar.

"James, listen," says Zan. "You had nothing to do with setting it up, right?"

"Setting up what?"

"The nanny."

"Sorry about that," he allows, "I know I told you I would—"

"Forget that," Zan says, "but then where did she come from?"

"Must have heard . . . " Brown thinks, scratches behind his ear, then shrugs. "Don't know," not finding it that interesting or understanding why Zan does.

Zan points out the window of the pub. "Our second day in London," he says, "or maybe it was the third, I forget . . . before I met you, before Viv vanished, the kids and I sat here at this same table and Sheba was watching someone right out that window, there across the street—and it was Molly, staring back. A day or so later, she shows up at the hotel and says, Here I am, the nanny."

"That *is* peculiar, isn't it?" says Brown.

Jesus, you think so? Zan wants to reach across the table and grab Brown by the lapels; the British diffidence is driving him nuts. "Now," he says, "Molly claims she heard we needed a nanny from Viv—who I haven't heard from at all. Nothing. No email, no phone call, I can't reach anyone in Ethiopia . . . "

"Viv is a resilient woman," says Brown.

"Will you stop saying that?" Zan hears his voice rise. "I know she's resilient. I also know she's *driven* about this thing with Sheba's mother, that this whole business has become a moral crisis for her—"

"She can hardly hold herself responsible—"

"I know that . . . "

"Right. Ronnie Joe . . . "

"Ronnie Jack Flowers . . . I know all this. Doesn't matter what perspective you or I hold on it, what matters is how Viv feels about it and whatever lengths she's compelled to go to in order to find or help someone who may or may not be Sheba's mother—and no sooner does Viv go looking for Sheba's mother and suddenly become incommunicado than Molly shows up."

The other man frowns. "Not sure I follow that last bit."

"Never mind," Zan shakes his head. He doesn't want to explain the crazy thing that's been in his head since Molly appeared. "What's important at this point is finding Viv."

"Of course."

"Until then, we're stuck in London," *and we have no money and we're about to lose our house* but he doesn't want to explain that either.

Brown replies, "Let me see who I can talk to."

First useful thing you've said, thinks Zan.

That night as both kids sleep, Zan surrenders to his insomnia and turns on the TV. The sound is down so low he can't be sure, but back home the BBC seems to find the new president somber before his time. It's a strange thing to witness from five thousand miles away, but Zan suspects that many people, from the woman on the plane to his anarchist friend in Texas, will take some satisfaction in this.

For his part Zan takes solace in the same presidential ego that others consider so intolerable; the new president hasn't merely a political sense of himself but an historic one. Mere elections are small potatoes for him. He's running for history. He's running for greatness, and in the eyes of history, whether he's a megalomaniac, as is entirely possible, depends only and entirely on whether he succeeds.

In his lifetime, Zan doesn't remember a president's very identity being such a point of political contention. He doesn't remember large segments of the public twenty-five years ago debating whether the president at that time secretly had been born in Ireland. The new president's race is part of his political identity; the two can't be extricated; and if, as some indicate, his racial identity is a creation, if he taught himself—even for purely political purposes—how to be black, how to talk or walk black, only to later teach himself how to be a little whiter, does that make his identity more a creation than anyone else's? Doesn't everyone choose aspects of his or her identity, or is race the rubicon of authenticity?

Zan began pondering race when he was younger only because he began pondering his country, and knew that it wasn't possible to understand his country without pondering slavery and it wasn't possible to understand slavery without pondering race. He considered how his countrymen from Africa were the only ones who didn't choose to be there; Africans were compelled to come and only once they were made to come did they choose to stay. Did that make them, then, the true owners of the country's great idea, by virtue of having accepted the country in the face of so many reasons not to? If the country is more an idea than a place then are those who were so compelled its true occupants, given how the country's promise to them was broken before it was offered?

When Brown calls, the expeditious response that should be reassuring seems suspicious in a way that even Zan knows is unreasonable, his mind reverberating with half-baked conspiracy theories even his paranoia finds far-fetched. "Look here," Brown says, "I got you a meeting tomorrow with the Ethiopian ambassador in London. If anyone can sort this out, I feel certain he can," and to Zan the "if" and "certain" seem conspicuously at odds with each other.

Only later will Zan consider how fateful is the turn of the following day when Parker insists on accompanying his father to the embassy rather than remain with Molly and Sheba. "I want to go with you," he declares in his newly adolescent way that brooks no argument.

"Why does Parker get to go?" Sheba asks, but Zan is struck by how perfunctory her protest is. "I promise," he answers, "you'll prefer being with Molly."

"You're not going, buttmunch," says Parker.

"Knock it off," Zan says to his son, but his daughter already has conceded the point more readily than she's conceded anything, and taken hold of the nanny's hand.

After the incident at Hampton Court and the maze, Molly's manner has vacillated between warmth and remove, her speech to Zan more terse as she becomes with Sheba more expansive. On this unseasonably warm morning she seems positively frail; having shed her voluptuousness, she looks as though she's lost ten pounds, and her skin pales to the color of sand and then ash. Since Zan and the children first saw her standing on the street outside the pub at Leicester Square watching them back, she's been diminishing. In her approach up the street, she's exhausted.

M ost notably the music from her that filled the hotel room the first day fades, phasing in and out in wails and trebles. "Are you all right?" Zan says.

"Yes," she says. She rubs her finger against Sheba's cheek.

"Parker and I are going to the Ethiopian embassy. I imagine you know where it is."

"Why would I know where it is?" says the woman, and Zan thinks to himself, Did I say something so offensive? "It's on Kensington Road," he answers, "across from Hyde Park, a little west of Knightsbridge. I don't know what's around there to do with Sheba but we can meet in the park afterward or if you want to take her on a walk, maybe we can eat something or get a soda for the kids at the pub where we first saw you. Parker will be hungry."

Molly says, "What pub?"

"The one off Leicester Square that—"

"I don't know it," she says.

He says, "You do." Did they ever actually talk about that afternoon they saw each other there, or is this a conversation that took place in his head, so vivid yet never in fact spoken? "You've been there," he persists, "well, maybe not inside, but outside."

"I don't know it," she says firmly.

The tone is becoming antagonistic. "Let's meet then," Zan says, "across the street at the park."

"It's a big park," she says.

"The embassy is at Kensington and Exhibition Road."

Actually it's on a small sidestreet called Prince's Gate. Zan has imagined a consulate out of the movies, a compound with a yard and guards everywhere; but the Ethiopian embassy doesn't even occupy the whole building, rather the middle floors where there's a single security entrance that's more intent on not seeming rude than secure.

The display case in the lobby features not the usual artifacts but different kinds of coffee. Parker hoped to see weapons, shrunken heads, the poisoned tips of pygmies' arrows. "They don't have pygmies and shrunken heads in Ethiopia," says Zan.

Zan expects an ambassador out of the movies too, formal and in a coat and tie, with cufflinks gleaming so bright Zan can see their glow from beneath the coat sleeves. Rather the ambassador wears a cardigan, with sleeves pushed up his arms. If this were L.A., thinks Zan, he'd be in a t-shirt.

The ambassador listens intently. Watching Parker out of the corner of his eye, Zan calibrates his case, trying to say something that won't alarm his son while still striking a tone of urgency. The ambassador, Zan is impressed to note, seems to grasp the situation and rather expertly registers measured and not undue concern. This is why he's a diplomat, Zan realizes. "You understand," the ambassador says sympathetically, "that my country still has its technological challenges, and so therefore sometimes internet service, for instance, can be down for days. And mobile service . . . " He shrugs. "It's not so unusual for you to not have heard anything."

"I can't help worrying," Zan says.

"Of course not. I will ring up people and make inquiries."

"Thank you."

"We will begin with the hotel where Mrs. Nordhoc was staying and go from there. We will talk as well with the birth-family of your daughter. Can you give me their names? Or we have records that I can check, if you don't have them."

Zan hands over a list with the names of Sheba's aunt, grandmother and father. He's gone back and forth in his mind whether to include the father's. "The last thing I want," he says, "or that I know my wife wants, is to cause problems for Sheba's . . . Zema's father or family. I think Viv is distraught at the prospect that trying to find and help the girl's birth-mother has created trouble."

"It was a natural impulse," the ambassador says.

"It's just that someday Sheba will want to know. Zema."

The ambassador laughs. "Sheba."

"It's . . . just a nickname," explains Zan.

"Of course. She has a royal presence," he jokes.

"Very headstrong," Zan agrees, "a 'professional,' she would say."

"Later on this will serve her well."

"That's what we keep telling ourselves. Uh . . . also . . . "

"Yes?"

Zan points at the list of names. "We've sent some money to her family in Addis when we can manage it financially. Only recently have we realized this could be construed the wrong way. It's only been to help them out."

"Of course," answers the ambassador. "I assure you that no reasonable person could see this as anything but an act of generosity, the same generosity that led you to open up your home to your daughter in the first place."

"Thank you. I hope so."

As the ambassador walks the father and son to the door, Zan presents him with a gift. "I hope it doesn't seem completely vain," Zan mutters, "it's . . . "

"Yes!" the ambassador exclaims appreciatively, examining the book. "Mr. Brown told me that you are a novelist of repute."

"Uh, well, ill repute maybe. I *used* to be a novelist, fourteen years ago . . . "

"But you have written a novel," the other man protests, "therefore that makes you a novelist."

Zan smiles. "That's what my wife says."

"I shall let you know what I learn, Mr. Nordhoc."

"I'm extremely grateful for all your time and trouble."

"I know that you are worried but I believe it shall be for naught and all will be well. And by the way, congratulations!"

"Oh . . . " Zan thinks he's referring to the book. "It was fourteen—"

"Yes!" the ambassador exclaims. "For what is happening in your country! Its great new adventure!" but to Zan, the election already is beginning to seem a long time ago.

Across Kensington Road, Sheba and Molly are nowhere to be found in the park. It is, as Molly noted, a big park, so Zan and Parker spend the better part of an hour south of the Serpentine searching everywhere. Zan remembers that the last time he was in this park, almost thirty years ago, an IRA blast killed eight people. "Probably," Parker suggests to his father, "they went back to the hotel."

"Yes, I'm sure you're right," Zan answers uneasily. The two head east along the edge of the park, crossing Carriage Row. Bloomsbury is a half-hour walk. For all the Tube's gleaming futurism, Parker still hates places close and dark; but a growing dark seed in Zan trumps the boy's protests and they catch the Piccadilly line at the Knightsbridge underground. By the time they ascend—as evening falls and their neighborhood comes alive with light and people—and arrive at the hotel, Zan almost persuades himself that the woman and girl will be there.

Zan is overwhelmed by people vanishing. He's angry at himself for not having bought Molly a cheap, temporary cell phone even though he doesn't have the money. Everything now tumbles into the realm of scenarios that make no sense; in the clamor of Bloomsbury, he's having a hard time focusing or thinking clearly. He convinces himself of increasingly unlikely outcomes. When there's no sign of Sheba and Molly in the hotel lobby, he asks Parker, "Did I give Molly the key?" and sensing in his father a looming panic, the boy doesn't answer.

Standing in the small hotel room gazing around them, as though within its few square meters the girl and woman could possibly be undetected, with revulsion Zan realizes that he struggles for composure, realizes that in front of his twelve-year-old son he's on the edge of breaking down from everything, Viv gone, no money, no prospects and now his missing daughter. As the evening passes, Zan waits for a knock at the door as sudden and without warning as the first time Molly appeared and Sheba answered, staring up at her in a silence that for the small girl was as uncommon then as it seems foreboding now.

Zan and Parker have a fight about going out for food. "I'm hungry," Parker says.

"I'll run down to the corner," Zan mutters, "get us some fish and chips." Parker wants to go to a sushi place a few blocks away, where little dishes circulate the restaurant on a conveyor belt and diners pick out what they want, but the boy realizes this isn't going to happen tonight. "I want to go with you," he says instead.

"Stay here. In case—"

"I want to go with you," the boy insists.

"You need to stay. Someone needs to be here."

"I want to go!" yells Parker, and Zan realizes the boy is scared too of how at loose ends everything in his young life has come to feel. Zan puts his head in his hands. "Then we're staying," he says, immediately ashamed of how petulant it is, punishing his son by making him go hungry. After a while Zan writes a note and sticks it in the door and the two make a mad dash for the grocery store around the corner, buying sandwiches and sodas.

That night Zan barely sleeps. His head explodes; along with everything else, his doctor back in Los Angeles holds hostage, over an unpaid bill, a refill of Zan's migraine medication, and now he's down to only a few pills. Parker prowls the internet on Zan's laptop until finally collapsing into his own restless unconsciousness.

They remain in the room the next morning waiting. Zan calls J. Willkie Brown and gets a voice-mailbox, disconnects without leaving a message, calls back again, leaves a message. Around lunchtime he leaves his cell number with the woman at the hotel's front desk who asked on the day they checked in if he was Alexander Nordhoc the novelist; and then the father and son walk to the police station at Russell Square ten minutes away. Past a door next to the underground, the police bureau is down a long white hall that might be mistaken for a hospital or asylum.

Taking Zan's information, the constable's manner disavows empathy. "But you say," he asks, trying to get it straight, "that your wife has gone missing as well."

"My wife is missing in Africa," Zan explains as calmly as he can manage, "and now my daughter—"

"You best need to speak with the consulate general of the country where your wife—"

"I'm not here about my wife. I'm explaining how the situation came about . . . "

"Sorry?"

"How the situation came about. My daughter has gone missing with her nanny."

"I see," says the officer. Zan may be imagining the tone of accusation, but given his own sense of guilt and accountability it doesn't matter: If I just had talked Viv out of . . . out of . . . what? Going to Ethiopia? Hiring someone to find Sheba's mother? and he's swept by nausea, certain he's going to be ill in the middle of the station. He looks at Parker in the chair next to him, slumping as though to disappear down whatever hole might open up underneath and deliver him from this situation. "It happened yesterday," says Zan.

"And you chose not to report it before now?" the officer says.

"I keep thinking she'll come back."

"Perhaps she will."

"I just made a report yesterday to the Ethiopian embassy concerning my wife—"

"Mind, Mr. Nordhoc, we're not the Ethiopian embassy."

"I know that," Zan says, breathing as deeply as possible, "I'm trying to explain why . . . what my . . . *state of mind* . . . "

"State of mind?"

"What my thinking was . . . that she might come back—"

"What's your business in London, if I may ask?"

"I gave a lecture at the university."

"Can you describe the girl?"

Zan blurts, "She's black." Not "She's wearing this or that," not "Her body transmits music from far-flung stations of the universe." He goes on, "She's four. Years old."

"Mrs. Nordhoc is black as well, then, I take it?"

"No," but since the constable has made it clear that Viv

isn't the London police's concern, Zan isn't sure why this question is relevant. He explains, "We adopted Sheba. Zema."

"Zema?"

"Her name's not really Sheba."

"Is it Sheba or Zema?"

"Uh . . ."

"You last saw her yesterday in Hyde Park near Kensington."

"Yes."

"It was Hyde Park proper rather than Kensington Gardens?"

"What?"

"It was Hyde Park proper rather th—"

"I don't know. It was the park. She was with her mother, they were supposed to wait for us to come back from seeing the Ethiopian ambassador."

The officer frowns. "Her mother?"

"What?"

"Her mother?"

"What about her mother?"

"You said she was with her mother. Your daughter was with her mother?"

"I said she was with her nanny. They were waiting—"

"I'm sorry, Mr. Nordhoc. But I assure you that you said her mother."

"Are we," Zan says angrily, "going to start arguing about what we said, like I have to do with the bank? My wife is missing. My daughter is missing. Why do I have to argue with everyone about what they said?"

"We're not arguing about what I said, are we?" the officer answers calmly. "We're arguing about what you said."

"Dad," Parker says quietly from his seat, "you said mother. Sorry."

Helpless, Zan and Parker return to the hotel. Now everywhere Zan goes, every corner he turns, he hopes against hope that Sheba will appear before him. He feels himself sinking. His son watches him and whispers, It will be O.K., and Zan thinks, I should be telling *him* it will be O.K. Glancing at his cell, he notes that he's missed another call from Brown, whose message is brief: "Alexander. James here. Ring me when you can," but when Zan returns the call he once again gets Brown's voice-mail.

Parker is on the laptop and Zan stands at the hotel window still thinking any moment he'll see Sheba coming up the road, with the nanny or without her, when his son says, "The heck? Zan."

"What?" says the father.

"Look at this."

Zan surveys the website on the laptop where Viv's name appears. "I don't know what it means," he says.

"It means," Parker explains, "Mom has posted a message."

Zan says, "It's an email?"

"It's a posting," says the boy, "nobody emails anymore."

"Mom sent us a message?"

"Not exactly a message, not exactly to us."

"Parker," the father quietly implores, "I don't understand."

"It's for anyone who sees it." In place of text is a photo. In the background of the photo is a monumental structure, six columns—though there are more corresponding columns behind the six—capped with a massive stone ledge. On top is the sculpture of a chariot, drawn by four horses and driven by a winged woman carrying a long scepter. At the end of the scepter is an Iron Cross, and above that a mighty bird spreads its own wings.

Zan knows he's seen this structure. Out of it pours into the foreground of the photo a wide boulevard dotted with passers-by, one of whom, at the image's forefront, is a woman disappearing off to the side of the photo. Though she's slightly blurred, Parker says, "It's Viv!"

Zan nods. "It does look like her."

"But who's taking the photo?" says Parker.

Zan says nothing, brooding over the image.

"Is that Ethiopia?" asks Parker. "Those people don't look like Ethiopians." He means they're white.

"It's not Ethiopia. I've seen this." He points at the photo. "I don't mean just pictures of it."

"It's London!" Parker exclaims. "Didn't we see this the first or second day here, when we went to that über-creepy place below ground that wasn't below ground and then that other creepy place they cut off the heads? Mom is here in London!"

In Zan, a flash of exhilaration wars with confusion, and loses. "We know it's from Viv?" he says. He shakes his head trying to make sense of it when it hits him. "That's not London," he says, "that's the Brandenburg Gate in Berlin."

Zan collapses onto the bed. On his back he stares at the ceiling. "Where's Berlin?" says Parker.

"Germany," says Zan.

"Germany's its own country, right?"

"Yes."

"Why's Mom there?"

"I don't know."

"Why would she post a photo?"

"I...well, she's a photographer . . . "

"Dad!"

"I don't know."

"If she's not in Ethiopia, why doesn't she call? Why doesn't she—?"

"Stop, Parker," the father says, covering his face with his hands.

Parker says, "Do you want to answer?"

"What?" says Zan.

"Comment? On Viv's photo? Post a reply?"

"You can do that?" and his son sighs deeply. The photo feels to Zan like a bulletin, a flare shot into cyberspace— "like," Zan says not really to Parker but out loud, "I'm supposed to go get her."

"How far is Germany?"

"I'll take the train," Zan is thinking out loud, "I don't have the money for a plane ticket . . . "

"I, I, I," says Parker, "what, you think you're leaving me here?" because momentarily Zan has forgotten he doesn't have a nanny: and then he realizes, But what about Sheba? *This cannot be*, he silently prays to the choice before him. He can't leave his daughter who already has been passed off three times in her short life and feels herself stranded whenever anyone exits whatever room she's in. *You left me in London*, he already hears someday's cry of betrayal.

Viv never would want him to leave their daughter here. If I go find her, Zan thinks, she'll hate me for leaving the girl; he remembers a talk they once had shortly before Sheba came— wasn't it before?—when a fire threatened the canyon: If ever there was a decision to be made for either mother or father to save each other or their son, they would save their son. It was the easiest thing they ever agreed on.

B ut Viv doesn't know Sheba is missing, and now the choice doesn't seem so easy. Zan can't ignore what's plainly a message from his wife, and—reminding himself that he still has Sheba's passport and no one can take her from the country—never in the previous twenty-four hours has he believed the girl to be in danger.

Of course this leads to the next thought which finally it's time to express if only to himself. With the sound in Zan's ears of the lost Sheba constantly calling Molly's name in the Hampton maze, and with the scene playing out in his mind's eye of Sheba turning to Molly in the maze and racing into the woman's arms, finally it's time to say the crazy thing that's been in his head since the moment Molly appeared at that door— Zan looks at the door now—and stepped inside.

In no way does it make sense, and in every way does it feel true; and who's to say no to it? And if it is true, then who's to say Molly shouldn't have her? Who's to say that at this moment Sheba isn't reunited with the very person in search of whom Viv has vanished in the first place? Zan thinks, When there's no other obvious option, sometimes you can only follow the signs. They can ignore Viv's posting and continue waiting for her while they try to search London, and a month from now be exactly where they are at this moment with not a thing different. Sometimes life calls for a catalytic instant.

Father and son spend the next day packing. Zan moves by rote; he can barely think at all. He arranges with the front desk to leave their bags behind; he has no idea how to explain that he can't settle the bill. Ruling out the clandestine escape in the night, nonetheless he can't stand the prospect of humiliating himself before his son.

The woman at the desk says, "Yes, Mr. Nordhoc, it's taken care of."

"What?" says Zan.

She looks at the computer. "Mr. Brown has taken care of it," and Zan is too relieved to feel bruised. Well, you're all right then, James, he thinks to himself; maybe this is the first sign of straits at their most dire, when pride dies.

Their last night in London, Zan and Parker return to the pub that used to be the Ad Lib, where everything began with Molly, in one last hope Sheba will be there. Stepping inside, Zan closes his eyes thinking he'll hear the girl and woman in front of him; but in the dark of his eyelids he knows the pub's music isn't theirs.

They take the table by the window through which Sheba saw Molly the first time. On the tabletop Zan counts his money before he orders a sandwich for his son: "You haven't," he struggles to ask the bartender, "seen a woman and small girl, have you? Today or yesterday, or the day before."

"Well, that could be anyone, couldn't it?" says the bartender. Examining the shaken man in front of him, he says, "Are you all right?"

"They're black." Now it seems like a magic word.

"How's that?"

"The little girl," Zan mutters.

"Still doesn't narrow it down much," the bartender answers.

In a hoarse whisper the father says, "Can I leave a number with you?" He writes it on a cocktail napkin. "It's very important. In case they show up?"

The graying bartender looks at it. "I'll be straight with you, mate," he says, "forty-three years I've gotten a lot of napkins with a lot of numbers, and never wound up calling any of them." Back at the table, pressed against the glass of the window and peering out one last time, Zan whispers, Sheba, forgive me. I didn't even get your hair done like I was supposed to. I've failed you completely; and once again he has to pivot sharply so the boy won't see him break down. "Tell them we'll be coming back," he chokes to the bartender over his shoulder, who doesn't hear, or maybe Zan never really gets out the words.

Forty-three years ago, at this same table where Parker eats his sandwich, another Yank passing through town on his way to somewhere else, who feels every minute as old as Zan even as he's almost twenty years younger, gazes at the front page of a newspaper that someone has handed him in the street.

The newspaper is an unseemly mess of text and image, as anarchic as the sensibility it means to convey. The black ink comes off on his fingers, with streaks of headline-red, and the Yank frowns at its front page, which has the picture of a nun who appears to be at some sort of social occasion. She's surrounded by people who have the look if not of familiarity, of celebrities, young men and girls with hair longer than his, and caught by the camera from the back, she reveals a bare bottom.

He glares at the tall ale he's barely sipped. Lately he's heard that everything in London is spiked with a new and dangerous intoxicant. He brushes a brown lock of hair off his forehead.

If he allowed himself to say so, he would admit it's an impressive bare bottom—and only when he spies the ends of blonde hair peeking out from under the rather chic habit does he fully realize this can't be a real nun. In another lifetime, as a devout Catholic he would have had to stifle a flash of anger; now it only embarrasses him. It isn't that he's no longer given to flashes of anger in his life. It's that over the past two and a half years the anger has become reserved for outrages greater than the irreverence of young people, when the anger isn't subsumed by grief.

Brushing the hair out of his face has become a nervous habit, almost a twitch. *it:* reads the newspaper across the front, above the altogether too comely nun, in the large red lower-case letters which he discovers inside the newspaper stand for "international times." Sounds communist, he thinks, which also once would have provoked anger: subversion and heresy in one swoop—and he manages the smallest and most rueful of smiles. Though he knows little about the current music, he recognizes under the masthead the variation on Plato that serves as the newspaper's motto, and can't help feeling his admiration stirred: *When the mode of the music changes, the walls of the city shake.*

It's been nearly an hour and a half since he slipped away from the house. I wonder if they're looking for me by now, he thinks. Perhaps I should go back.

The Yank lays the newspaper on the table. The music from the Ad Lib upstairs, which can be accessed only by a somewhat secretive elevator, is a muffled throb, and from behind the downstairs bar comes a pop tune on a radio or record player— *in dollhouse rooms with colored lights swinging . . .* —he can't tell. Sipping the tall ale in front of him, his first and last of the night, he finally notices the young English couple at the bar that have been watching him, and he's only surprised he got away this long without being recognized.

"Too old to be a musician," says the young man standing at the bar. The Yank at the table is familiar, and the man at the bar, white and in his mid-twenties with long hair, and the younger black woman, her hair already in dreadlocks that aren't typical yet, are trying to place him. The woman teases, "But not that much older than you, is he?" and her companion exclaims, slightly outraged, "Are you serious? He's *much* older!" and the woman bursts into laughter.

He realizes, "You're having me on." Maybe she knows he shaved four years off the bio he gave the record company. He calls to the bartender, "Jonesy!" with no reason to believe the bartender's name is Jonesy, then turns to the young woman. "So, this the night then, Jaz?"

She says, "Shut up."

"A tumble would inspire me for tomorrow's session, yeah?"

"We both know," Jasmine answers, "that *no* tumble will inspire you all the more, don't we?" Even by lead-singer standards, she thinks, Reg is lascivious; his songs are a nonstop orgy. The bartender brings another. "Dead night," Reg says to him.

"Monday," the bartender says, "theatres are closed."

"Everyone's at the Indica or Marquee," says Jasmine.

"Never heard of the Indica," pouring the drink, "but then I'm new."

"Me too," says Reg. "In town, I mean."

"Hear the Marquee lot used to come in straightaway after the shows."

She says, "Too late for the Marquee."

"Don't know why they stopped. Coming after the shows, I mean."

"Soft Machine's on the bill, yeah?" says Reg. "Should be a bit of a crowd, then."

"That's Sunday night," says Jasmine.

"Never heard of the Indica," the bartender says again.

"Next to the Scotch, over on Mason's Yard. It's not a club, it's a gallery. The Marquee moved."

"Yeah?"

"From Oxford over to Wardour now."

"Jonesy . . . " says Reg.

"So if you're waiting for the lot from the Marquee," says Jasmine, "you're going to wait awhile. Everyone heads for the Crom now, or the Ship a few doors down."

"Jonesy."

"But you got *us*, don't you?"

"Oh," the bartender assures her, "I got more than you two—"

"But Jonesy," Reg finally says emphatically enough to stop the other conversation, lowering his voice and leaning across the bar, "who *is* that?" and points at the Yank across the room.

When they reach his table, the Yank speaks first. "Are you a Beatle?" he asks Reg so abruptly it can't help sounding accusatory.

The young man and woman laugh. "No," says Jasmine, "he's Elvis Presley."

Bewilderment flits across the Yank's face. He narrows his eyes, studying them on the other side of the ale he's barely drunk. "You're not Elvis Presley," he decides; they laugh again. "I don't think he's in music, then," Jasmine says to Reg, who worries, He's *much* older than I. She was just winding me up. For a moment the other man seated at the table is uncomfortable, slightly irritated before he forces himself to laugh as well. "You're not him," he declares with more certainty.

"Not Elvis, anyway," Reg says.

"Not the Presley part either," says Jasmine.

"Hey, you lot in management came up with *that*."

"If you're not a Beatle, then you might as well not be anybody," the Yank says, and it isn't clear to Jasmine if he realizes or cares how rude it sounds, though he does feel bound to add, "What I mean is, you might as well be a Beatle, for all that I know."

He speaks in a whine. Over the gray noise from upstairs, the other two barely hear him. "Reg and Jasmine," Reg tells him. He says the names like they go together but the woman decides to let it pass. There's a slight hesitation from the Yank: "Bob," he says as though giving an alias, or as though he's got different names for different circumstances and has to decide which sort these are—circumstances, that is. He reaches out his hand. His handshake is almost womanly and Jasmine is put off by it.

It's a small hand like a child's that barely reaches all the way around Reg's. When he takes it back, Jasmine sees how it shakes. The Yank sees it too and tucks the hand under the other arm to hide it. Since it doesn't seem to occur to him to invite them to sit, Jasmine does it on her own and Reg follows. "So, Bob," Reg says, "not into the music then, are we?"

"I, uh . . . " the Yank begins and the other two have to strain to catch what he says, "like . . . the Broadway tunes . . . " and smiles, "'The Impossible Dream.' Do you know that one?"

"No," Reg says, "who did it?"

"As he said," Jasmine answers, "it's from a show. Broadway. Don Quixote, right?"

"Yes," says Bob.

"Hey, it's a groovy song," Jasmine allows, "good message."

"I, uh, think you're being polite," the Yank says.

He's out of place. In the dark of the club, Jasmine still can't place him; he looks like a fifty-year-old teenager but in fact has just turned forty, aging a decade in the last few years. With his rabbit's teeth and long brown hair already turning gray, all of his features are too big for his head. He's still growing into himself, still in the process of becoming who he'll be, and he has a perpetually distracted quality that seems interrupted only by concentrated doses of discomfort, self-amusement, a secret. He takes everything personally.

There's a calm about him but it's not the calm of sanguinity. It's the calm of something too damaged to be grace, let alone peace; Jasmine already has decided he's the most intense person she's ever met. She says, "What are you in London for, then?"

"Passing through," Bob answers, voice dropping back to his nasal whisper, "here tonight, then leave tomorrow," and adds, "I never sleep well so I . . . thought I would go out, not wake my wife . . . "

"Get a bit of time for yourself," observes Reg.

"Sometimes," he says, "you're most alone when you're not." Reg nods uncomprehendingly. "Where's home, then?" asks Jasmine, and the man smiles his little-kid smile. "New York," he says, "sometimes. Boston. Washington . . . no," he shakes his head, "not Washington. *Never* Washington."

Pushing away from the table, he gets up. "I, uh, should head back. They're looking for me by now." He hesitates. "Want to walk?" No, Jasmine realizes, this isn't a man who fancies being alone; when he can, he bullies his way through his reserve, when he gets through at all. She says to Reg, "You have your session tomorrow," and looks for a clock on the wall but there is none. "Or today, I mean."

Reg answers, "Not till noon," passing up the out she's given him, or too dim, she thinks, to realize she's given it. Bob gets up from the table and he's small like his hands; inside his clothes, his small frame sinks with exhaustion. "Don't fancy a taxi?" asks Jasmine.

"No."

"Where you staying?" asks Reg.

"Over near the park," says Bob, and both Brits laugh again. In the dark of the club the Yank flushes again, and again has to compel himself to smile at whatever he's said that they find so damned ridiculous. The three step outside the pub. In the late-night hours there's still scattered traffic and taxis gliding by. "We're in London," says Jasmine, "more than a few parks. Not like New York where you might say 'the park' and everybody assumes you mean the big one." Bob nods. "Right," she says, "so you know which park?"

"I can never remember the name," says Bob.

Reg says, "Hotel?"

"I'm, uh, not at a hotel."

"Residence," says Jasmine.

"Yes."

"Hyde Park," she says.

"No."

"Green Park, over near the palace."

"No."

"St. James."

"No."

"Regent's."

"Yes."

"You think it's Regent's?"

"It's Regent's," the Yank says.

Outside the pub is another song from one of the city's windows that are lit up like reverbed fireflies. *Over, under, sideways down.* Bob appraises the remnants of the midnight legion that cross the curbs and brush past; they wear lace and silver trench coats, brilliant-red braided Hussar coats and Moroccan boots. Their wide Edwardian ties have images of fish so radiated with color that all the people in the street appear to be aquariums. *When will it end?* Everyone in the world is young, suddenly.

Each road is a vortex. In the wet nighttown gleam, there drifts past the three of them on the sidewalk a Rolls Royce the color of a prism, the aurora borealis on wheels. The window is down on the passenger's side and they have a clear glimpse of who's in back. "See who that was?" Jasmine says to Reg.

"Bloody right," Reg answers.

"Who was it?" says Bob.

"Who I'm not."

"Elvis Presley?"

"Better."

"These days," says Bob, walking now, "London isn't the way I remember."

Jasmine says, "These days, London isn't the way anyone remembers."

"Are you a Beatle too?" he says to her as they stroll, only because it's a time when such a thing can be believed.

"Assistant for the management of Reg's band. Studying journalism at Kingston Hill."

This seems to interest the Yank. "What kind of journalism? Politics?"

"Not politics," she shakes her head. "Politics as it's presently practiced doesn't matter much these days, does it?" She's aware this sounds pompous.

"My brother considered journalism when he was young."

"What happened?"

"He went into politics," Bob laughs almost bitterly.

"Sorry."

"You've been to London before, then," says Reg.

"I grew up in London," says Bob.

"Seriously?" she says.

"Only a year or two. After the Blitz, before the war. I was twelve." He shrugs. "The other war, of course. Not the one now, in Southeast Asia."

"Your war," says Jasmine, "not ours."

Reg says, "I was four when the war ended. Think I remember listening on the radio, Churchill and the King waving to the crowd from some bloody balcony or other. The palace, I imagine."

"You, uh, wouldn't remember the Blitz," says Bob, "not if you were four. The Blitz was over by the summer of '41."

"'That's when I was born," and Reg immediately realizes he's just blurted his real age. Missing nothing, Jasmine laughs. "Anyway," he says, looking at her sheepishly, "I wasn't in London. I'm from Andover, in Hampshire."

"So how is it you were living in London?" Jasmine asks the Yank, still laughing at Reg.

Always uncertain what's so damned funny, Bob answers, "My father worked here."

"What sort of work was that?" says Reg. He lights a cigarette and offers one to the other man, who waves it off. "Right," says Jasmine, "it's a bit of a walk from here to Regent's," and the three stop, gazing around. "Not really me town," Reg explains to the Yank. "She's the native."

"I'm not a native. I'm not even English."

"You're English," he puffs his cigarette, "you've been English since you were bloody two years old."

"Well," says Bob, "I know I walked to the pub where I met you."

"Not saying it can't be done," she answers, "and, you know,

the longest way round is the shortest way home, eh? Did you realize you had gone that far?"

"I suppose not. I was looking for the theatre district." He says, "I don't mind the walk," the three still stopped in the street. "I'll, uh, be able to get some sleep when I get back. I won't on the plane tomorrow. I understand if you two want to take off."

"Going back to New York, then," says Jasmine.

"No," and Jasmine can see in the dark the provocation of the Yank's blue eyes as they regard her, his hands in his pockets like it's the most casual thing in the world—in some ways it's the most casual he's been all night—when he says, "South Africa."

As if he's taunting her—and finally her ambivalence about him metastasizes to dislike. *He's trying to incite me* and, jolted as much by the way he's said it as what he's said, she wants to walk away. His idea, she wonders, of taking the piss? Delivered with the same bullying bluntness as everything else he's said tonight? An insensitive, even cruel retaliation for . . . what? good-natured teasing about not knowing who Elvis Presley is?

Of course it can't help feeling like a violation. She's restrained from leaving only by the regret she'll feel not having told him to sod off. "On business?" Reg says with an obliviousness that would infuriate her more if she weren't so used to it: Jasmine may not be political but Reg is hopeless. *He doesn't know South Africa from South Antarctica* and now she's not sure which of them to be angrier at. "Yes," Bob says, not taking his eyes from hers, still the taunt, "business," and then turns to continue walking. Reg follows. She hangs back and Reg turns to look. "Can we leave?" she says.

Reg insists, "Let's walk a bit more." In the early-morning hours the three make their way up Charing Cross along Soho's eastern border. Looming before them is the head of an incandescent African woman, painted on the side of a seven-story building; she has crouching day-glo lions for eyes and, like Medusa, her skull flames with bright violet dreadlocks that glimmer from the rain and appear to slither up the street. The words *Abyssinia* and *Queen Sheba* wreathe the woman's face like smoke. "Right," Reg says, practically jaunty, "so what was it took you back to Leicester Square anyway this time of night, Bob? A little late for the theatre." He glances up at the huge painting of the woman's lysergic dreadlocks and peers back over his shoulder at Jasmine, who walks along behind glaring at the ground, arms folded.

Bob never looks up from the ground. "A little late for the theater . . . " he nods.

"Never fancied the theatre myself."

"Retracing steps . . . "

"How's that?"

"From, uh, an earlier trip."

"Back when you were living here."

"No. After the War."

"So you've been back since?"

"I met an actress then, in one of the shows."

"Not your wife?" Reg says. Jasmine still lags behind alienated, head full of her own voice.

"No." He stops to look up at the sky.

"Fancy being married?"

"Sure." The Yank holds out his palm.

"Kids?"

"Lots." Still looking up, "It's about to rain."

"Right, I felt something too."

"So we're checking out the haunts of old flames," says Jasmine, "brilliant," and Reg looks at her.

"I suppose," Bob answers quietly.

Reg says, "London bird then," still looking at Jasmine, finally sensing her mood. She stares back defiantly and Reg tears himself from her stare.

"She was in a show playing my older sister who, uh, just had been killed in a plane crash."

"Hang on," says Reg. "The actress you were dating was playing your sister?"

"It's queer, I suppose."

"You *suppose* it's queer?" says Jasmine.

"It *is* bloody odd," agrees Reg.

"Fancied a woman playing your dead sister?" Jasmine says, taking some satisfaction from her own tactlessness.

"What happened?" says Reg.

"My father strongly discouraged it." The Yank adds, wryly, "He, uh, knew something about showgirls."

"Or perhaps," says Jasmine, "just showgirls playing your sister."

I'll bet, she thinks, that he married the very next girl he went out with. So when Bob laughs, "The very next girl I went out with, my brother stole—the girl after *that*, I married," she's startled: Did I say it out loud? she wonders. Turning to her slightly, Bob doesn't break his stride. "Well, then, mate," says Reg absently, stopping in the street to look around or maybe just slow the pace, "you needed to nick one back from him. Jaz, is this the way?"

On the corner is a closed Wimpy Bar. "Nearly did once," says Bob. No, I didn't say it out loud, thinks Jasmine. "But he wasn't the sort—"

"She's the native home-town girl," Reg nods at Jasmine.

"—who had girls stolen from him." The park comes into view.

"I'm not a native and yes it's the way and," says Jasmine, "there's the park." She turns to Reg. "Can we go now?"

"But let's walk him the rest of it," says Reg.

"I want to leave."

"Where are you from?" Bob says to her.

Oh don't bloody bother. To Reg, "I want to leave."

"It's all right," Bob says to Reg, and points through the trees of the park at a large house lit from the outside, red brick and white columns visible in the lights. "That's where you're staying?" says Reg. As the three stand in the street peering at the house, a downpour opens up above and Reg dashes to the Wimpy Bar to take cover under the overhang; Bob follows, though never breaking from his determined stroll. Jasmine remains in the road. "Are you daft?" Reg calls to her. "Get out of there," but the rain comes down and Jasmine doesn't move, staring at him, arms folded.

"I'm going home," she says.

"What?" calls Reg. A few feet away, he can't hear her for the rain.

"See you at the session," she says and turns on her heel and walks off, and when Reg calls after her, "Cheers," she doesn't answer. When Bob calls, more softly, "Goodbye," she doesn't answer that either. Bloody hell, she thinks as she splashes down the road in the rain. The Bloody Impossible Dream. She shakes her head and soon is gone from the men's sight.

Reg shrugs to the Yank under the Wimpy Bar overhang. "She's upset with me," he says, "we'll sort it out tomorrow."

"I'm the one she's angry at," Bob says.

Reg is surprised. "Why would she be angry at you?"

It's becoming cold in the rain. Reg pulls his coat around him closer, but the other, barely noticing, says, "Evil has become a quaint word, hasn't it?"

"Uh," says Reg, "well. 'Evil'? Don't suppose I've heard it since Church, whenever the last time that was."

Watching Jasmine disappear in the distance, Bob says, "How long have you been together?"

"Not that long," says Reg. Now he doesn't want to tell the other man they're not really a couple. "Met her through the record company. She's there to keep an eye on us in the studio, and soon I suppose I was keeping an eye on her."

"What were you doing before you made records?"

"Laying bricks back home. Started the band with another bricklayer. Still me day job, construction."

"Do you write your songs?"

"Sometimes. One we're doing tomorrow is by a cat from your hometown, New York—"

"I don't have a hometown . . . "

"—but sometimes I change a lyric or two . . . "

" . . . anymore."

" . . . if I think we can get away with it. Make it a bit our own, you know?"

"No one gets angry at music."

"Are you having me on? People get angry at music all the bleeding time."

"No one will kill you for it, though."

"Not yet." In the shadow of the Wimpy Bar, the Brit sees the same blue glint of the Yank's eyes that Jasmine saw. Bob says, "You, uh, don't have to go the rest of the way."

Doesn't occur to him, thinks Reg, to spot me a few quid for a cab. "So what is it then," he says, nodding at the large house through the park trees, "if not a hotel?"

"Ambassador's residence."

"You're staying with the ambassador?"

"I lived there as a boy. Queer to be back."

"You lived in the ambassador's house as a boy?"

"The scene of . . . " says Bob, and stops. "Whatever can be redeemed, I suppose," he finally finishes. "But then my religion would make me believe that even if I didn't want to. My father, uh, his judgment in world affairs was something less than his judgment in showgirls."

They continue watching the rain come down from under the Wimpy Bar overhang. Still pulling his coat close, Reg lights another cigarette. Bob says, "What's your girl's name again?"

"You're not making a move on me old lady, are you?" Reg says it like he's joking.

Bob snaps, "No."

"Just winding you up a bit. What with stealing birds from your brother and all. Jasmine."

"Nearly stole."

"Right, nearly."

"Didn't I say nearly?"

"You did," Reg assures him.

Sticking his head out from beneath the dripping overhang, Bob surveys the skies. "She's African, isn't she?"

"What?"

"Your girl."

"Oh. Yeah."

"From South Africa."

"Don't remember, mate, I get all those places confused, if you want to know the truth. Same thing, aren't they? No, she's from that country with the emperor cat. The one the rastas think is Jesus."

"Haile Selassie."

"Yeah."

"Ethiopia."

"That's it."

"Abyssinia. The beginning of the world. He was at my brother's funeral."

"What?"

Bob says to Reg, "My brother was better in *every* way."

"The emperor of Ethiopia was at your—?"

"But he had his weaknesses, and she was one."

"Bob? I've sort of lost track who we're on about."

"And we couldn't have it anymore. And when she didn't want to let him go—"

"Right. We're not talking about the London bird from the theatre anymore."

"—she came to me," but he stops, a man who resents having to explain anything to anyone. "I made her heart sing, for a few hours."

"She said that?"

"She's gone now. He's gone too."

B ob says, "I was the one . . . not born with gifts. I was the one about whom people said, This is a boy without gifts. I wasn't the son meant for anything, I was never meant to be the great man. Runt, they called me, sissy they said. Mama's boy, what shall we do with him? Not born with gifts, I had, uh, only my will. My brothers and sisters were born with gifts, then one by one they were gone and left no more shadows in which to hide. No longer were their gifts for me to serve, when I no longer was a middle brother but the oldest . . . when I was left by default then I made out of my will what I could. You know, most of my life," he says nodding at the house in the distance, "I would have beaten any man who said or hinted that my father had anything to redeem," and up until he says it, Reg wouldn't have imagined this small man beating up anyone; but now he can. Bob turns to Reg. "Sooner or later you have to see the sins of the father for what they are. Your Mr. Churchill understood things more clearly. It doesn't mean I don't love my father. It doesn't mean I didn't spend my life trying to make him as proud of me as he was of my brothers and sisters." He looks back at the house. "I do worry if tomorrow is a mistake."

Reg says, "Look here, is this about Jaz being a colored bird?"

"Giving a speech to some students," says Bob, "but, uh, I'm not sure what to tell them—I don't think there's much I *can* tell them," in his high nasal voice, "and the government doesn't want me coming. I mean *their* government but mine too, I suppose. Will I only succeed in giving the white government a, a . . . an excuse to arrest black Africans? Am I only making trouble? Do I become the . . . *rationale* by which more blacks are oppressed, beaten, brutalized? Is this about my damned ego? Is this one more test I put myself to, for which other people pay the price, as my brothers paid the price for my father? I keep going over the speech. Taking the anger out. Putting it back in."

"What is it these students want from you, then?"

For the first time tonight the hair-trigger altar boy becomes all of a piece with his sad burning eyes. "I don't believe one man changes everything," he says, "maybe no one man changes *anything*, least of all me. I'm an *accident*. But I believe there are times when even men who aren't great must find a way to try and do

great things. People think I'm afraid of nothing when the truth is
I'm afraid of everything, and not so long ago I vowed before a
God I love and trust a little less than I used to that I would do all
the things I'm afraid of, because I do believe anyone can change
part of something, and that part of something changes something
else, and soon the ripple in the lake is the wave on the beach."

A t Olympic Studios off Baker Street the next day, the
session starts late. The band spends most of the morning and early afternoon waiting outside in a van for
another session to finish; Reg and Jasmine don't speak. He
tries to tell her about the conversation under the Wimpy overhang in the downpour, but she doesn't want to hear about it.

Once in the recording studio, there's further delay over
the tuning of the guitars, and discussion about replacing a
whistle in the song's middle-eight with a flute. Because there's
no time left, the session is necessarily brief, two takes, the second in the can. "You changed one of the lines," Jasmine complains to Reg and he explains, "Made it a bit our own, yeah?"
and she says, "Yeah, well, the bloke who wrote it has this
funny idea the song is his." She's bitching about everything
today, thinks Reg.

N ear the end of the session, she ducks out of the studio
and stops on the way home at the pub below the Ad
Lib, where Jonesy buys her a drink and she's stunned
by the BBC interview on the telly above the bar. "Bloody hell,"
she mutters into her glass, staring at the screen.

"Hey," says Jonesy, remembering the night before, "isn't that . . . ?" How can I be so dim? she thinks. And I'm studying to be a bloody journalist. "Doesn't really look like that in real life, does he?" Jonesy says. "A lot older in real life." A week later over a cup of tea, she reads in *The Times* an article about him in South Africa.

The article describes him arriving at midnight at the airport outside Johannesburg to no state reception whatsoever, the government having decided to ignore him. Because no one representing the government is there, the airfield is stormed by hundreds of black South Africans to greet him. A few days later at the Cape Town university where he's scheduled to speak, the government cuts the speaker cables; he speaks anyway—"It's from numberless diverse acts of courage and belief," he murmurs, barely audible, "that history is shaped"—stumbling through his address in his high nasal whisper, to silence that precedes the thunderclap of ovation. He rides in the backseat of an open car, recalling for those few reporters able to cover the story, the vast majority having been denied credentials and travel papers, an image that leaves them unnerved. In defiant response to that image, he stands in the backseat rising from the sea of black faces that grows from day to day and town to town.

He faces down protesters who claim to base their views on Judeo-Christian beliefs by asking how they can be certain God isn't black. He walks through black villages and the immense crowd doubles, triples, multiplies in what seems unquantifiable exponents; he shakes every black hand that never before has been offered a white hand that didn't have in it a stick.

Each rally becomes so large as to leak into the next until it's as if the entire country is a rally. For everyone who sees him, the astonishing courage of the small shaking man with the limp handshake who said to Reg, "People think I'm afraid of nothing when the truth is I'm afraid of everything," has about it the force of revelation. "We felt small and meaningless," the article quotes one of the student leaders, a young woman Jasmine's age, "and he's the only man to come tell us we're not alone. He has reset the moral compass."

Over the next year, pursuing her studies in London and continuing to work for the record company, she keeps the *Times* article as it makes its folded way from one textbook to the next.

She doesn't forget the night she met him. She follows his career and speeches back in his own country, alert to any mention in the press of a return to London. In the fall of 1967 she applies for a visa and quits both her job and school, and flies to New York, remaining forty-eight hours before she catches a train to Washington, D.C.

As a low-level secretary and receptionist, she has worked on his staff for three months before he notices her. By then the Washington office has sent her back to the New York office, and over the course of those three months he brushes past her desk twice, even nodding at her routinely without recognizing her. Then the third time something he can't place breaks his stride as he passes, before he keeps going. The fourth time, he stops and stares at her.

Almost puppyish he cocks his head, studying her. To her irritation, having been in his company a couple of hours in London and felt no intimidation, now she's a bit terrified of him. "You're new?" he says.

"About three months," she says. "I was put on staff in September."

Then he remembers: It's her accent, she realizes. "London," smiling the small smile as he walks away, "you were angry at me." A week later Jasmine sits at her desk daydreaming about Christmas trees and spending her first holiday abroad when the woman who hired her calls her into a cubicle. "Just how settled are you here?" says the woman.

"What do you mean 'here'?"

"New York."

Jasmine shrugs. "Fancy getting a proper little Christmas tree."

"Get a proper little Christmas tree in Washington. They want you back down there, maybe for a while."

By ten o'clock that night she's back in Washington. For a few days she's doing the same work that she was in New York. On the weekend she takes the train back to pack the rest of her things and hasn't been in her flat twenty minutes before the phone rings. "What are you doing here in New York?" says the woman who hired her, on the other end of the line.

"Sorry?"

"Didn't I tell you to get down to D.C.?"

Jasmine says, "Right, well, I came back to get the rest of my thi—"

"They're looking for you down there."

"I've been there all week."

"The senator was looking for you this morning," huffs the woman, slightly irate. "Get back there this afternoon."

"On a Saturday?"

"You know, this isn't a normal job."

J asmine returns to Washington that afternoon. She goes to the office and finds it closed. "But where is everyone?" she says to somebody passing in the corridor of the Senate building. She returns to the office the next day, Sunday, and it's still closed; she reports Monday morning. Making no effort to hide her pique, she says to her immediate supervisor, "What was the rush, then?"

"How's that?" He has long red hair and glasses and isn't much older than she is.

"I'm trying to move my belongings. Half of me still is in New York." She storms back to her desk and half an hour later the supervisor comes over. "He wants to see you," indicating the door over his shoulder, down the carpeted hall. She walks down the hall and knocks at the door and, when she doesn't get an answer, opens it anyway.

L ater she'll realize he's not as small as he seems. Standing upright to his full height, he comes within a couple inches of six feet. But now behind his desk, the chair he sits in yawns as if to swallow him.

Everything sags from his eyes to his clothes. His coat is off and his tie barely tied; his shirtsleeves are rolled up and she's surprised that his arms are distinctly hairy. He wears dark rimmed glasses that she's never seen on him. He swivels slightly in the chair eating a bowl of chocolate ice cream, a man who once arrived at his own swearing-in for a job by sliding down the White House banister. In the last few years he's grown old too fast, bowls of ice cream at odds with the black cloud he brings everywhere he goes.

Jasmine isn't sure whether he answered when she knocked and she didn't hear, or he just didn't answer. She feels like she's been standing in the doorway several minutes—though she knows it can't have been that long—before his gaze wanders from whatever he's fixed on in the air before him.

Except for the swirl of papers on his desk and the children's drawings tacked to a cork bulletin board over his shoulder, his office is no more settled than her apartment in New York, though he's been here not three months but three years. In any event it's not the space of someone planning to stay long. He swivels back and forth a bit manically, brooding at nothing she can discern; his hand holding the ice cream spoon, with his sleeve he brushes the forelock of his hair from his face. "I hear you're, uh, still upset with me," he finally says. He points at a chair on the other side of the desk from him and she takes it.

"Just trying to sort out where I'm supposed to be," she says.

"You're supposed to be here," he says.

"Good to know." She adds, "I'm not always upset."

"I remember," he nods, "you did have a sense of humor. Mostly at my expense."

"Well, sir, as I recall, you don't know Elvis Presley from Paul McCartney."

"Yes, I'm sure anyone would find that uproarious. I know

who Frank Sinatra is," he points out with the ice cream spoon. "It's queer after that night," he says, "for you to call me sir."

"Doesn't feel proper calling you anything else."

"Probably not," he agrees, "not around here anyway. So I've, uh, been asking everyone the same question—practically, you know, stopping people in the street . . . " He looks out the window toward the street.

"Yes."

"Do you know what the question is?"

"Yes."

He waits a moment, turns back to her and throws up his arms as if to say, Well? "Whether to run for president," she says.

"Yes," he says.

"Yes," she repeats.

"Is that, uh, 'yes,' as in, Yes you know the question that I'm asking everyone, or as in, Yes I should run?"

"Yes you should run."

He takes off the black-rimmed glasses. "That was straight-forward," he allows, at once relieved and vexed.

"Do you fancy running for president?"

"Fancy it?"

"Yes."

"Well, *that's* the question"—and now the kid in him swivels all the way around in the chair—"everyone asks *me*." He stops before the window and the trees along the Mall in the distance. "Know much about presidential politics?"

"No."

"Still studying . . . it was journalism, right?"

"Not in a while."

"Still think politics is, uh, whatever it was you said that night? A waste of time."

"I don't think I put it that way, sir."

"Pretty much." He glances at her over his shoulder. "What changed?" and she doesn't answer but, as if she did, he returns to the window. "Do you have family?"

"Dad more or less disappeared when I was young. Mum died three years ago."

"Brothers or sisters?"

"A brother. Don't see him much either. He's older."

"How much?"

"Eight years."

He murmurs, "My brother was eight years older. I keep wondering what *he* would say but perhaps that doesn't matter—he thought everyone else should be careful except him. He wasn't careful." The bowl of ice cream finished, he swivels back to put it on the desk. "No modern president's ever been denied the nomination of his political party. You have to go back to, who? Cleveland?"

"I wouldn't know."

"Truman was the most unpopular man in the damned country by the time he ran. The children of Franklin Roosevelt, the man who appointed him, tried to take away the party's nomination and give it to Eisenhower, who didn't even belong to the party. Eisenhower only saved the world—and they still couldn't do it. Theodore Roosevelt, most revered president since Lincoln, tried to take the nomination of his party from President Taft, who nobody liked and came in third in a three-man election," he leans over the bowl on the desk, "and Teddy Roosevelt couldn't do it," and stares into the bowl as though it's bottomless. "I need more ice cream."

S he says, "Times change?"

"Yes times change," he agrees, "but the system changes last, after everything else. If I run, it will be Bad Bobby again. Ruthless Bobby. Everything that those who hate me have ever said about me, it shall all be true. Selfish Little Son-of-a-Bitch Bobby who can't wait to get back in the White House. Every damned office-holder of my party, which is to say those who control the party, will hate me because it will just complicate the hell out of their lives and their own political fortunes. And when people are for me, they won't be for *me*. They'll be for *him*."

"You're wrong," she shakes her head.

"On the other hand, there's Dante."

"Dante?"

"Uh, 'the hottest place in hell . . . ' etcetera."

"Etcetera?"

"Is reserved for those who do nothing when faced with a moral choice." He blurts, "Whatever I do, I need your help."

"Right. Of course. I would be honored." It sounds funny but she means it.

"Not *too* honored. I don't deserve that."

She rises from the chair and at the door stops, the thought tripping her up. "Is it because I'm black? I mean, I don't know what you have in mind, do I, but whatever it is—?"

"How can you wonder that," he says, "if neither of us knows what I have in mind?"

"I've never been all that conscious of that part of me. With these white woman's gray eyes, I suppose."

"Ethiopia."

She's impressed. "Did I tell you?"

"I don't remember."

"Folks moved my brother and me when I was two—Dad was a med student. As I always heard it, the idea was eventually to come on over here. They got as far as London before they split up."

"If we do this, remember to bring the angry woman with you. I'll need her."

"I'm not an angry woman."

"Bring the one with the sense of humor then."

"I'll bring them all," and with a start she's unsettled by how much he already looks like a phantom. "There's more than one."

"Yeah? Try being *me*."

He already looks like a phantom, and on the campaign trail over the next four months, he forever seems on the verge of falling apart. When he speaks to crowds he shakes, rushing through speeches when he's not stumbling; sometimes the words run into each other as if spoken by a drunk man or, worse, a man seized by a stroke. On planes and buses after each rally, he crumples into seats, passing out in a sweat, fevered by dark providences and the irredeemable. He's bleached of color, seems to be disappearing before everyone's eyes. He already was old before his time when she met him in London nearly two years ago and now he's older still.

But then he gathers intensity, prying himself loose from the grip of whoever he was in the past, now in pursuit of something inside him that he no longer can refuse to believe in—and finally catching it, though he can't be sure that it hasn't caught him. He holds out to the crowd his open hand as if it's filled with a beating heart pulled from his own chest, and his persona is made raw; the motorcade moves down the street and men twice his size, their knees and hands bloodied, have to hold him around the waist so he's not pulled away by the crowd who would disrobe him, pick him clean of his cufflinks and tie and shoes, benignly strip him as naked as their feelings for him and his for them or, more ferociously, divide him up among them in pieces. He refuses to allow about the campaign the air of celebration on which campaigns depend. When he whispers to her at a rally in Los Angeles, *These are my people*, it's not a boast; he derives from it as little exhilaration as he does from the rest. He won't reconcile himself to the old rituals of politics or to even the rituals of new politics that he in part invented. He's come to be mortified by the political truisms to which he once devoted himself.

The campaign is shambolic, a moving pandemonium. More than anything it resembles an act of penance, the lashed slog from one station of the cross to the next; when he unconsciously touches the heads of poor children, brushes their cheeks with a finger, it's more priestly than political. Jasmine can't imagine how, if he manages to get elected, he'll survive the job—not because he isn't tough enough, certainly not because he isn't committed enough, but because he's altogether too committed, because he gives altogether too much, beyond what any sane self can stand or give. Retreating to the edges of staff meetings where he lies on a couch saying nothing as some point of strategy is hashed over, he ends arguments with decisions so succinct and raging ("Indiana is essential, we need to not just win there but *crush*") that Jasmine can only be mystified by the method and math of democrazy that she's come to spell with a z.

Wild and frenzied from kansan desolations that no foreigner can imagine short of the moon, where white college students chase the bus and train just to call to him the goodbyes that will be unbearable to remember in three months, to indianan victories not crushing enough, to oregonian defeats that leave him precarious on the edge of political oblivion, little of it seems to have bearing on what he speaks of to privileged and working-class alike: the rats of the black tenements and the self-killing grounds of Indian reservations, delano daughters with hands stained by the vineyards on which they barely subsist and delta sons with bodies misshapen by hunger. This is prosperity, he bays at them beneath montana nights, calculated as much by what's polluted, what's killed, what's secured and incarcerated, but never by a child's delight, a poem's spell, the immutable power of a kept promise. It's a prosperity that measures everything that means nothing and nothing that means everything. It tells all of us, he concludes to the crowds, everything about our country except why it's ours.

There's another sort of murder, he warns—and does he intend it as prophecy? or does the prophetic just come naturally, not by virtue of what he foresees but what he knows in his bones—a sort of murder as fatal as the sniper's gunshot, and that's the violence of the institution that never sees the poor in their rags or hears the sob of the hungry or feels the touch of the forsaken. This violence shatters the spirit. It not only accepts but advances the premise that this is a country where it's acceptable to succeed by destroying people's dreams and breaking their hearts.

Jasmine has no way of knowing that this campaign is singularly different from any other. It reminds her more of a concert tour not just in its organization but its entropy. Glumly assessing a campaign poster of himself, he says, "Am I a Beatle?" and winks at her about the inside joke; but when the crowds tear his clothes and steal his shoes, wanting a handful of his hair that grows longer, she realizes this is on another level from what she's expected let alone known. "Are all campaigns over here like this?" she finally asks an aide in one of the Los Angeles suburbs. This is on an afternoon when, casting aside her clipboard, she pulls to safety a teenage boy a few years younger than she is, who's been lifted off his feet by the crowd and nearly pulled under to be trampled or crushed. The aide doesn't have to answer, given the look on his face, but does anyway. "No campaign," he says, "has *ever* been like this," and in his face she sees the terror at what's been unleashed that no one can control.

Pulled from the crowd, the teenage boy hears Jasmine—leaning close to his face—whisper in his ear a single word; and though Jasmine wouldn't dispute that she did so, she has no distinct recollection of it though it isn't a word that would surprise either of them if they could relive the moment, stop and catch the word in the air and hear it again.

There's more than one of me, she said to him that afternoon months before, back in the capitol, and he answered, "Try being me," and she sees all the versions of him in the room of an Indianapolis Marriott on an early-April night of murder that can't help feeling to everyone like a foretelling. The network reportage from the television in the other room is on a kind of loop, delivering the same news over and over so as to try and shake off the shock of it; and dozing on the bedroom floor she still can hear people crying in other parts of the suite but she's moved most by the silence from outside, since alone among all cities tonight, on this particular night this particular city isn't gripped by riot because the man who lies on the bed a few feet away in the same room dared to go break the news to a black crowd in the ghetto a few hours ago, a few miles away.

It was cold that night but the rain was fine and dry like ash blown in from the southwest all its way from that motel balcony in Memphis, and the torchlight was still the red haze of the mind's fires not yet lit. When they first drove up to the rally it wasn't clear how many had heard the news, only that most hadn't, especially those who came early so they could be within touching distance, or spitting distance a few feet back, or shooting distance a few more feet back.

An aide hurriedly scribbled some brief remarks for him— *and then please Senator let's get the fuck out of here*. But stepping from the car, taking the first step up to the platform to address everyone, each and every face before him black, he crumpled the speech and stuck it in his overcoat pocket and just went up and told them. He's dead. Shot and killed tonight, he told them—and then he talked not for a minute or two or five but nearly ten, talked over the roar of gunfire heard in his mind's ear four and a half years since Dallas, "so go home tonight," he told them, "and yes say a prayer for Dr. King and his family, but say one too for our country that we love," and for those close enough to see, the pain in his eyes was his passport to theirs, the signal of truth and his right to say it and theirs to hear it.

Then however many hours later it is, from her place on the floor in the room at the Marriott she can't tell at first if he sleeps or just stares at the ceiling. Nevertheless all his versions of himself are there on the bed with him: that man of thoughtless courage who broke the news to the ghetto tonight; the man who presumed in such a mean moment to quote Greek poets and call for the taming of men's savagery and making gentle the life of the world; the petty man possessive of his own calamitous heartbreaks who afterward admonished those around him for their sorrow, snapping that this wasn't the greatest tragedy in the history of the Republic, as though this murder of a black Atlanta preacher had the temerity to move anyone as much as another of a president fifty-five months earlier; the blunt man who practically spat at Jasmine in the early morning London hours "South Africa" as though to provoke her, as though to dare her to engage his conscience and expose her own; the guilty man remembering that in another life not so long ago he approved electronic surveillance of the black preacher now dead in Memphis; the stirred man who called the victim's widow to offer solace, a word he prefers to "comfort" because it sounds less secular; the newly afraid man, corpses of fears he hoped he had killed still fresh, maybe not even corpses. The man who hears the echo of a future already fired and on its trajectory.

All of the versions of him lie there on the bed and then she hears one of them in the room's fading light. "The pain. The pain that can't forget," he says, "must find a way to rain forgiveness on the heart until there grows a wisdom and grace as close to God's as we can manage. The Negro in this country understands the country's promise better than anyone because he's felt its betrayal. I don't have the right to ask them to believe me. No white politician does. Six years ago when I was Attorney General and the Freedom Riders took their buses into Alabama and they were beaten and hosed down and run down by dogs and they asked me to protect them, I just wanted them to stop making trouble. Just stop, I said. You're making trouble! Don't be in a hurry! That seems a different life now. That man . . . seems a different man, or I hope he is, anyway. So many times in this country, faith has been asked of the children of slaves to only dishonest and treacherous ends. The children of slaves took a leap of faith six years ago out on that Mall in the shadow of our most haunting memorial and now, now that he's been shot down, we ask them to take another leap. If it's true that the promise of this country can't be kept until white begs the forgiveness of black, it's as true that the promise can't be kept until the black man decides whether to extend that forgiveness—and slavery's child is under no obligation to do that. In our hearts on which rains the pain that we can't forget, we know that. Who knows how such a thing can happen, the request for forgiveness and the granting of it? What historic moment can represent that? A black man or woman someday running, perhaps, for the office that I run for now? But we can't tell the slave's child whether to forgive. We can't pretend it's incumbent on blacks to do that. One more time the fate of the country and its meaning is in the same black hands that built the White House, the same hearts broken in the country's name. We'll be only as good a country as the black man and woman and child allows and only as redeemed as black allows white to redeem itself. But the slave's child owes no one that redemption."

All the versions of him collapsing into his exhausted frame, he says, "I know it could have been me. Everyone knows that. No one knows it better than I. Perhaps if it were, it would have mattered as much, perhaps not. Perhaps it would have been better."

"Don't," she whispers.

"I don't know how much time I have," he says, "to become the person that I hope I am."

One night on the campaign train she overhears one of the reporters say, "Someone's going to kill him too." She's passing through the press car when the reporter says it over a shot of bourbon and a hand of cards where black Jacks are wild, and it stops her in her tracks.

In the late-night light with everyone else on the train asleep, it sounds louder than he actually says it, and the reporter looks up at her and all the reporters turn to look at her; and everyone wants to take back what's been said but they can't. The reporter's eyes are wet. He looks at her, they all look at her, then he looks back at his cards. "Someone's going to kill him too," he says again with quiet fury, "and everyone knows it, and it's all just a dirty trick, him running like this, him raising people's hopes, as though his election is a scenario the country can actually believe in."

"Don't," she whispers again, too late.

South Africa, he said to her that night in London that she first met him—the glint of his blue eyes catching some light off the street—with every intent, whether he realized it, to infuriate her: purely an act of provocation; and now she watches him provoke everyone, most particularly those who would presume to be on his side, those who would presume he's on theirs. Those who would presume to take any sort of comfort in their own righteousness or liberalism: He would

186 · STEVE ERICKSON

make the world as anguished as he is, not out of narcissism but because no truth is worth anything to him without anguish. Everything that would presume to be true must prove itself to him by fire. He no longer accepts that, in political terms, he's no one if he's not who the public thinks he is. He's come to insist that he's who *he* thinks he is.

He provokes those who would presume to be indifferent. "There are more rats in New York," he tells one audience in the Midwest, "than there are people," and they think he's joking until they laugh and he hisses, "Stop it." He provokes those who would presume that he's indifferent. Meeting militant blacks in California, he stoically submits to their torrent of abuse until it's exhausted and they're left with nothing but their respect for him and the exceptional instance of a white man who will come to them alone and listen, and listen, and listen.

But more than anyone, he provokes the killer out there. More than anything he provokes his own fate. Campaign assistants draw the curtains in hotel rooms, and she watches him get up and open them and frame himself in the window: I'm here. You out there on one of those rooftops, here I am. *Ready, aim.* Here I am, take . . . me . . . out. Stepping from a doorway out onto the sidewalk, his bodyguards trying to bustle him into the waiting car, she sees how he resists, stops, lingers a moment at the street's edge: You. Up there in one of those windows—I know about high windows. I know about their vantage points. *Fire.* I know about high-powered fifty-two millimeter Italian Carcano rifles, I know how the flimsiest of men and circumstances can change the world.

She made my heart sing.

Wild thing comes from the radio through the open back

door of the car waiting for him: He provokes the future, thinks
Jasmine, that the New World has claimed for itself for five hundred years. With every bit of the future that he passes through
unscathed, he would inoculate himself to all the ways that the
present threatens him, all the ways the past haunts him.

O f course she'll remember all of this on the night in Los
Angeles two months later, in the back kitchen of the
old L.A. hotel where the Academy Awards were held
several decades before. She isn't sure whether she actually
hears the shots or just imagines hearing them, not knowing
exactly where they came from except close by; the one thing
that the television footage can't or won't capture is the amount
of blood a single handgun can spill. "Is there a doctor in the
house?" someone with a microphone screams over and over;
and over and over are the wails of "Nooo, noooo!" and "How
could this happen?"—but how could it not? will be the question later.

F or a moment she sees the man behind the .22-caliber
gun, dark and small, no bigger than his target, twenty-
four years old, half of them spent growing up in
Palestine and the other half in Pasadena fifteen minutes away.
He's cased the hotel for the last several days; his diaries will
reveal that his planning was methodical. In the months to
come, Jasmine will try to establish some connection, something
about the man to relate to, though why she needs to understand anything about him, she doesn't know; she wonders

what music is in his head when he perforates the target with the four shots from the gun—don't assassins have music in their heads?

There in the ensuing tumult of the hotel, fear dies along with her dread, and anticipation along with her hope. She feels like she might go under the madness like the teenage boy she pulled from the frenzied crowd a few weeks ago, not caught in others' current but rather a current of her own in which she now not only expects drowning but desires it. "We're a great country," are practically his last words, "we're a selfless country, a compassionate country," and before mounting the stage he confides in her, "I've finally become who I am"—but in an instant, politics reverts to meaninglessness again. "Don't think," she answers to his memory afterward when no one is around, sometime when she's alone in a room, sometime on a bus, sometime walking along the sea, "that your death inspired anything. Don't think," she cries, "that I believe yours was anything but a freak flame in the dark, one random flash of beauty that happens not because it means anything but because in a universe of such chaos even beauty is going to have its moment, by sheer chance," and finally she slips from his hold on her, mostly.

At first she's determined to remain in Los Angeles, but at the request of the campaign, purely for organizational purposes she accompanies the body on its flight back to New York to lie in Saint Patrick's Cathedral, which she can remember walking by during the short time she lived there, never suspecting this. Four days after his murder the coffin is carried by train from New York to Washington and she tries to hide herself in one of the cars, hide from the widow he married after dating the actress who played his dead sister, hide from those who were part of the campaign, hide more than anything from the hundreds of thousands along the track, old men with flags saluting and boy scouts with caps over their hearts, home-made signs that urge GOODBYE GOODBYE GOODBYE to the train that only proceeds more slowly as the crowds swell. Those are the ones she can't stand to look at—until finally she looks and it's at the sight of wet black faces sobbing more for him than any white man in memory that she bursts into tears. When the train passes an anonymous young woman fallen to her knees in the grass holding her face in her hands, Jasmine wonders, Do I have the right, as a woman from another country who hasn't borne what they have, to hold my face in my hands? and then thinks No, and holds her head anyway.

In the late hours the train arrives in Washington and the coffin is eased from its car and taken from the station down Constitution Avenue along the Mall's northern border to the Lincoln Memorial where people sing, then to the cemetery to lie alongside the buried brother. She's never seen a night funeral before filled with torchlight: All funerals should be at night, she concludes, it's the only beauty bleak enough to be worthy of funerals. Next to a plaque that quotes from the speech he gave in South Africa two years before, in that moment that first so alienated her and then so moved her to give him her heart, there's only a small unassuming white cross.

few weeks after the frenzied campaign rally where he almost is trampled to death, an eighteen-year-old boy recognizes on television the woman who pulled him to safety from that terrible sea of human hope and then whispered in his ear something he'll never forget, even as he has no idea what it was.

It's late on the night of the state's primary election. The news pictures are broadcast from the back kitchen of the old L.A. hotel that several decades ago hosted movie stars and presidents nearly as notable, where the Academy Awards took place; in the early-morning hours of this night, the unspeakable thing that's on everyone's mind finally happens. He lies in bed in his dormitory room at the university, listening to the primary returns on the radio. He's about to turn it off, the candidate having given his victory speech, when the newscaster reports hearing shots.

ot knowing where the shots are fired or exactly where they come from, the newscaster audibly trembles. Some semblance of professionalism in his voice struggles to keep catastrophe at bay.

Zan gets out of his dorm bed and pulls on some clothes and goes into the room next door where other guys who live on the same floor play cards. Without asking, he turns on his neighbor's small black-and-white television and there's the young black woman in the tumult, none of the fear in her eyes that Zan saw that afternoon weeks ago but rather now a dead release. "What's going on?" one of the guys says looking up from his hand of cards, and Zan says, "Something's happened."

Forty years later, the original exhilaration felt by the country that greeted the new president on his election is supplanted by an opposite hysteria for which Zan can only wonder if the first hysteria is in some measure responsible. On the express Eurostar that pulls out of London's St. Pancras station off King's Cross and hurtles beneath the Channel toward Brussels and Paris, while his son, wreathed by a rare quiet, stares out the train window at the Chunnel walls, Zan reads newspapers scooped up beneath the skylights of the station arcade and, from the dispassionate vantage point of foreign shores, realizes that his country has lost its mind.

At citizen meetings in towns around the country, people are becoming unhinged about . . . everything. These are people who were not part of the small era of good feelings that followed the election; these are people who held their tongues. The hysteria isn't really about what's proposed or opposed or the facts of these things, no more than was the original hysteria. As was the original hysteria, it's about the president himself and how into a time of tumult and anxiety has come someone that some regard as so alien that now the emotional tenor of every debate is separated from reality. It's the dark nihilist brethren of the euphoria that greeted the new president's election, the commensurate response to a hope and promise too uncommon and maybe delusional to last any longer than fleetingly.

In the dark of the Chunnel, the train comes abruptly to a halt. As they wait for the train to begin again, Zan mulls the article in *The Times* that reports death threats against the new president up four hundred percent. Over the months that have followed his assumption of office, first there have been openly

expressed hopes that he'll fail, then accusations that he's a radical, then questions whether he was born in the country and
really is president at all. "When are we going to move?" comes
Parker's voice out of the dark.

Then he's accused of hating white people. Then he's
accused of fostering a presidency under which white
people will be attacked and beaten. Then it's claimed
he's setting up death tribunals that will condemn old people
to termination. Then he's compared to fascist dictators, then
people bring guns to events where he speaks, then a widely-
read blogger calls for a military coup, then a minister in
Arizona calls from the pulpit for the president's death. A popular website runs a poll asking respondents whether he should
be assassinated.

Following such a linear progression, Zan asks himself in
the dark two hundred feet below the surface of the English
Channel, what else could be next? Or, put another way, what
possibly could *not* be next? A new source of dread invades
Zan amid all his other more prosaic trepidations. While this
has been a country of murder since Zan was a teenager, and
though Zan has lived through other assassinations and seen
the country find a way to go on, he's uncertain whether this
time the country could endure such a thing: Too much history
attends this presidency. However much anyone resists it, this
president is too much the asterisk of the dream's last four hundred years; he wears asterisks like a crown of thorns. Zan feels
vested like he hasn't before—no doubt, he thinks in the dark,
to an extent that's unhealthy, politically and any other way.
But he isn't the only one so vested and then there are those
vested in the man's fall—so should the unspoken thing hap-

pen, then how does a country that has invested so much stand it? Or does the very improbability of his rise suggest that he's fated to be martyred.

Zan knows he's not the only one contemplating this. He's not the only one nursing a fear terrible enough that no one wants to name or give voice to it, just as few could stand to name or give voice to the fear that accompanied another prospective president forty years ago whom Zan, as a freshman, saw in the campus quad. Something about such men lets loose in the country a fury which no one names and to which no one gives voice; but then if it comes to pass, will everyone be left to wonder whether it would have been better to say it out loud after all? Now some do, in whispers so that fate might not overhear. From the flattest part of the Texas Panhandle, Zan's anarchist friend writes, *I can't stand him—and I pray for him every day.*

Zan wonders if they should get off the Eurostar at Brussels and change trains there for Germany. But the disadvantage of changing in Brussels is that it would involve yet another change of trains in Cologne; if the father and son continue another hour south onto Paris, they can catch a direct overnight train heading to Berlin. Zan was planning to get a couchette for his son on the Paris-Berlin train but the boy insists he doesn't want to be in one part of the train while his father is in another, and Zan remembers years before when he went to Berlin, during his breakup with Viv before Parker was born, learning the hard way that european trains subdivide in the night while you sleep, whisking you off, if you're on the wrong car, to somewhere else.

The flaw of Zan's Paris-connection plan is that there's only half an hour between the Eurostar's arrival at the Gare du Nord and the departure of the train to Berlin from the nearby Gare de l'Est. Counting too much on the newly teutonic timeliness of London trains, including the sleek Eurostar, and the ease of maneuvering the ten-minute walk between stations, Zan leaves his plan behind him in the dark of the Chunnel, once the express finally begins to move.

Not even taking into account the time they've been stuck under the Channel on the Eurostar, the folly becomes more evident in Paris with the father and son's arrival. Thirty minutes to not only change trains but stations? A vanity, Zan understands now, born of younger days and a sharper mind back when—long before Viv and children—he lived in Paris with crazy taxi-life Trotskyites and their aristocratic tastes, who thought, like Ronnie Jack Flowers in L.A., that all the proletariat should have Blaupunkt sound systems. That was when he could have been airlifted into Paris blindfolded and determined within five minutes exactly where he was.

Ascending the vertical Gare du Nord with its transparent tubular walkways, Zan and Parker take half an hour figuring out where to exit. I'm becoming, the father tells himself, a confused old fart. Turning toward the Gare de l'Est, he and his son dart through the twilight across the rue Dunkerque between cars, Parker a few feet behind Zan, when a taxicab, the driver apparently beyond the control of anything but unexplained fury billowing from the exhaust pipe, barrels toward the boy.

Zan grabs Parker's hand so hard he can feel some small bone crunch. He remembers that this was the hand Parker broke the night he took the boy to the emergency room and then lost his car keys, railing about it afterward when his supernaturally wise daughter advised him from the backseat, "Poppy, let it go." Zan yanks Parker from the path of the cab much like a young black female hand once yanked him from a surging crowd except that, given the difference in years between older man and younger boy, the force is exponential.

The cab flies into the back of a limousine. Dimly through the cab's back window, the cab's passenger flies into the seat in front, grabbing her head; then the cab backs up and, the gear first thrown into reverse then into drive, hits the limo again. Then it backs up and slams into the limo still again. "Are you all right?" Zan says to Parker, who nods in shock; the boy is too wide-eyed at the spectacle of the cab reversing and crashing into the same limo over and over to bother holding his throbbing hand. Everyone stops to look. Finally the cab's passenger flees out the other side, leaving the back door open behind her. Later Zan realizes that in his own country, this scene wouldn't be nearly as insane, or rather it would be insane in a distinctly familiar, new-world way.

By the time they reach the Gare de l'Est, the last night train to Berlin has departed. Zan and the boy check into a no-star hotel on the rue d'Alsace that overlooks the trainyards below and a stubby stone wall that runs alongside. In the difference between the two stations, ten minutes by foot, lies the division between centuries and longitudes, the high-tech Gare du Nord they just left full of young people, western and futurist, the Gare de l'Est shabby and old like its travelers, refugees from Old Europe or those returning to it, fleeing millennial overload. Unable to find ice in any of the stores or bars, Zan wraps Parker's hand in a wet towel, his son finally slipping toward an ibuprofen sleep.

L ying in the dark of the hotel on the rue d'Alsace, the dank yellow lights of the Gare de l'Est coming through the window, Zan watches his son on the other bed. "Parker," he says after a few minutes, and the boy doesn't answer. "Parker."

"What?" Parker finally replies. He lies on his side, his back to his father.

"How's the hand?"

"It hurts."

"It will feel better when the ibuprofen kicks in."

"O.K."

"Are you all right?" says the father.

"I'm trying to sleep."

"What are you thinking about?"

For a moment Parker doesn't say anything and then, "If I had disappeared in London like Sheba, would you have left me there too?"

Z an inhales sharply. He turns onto his back in the dark and stares at the hotel ceiling: For forty-eight hours he's been struggling to keep composed in front of his son. He says, "We're going back for her when we find Mom."

"How are we going to find Mom?" Parker's voice comes from his bed.

"Molly won't hurt Sheba, and she can't take her out of the country." Zan doesn't say the other thing, the thing about Molly that he knows sounds crazy. "Do you think Molly would hurt her?" Only several minutes later does he hear from out of the dark, "No."

L ying in the hotel bed, Zan holds his head. Since his final forty-eight hours in London he's had a low-grade migraine that he treats with aspirin and caffeine—which makes the headache better until it makes it worse—and what modest quantity of codeine can be bought over the counter in Europe. If he can doze at all, the discomfort is bearable when he wakes in the morning before it spirals, over the course of the day, into the clutch of evening, when it's accompanied by nausea. Since the episode a few hours ago with Parker and the taxicab, it's become excruciating.

Zan and Viv used to joke that Parker was conceived in Berlin. When they split up years before and Zan ran to Berlin, it was where he realized he belonged back with Viv; not long after that, she was pregnant. Coming undone, Zan went to Berlin because it was the farthest place he could go before the act of traveling east turned into the act of returning west. But mostly he went because he got on the wrong car of the train. It was the aftermath of the publication of his last novel that somehow turned into a political weapon and cost another man his livelihood; those were the years when the sense of possibility that it once seemed his country might fulfill, the sense of possibility that reminded Zan what a fever dream his country could be when he was young . . . that possibility was on the run as well. The Berlin Wall was his country's final outpost. It was where presidents said, Tear it down, and, Let them come to Berlin, and where a future president said, not so long ago, This is our time.

A New World man hurtling into the heart of the Old World, Zan ran and ran in that moment of his undoing, guilt and failure so close behind that they weren't at his back so much as on it. Ran to Berlin and, where the Wall used to be, tore from his damned guilty novel its pages and shred them, and sprinkled them on the Wall's rubble as though that could absolve anything.

Now in the Paris hotel on the rue d'Alsace, Zan drifts, his dreams not quite dreams, somewhere between anxious dreams and figments of disorder. In the small cabin of his cross-Atlantic ocean liner, X plots his authorship of the Twentieth Century, having had the good stroke of fortune to stumble on its literature before anyone else could write it first. Not entirely unmoved by the ethics of the situation, he reasons nonetheless that in a sense writers always are plagiarizing something albeit unconsciously, things they've read or heard or seen that they re-manifest in some singular fashion that's the only true meas-ure of a writer's originality. As a man literally ahead of his time, X understands that "originality" will be a quaint notion in the next century, with its evolution to a higher philosophy about hybrids and appropriation: I can't be the first person this has happened to, he thinks, this going-back-in-time thing. Maybe all pioneers are out of time, bearers of the future to the past. I'm the first literary sampler, concludes X. I'm just sampling a whole novel, that's all.

And after all, if I produce the novel first, who's to say I'm *not* the author? If you get right down to it, how often have I felt I was onto something ten years before younger writers came along and got more attention for it? Who's to say that in another time the Irish poseur didn't himself get knocked on the head and wake up and steal the novel from someone else? In fact, who's to say that in another past, the Irishman didn't get knocked on the head and wake up and find *my* version of the novel that I'm copying now, dropped beside *him*? Maybe my version of time, thinks X, is the true prototype while the other is the clone.

To be sure, dilemmas present themselves. The first is that, thoughtlessly, the black teenage girl in Berlin who hid in the shadows while X was beaten neglected to deposit at his side, along with the one book, the rest of the century's canon, which X hasn't exactly committed to memory. Grimly realizing he'll have to write his own versions, he brightens: Who's to say I can't write them as well or better? But something else nags at X; he's not sure he can put his finger on it . . . but if the same words are written by a different writer, then are they the same words? Is it still the same book? Or is the text transformed by the experience and persona behind it? And as X imagines writing his own versions of these novels, he begins leaving out passages of the book he copies now—it just goes on and on and *on*, he groans—because no one can possibly miss them; and then it isn't such a far leap from cutting to editing to revising to recasting, enhancing, reimagining, *improving*.

This begs of X the most profound question of all. That question is whether it's possible for someone of his country to speak for the Old World. X is of and from a country that no sooner became the New World than it was time's other bookend, or floated outside time altogether; he is of and from a country that always has belonged to the rest of the world's imagination more than it belongs to its own. Now X labors to author the novel where the literature of the Old World discovers the vision of the New and waves goodbye to itself. Dublin? X would never be able to explain Dublin anyway. But if he doesn't know much about Dublin 1904, then let the story take place in the Los Angeles of 1989, seventy years early. Nighttown will be Twilighttown and Molly will be Dolly, and Bloom will be Zoom or Doom or Groom (as in a man searching for a bride) or Ploom (as in a column of smoke) or Woom (as in where a mother carries a child). Or Toom (as in where you're buried).

Zan wants to kill X. In his sleep, he seethes at the character with every passing word, growing more furious: This is why you're a failure! he screams at him silently in the dark of the rue d'Alsace hotel. You have a chance to be the greatest novelist of all time, author of the literature of the century, *and you rewrite it.*

With John's revision of Matthew, Mark and Luke, Zan tells the university seminar in London a week and a half ago, though it seems longer now, "the novelization of history replaces history itself." John's version of the narrative means to preclude all others. It means to banish from history those who are deaf to its music and to declare all other sins trivial compared to the sin of deafness. John's is the narrative as sustained hallucination, totalitarian in the manner of all great art. With paper and the printing press, the act of creation becomes an intimate one, the act of reading a private one, at which point storytelling is liberated from avoiding the forbidden in order to pursue it. The transformed imagination transforms the conscience. From John's novel there can only be one place to go, the Book of Revelation, "which isn't a novel at all," Zan tells the lecture hall, "but a rave."

Zan can't kill X. If he kills X, the rest of Zan's novel vanishes into the future. But as the ocean liner continues its way to New York, in the early morning hours a mysterious and unseen stranger bearing a strong resemblance to Zan himself breaks into X's cabin and beats him senselessly.

When Viv went to Addis Ababa the first time to get her new daughter from the orphanage, lying on the hotel bed and feeling the small girl next to her at night she heard the sax line of a song drift through the open window.

It was a song that Viv heard everywhere in Ethiopia; later Zan would play it on his radio show. "Tezeta"—meaning memory, or nostalgia, or reminiscence or melancholy—was not quite a title as much as a musical species like the blues, and in this land where memory is a euphemism for the blues, this curling melody always sounded the same to Viv's ears, whether played on sax or piano: smoke that got in your ears rather than your eyes. When the girl lying on the bed next to the mother ran her finger along the outline of Viv's profile to make certain she was there, it felt to Viv like smoke itself.

Now on her return to Addis to find Sheba's mother, when Viv stops in the labyrinth at the city center where the driver has led her and says, looking around, "No, this isn't right," she hears "Tezeta" rise mournfully in the distance like an answer. She has no idea what the answer is. The walls of the passages resonate with distant chants, the thunder of gathering storms, and Viv feels the past and future yearn for each other. Though she's almost certain the song she hears isn't just in her head, now she hears things in the Ethiopian memory-blues that she never heard the first time, lying on the hotel bed with Sheba beside her.

The song is ravenous for memory, and Viv hears in it every-thing that's happened to her and her family since that first time she came, the struggle of everything since Sheba came to live with them, the whispers between her and Zan in the night that somehow everything will be all right even as it becomes harder to understand how that can possibly be true. Lost here in these passageways Viv has a realization bordering on a small epiphany: It's the memory of how quiet Sheba was those first nights lying on the hotel bed beside Viv wreathed by "Tezeta," and how it wasn't until Sheba got back home that her own small body began to broadcast its music, as though a secret word was spoken that turned her up.

Jasmine hears the song on returning to Ethiopia for the first time since the age that Sheba was on leaving it. This is dur-ing Assassination Summer, riots as much about grief as rage sweeping the Chicago park where, forty years later on Zan's TV one November night, crowds greet the election of a new president whose only precedent is what forty years before was forsaken. Jasmine's sojourn follows a brief reconnection with her father, a retired medical orderly—who never became a doctor—hobbling with arthritis, and her brother, an eternal thirty-one-year-old student wandering the landscape of aspira-tions looking for his.

While she's angry at her father for abandoning her and her brother and mother, Jasmine senses this reconciliation is a fleeting final chance at something. The three take a trip to Addis together where at night she hears "Tezeta" wafting from the clubs and isn't sure whether what she glimpses is a memory from when she was two or a dream posing as one; but hearing this song is the only time Jasmine feels like she's home. In assassination's wake she sometimes aches for the solace—a less secular word than comfort—of the mosque; on the flight to Ethiopia, she wonders if she'll leave. Eight days later, with her brother she does, but her father does not, and she never sees him again.

Jasmine knows it should never have been about *him*, the small struck-down man. It should have been about what he stood for; she knows that. But she can't separate the two nor, she finally reasons, should they be separated. Democrazy, as she calls it, isn't about abstractions, it's about the humanity behind abstractions, the candidate's persona that becomes inextricable from accompanying convictions.

She doesn't believe that she has the right to leave Los Angeles, the scene of the crime. She drifts back into a music business that's on an altogether different level from when she was managing hardscrabble Andover bands in London trying to get a hit single; now everyone's an Artist. No one makes singles but rather magna opera with librettos delivered in spectacular gatefolds, right up to the altogether new pretension of librettos disappearing and gatefolds going blank. Her role never has been about aesthetics. It's about managing the lives that have gotten as extravagant as the product—bands with private planes, dressing rooms with liquor and drugs and candy of a designated color, naked girls of every color in closets wrapped

204 · STEVE ERICKSON

in red bows. On the rare occasion when someone tries to coax her from music back to politics, she answers, "No one's ever going to assassinate a songwriter, even in this country."

S he has an affair with a black session keyboardist who has a wife in Atlantic City. She breaks it off after eight months; to her surprise, since she never suspected such inclinations in herself, she has a longer relationship with a young white woman out of college named Kelly who designs album covers for artists that the public hasn't heard of. The covers fill the walls of the little house on the edge of Hancock Park that the women move into together.

Though the break-up takes a couple months, the relationship ends after three and a half years when Jasmine wakes in the middle of the night realizing she wants a child. "We can adopt!" Kelly wails desperately; but Jasmine already feels her womb invaded by the future. Hating herself, pulling away from the house with Kelly sobbing in the rearview mirror, she drives and keeps driving all night, trying to escape the melody of "Tezeta" in her ears until she realizes that the song comes from the vapor within her. "Are you a ghost?" the future mother cries out loud to the daughter who haunts her before she's conceived.

J asmine has been working for the record company four years when she's assigned its biggest client. "See what you can do with him," says the executive across the desk from her, in an office overlooking Highland Avenue, "this calls for personal attention."

"What do you mean personal attention?" Jasmine says suspiciously.

"At the rate he's going, he'll be dead within the year."

"Drugs."

"Kilos."

"He's a Nazi," she says.

"Those," sighs the executive, "were just silly things he said to an interviewer."

"Sieg heil from the back of a car at Victoria Station?"

"He loves black music!" the executive exclaims, and Jasmine stares at him stonily. "You've got to learn not to take these things personally."

"I once learned from someone," says Jasmine, "to take everything personally."

"Was he in music?"

"He ran for president. Does our rock and roll spaceman from Mars or Nuremberg or wherever it is this month still wear dresses?"

"That was one album jacket five years ago." Jasmine tries to remember if Kelly designed it. "He'll be back in town in the next couple days and has rented a house over off Doheny. Why don't you drive out there? Talk to Anna, his personal-assistant/backup-singer/girlfriend."

"So he does fancy girls then."

"He's always liked girls. Don't tell anybody, at least not yet. Our marketing on him is just entering its heterosexual phase."

"He's in his Nazi phase now," nods Jasmine.

I n the driveway of the house, she stops the car aghast. The abode is Southern Californian Egyptian—white pyramid with gas jets at the top spouting fire, a flaming sarcophagus. When she rings the doorbell, the woman who answers coolly appraises Jasmine half a minute before letting her in.

"Why did they send you?" asks Anna, lit joint between her fingers as the two black women make their way down the hall. She considers her manners long and hard before offering it. "No, thanks," says Jasmine. "I think they thought I might help."

"I'm sure they did," the other woman says, "but let me be fucking direct. His pasty white English ass likes the sisters. There was one before me and maybe one after but it sure as shit isn't going to be you."

"That's not what I'm here for."

"Groovy, but wake up. *That's* why they sent you."

"The last thing they want is more drama. They're worried about him."

Anna softens a bit. "Can't say he's not worrisome." She takes a chair and indicates the sofa across from her. "Coke," she says, "amphetamines. *Lots* of coke. More coke than I've seen a single human being suck up. Problem is he still does function, still gets it done. I know that's what they all say but in his case it happens to be so. Five albums in two years? And the last two sold best of all. It'd be better for him if they hadn't. Course I know you folks just want to squeeze another out of him before it's too late."

"They don't want to squeeze another," says Jasmine, "they want to squeeze another five. If they cared only about another they'd be less worried about trying to save him and more worried about getting him into the studio every available moment while they have the chance."

Anna leans forward as if divulging a secret. "*He's losing his mind.* You hear what I'm saying? Down that hallway," Anna points back to where the women came in, "behind that door is some extremely strange shit—black magic, voodoo, old nefertiti wah-wah," indicating the house with the sweep of her hand.

"I'm aware," says Jasmine, "that I'm house-mothering a Nazi."

Anna laughs. "I know—and he's with me? But the man," she says with some weariness, "is not a Nazi. He's not into the politics, he's into the *weirdness*. Maybe that's no better but when he's got it together, he's smarter than any musician I've known. Reads all the time, always onto whatever's coming next before anybody else—and someday if he hasn't killed himself he's going to look back on the Nazi nonsense and think, What the fuck? In the meantime he's coming undone. In hotel rooms he sees people fall from the sky. In the backseat of the car he hears kids' voices crying from the trunk. Swears up and down bodies are buried in the walls of whatever room he's in."

"When is the tour over?"

"Tonight's the last night. He's in . . . Denver? How he's managed to pull it off this long nobody can figure. Gets back day after tomorrow."

"Mind if I go meet his flight?"

"Flight?" Anna laughs again. "My dear, Mister Twenty-First Century travels by good old fashioned train."

Two nights later at Union Station, Jasmine waits at the end of the long amber tunnel beneath the tracks that funnel from the trains to the lobby. Disgorged passengers flood the exits. Only when everyone else is gone do two men appear, one small and wiry, cropped dark hair with a cap, the other emaciated in a black overcoat. The ends of his flaming crimson hair stick out from under a wide-brimmed black fedora; the last time Jasmine felt a man's handshake so weak, he changed her life. At first he calls her Anna, then stops with a slight start. "You're not Anna," he mutters.

"Anna's at home," she answers.

"Home?" he says, perplexed.

"The house. I'm Jasmine."

"From the record company?" and then, "This is Jim," introducing the other man. "Charmed," says Jim, kissing her hand, not exactly elegant but courtly. On the way back to Doheny the singer with the red hair announces sweepingly that Jim is "the greatest rock and roll singer in the world," but the only Jim that Jasmine has heard of flashed his willy at a concert years ago and is now dead. "Sings back-up," Anna snorts dismissively at the house after the two travelers have collapsed, one in the mysterious backroom and the other on the same couch where Jasmine sat a couple of days before. "I seem to remember that was *my* job before I started sleeping with the star. Jim made a couple of albums with his own band a few years back—lunatics . . . I won't even go into the fucked up shit that man did on stage. His raggedy junkie ass," she confirms, "is crazier than the other one," nodding at the room down the hall. "Was locked up in a mental ward over at UCLA before we sprang him."

"You," Jim announces from the couch without twitching a finger, startling Jasmine who thought he was unconscious, "didn't spring anyone. *He* did."

When Jasmine returns to the house the next morning, the front door is open. No one answers when she rings the bell. She walks into the house and down the hall, bracing for what she might find, which is Jim sitting in the chair wearing no shirt but owl-rimmed glasses, across from the couch where he passed out the night before. He drinks hot tea and is buried in the *Wall Street Journal*.

Five televisions are on in the room, three of them on the same channel, all with the sound down. Jasmine never noticed the TVs before and now that she looks closer she sees there are two more, turned off. She's trying to compute the incongruity of this not to mention the *Wall Street Journal* when—having in no other way acknowledged her entrance—Jim says from behind the newspaper, "Little doll with gray eyes. What it is." The only other person who's ever commented on her eyes was Kelly. "Primordial," she called them, "from the beginning of time."

"Everything all right, then?" she says.

"Anna left," now peering at Jasmine for a moment around the edge of Dow Jones before disappearing back.

"Left? You mean left left?"

"Yes she did."

Jasmine pokes her head into other rooms. "Why?"

"You'll have to discuss that with her or, more likely, him. I believe," Jim says, "they had a falling out." He adds, "The Communists won an election in Italy."

"They had a falling out because the Communists won an election in Italy?" Jim looks at her around the newspaper again to see if she's kidding. "Shots weren't fired?" she says. "Knives drawn?"

"Oh, worse," Jim answers, *"words were spoken.* Everyone's still alive, though, if that's what you mean—or *she* was, anyway, last I saw her. Being the shiny red cockroach of rock and roll who will survive atomic meltdown, he is as well, I assume."

Jasmine walks down the long hallway to the room in back and knocks on the door. "Hello?" Pressing her ear to the door she can hear music playing, and knocks again more assertively. "Are you all right in there?" The song she heard before begins playing again. "Look here," she says, "I'm going to have to ring the police if you don't answer—"

The door opens abruptly. He wears a thin burgundy robe undone at the waist that he ties now; in the dim hall he shields his eyes as if from some blinding light, though she can barely see in front of her. "Oh," he mutters. He pulls open the door.

"Sorry to bother, just want to make sure you're all right then . . . Mister—"

"No, no, not *Mister* Anything," and he has to muster up a tone of insistence, "come in." There's the scent of smoked Gitanes, and on the drawn window blinds that allow only a brown light, pentagrams have been scrawled. One is drawn on the floor as well. A row of small stubby candles burn on the shelf perilously near books that age has rendered immediately flammable; a couple of other candles burn on the floor. A guitar resting against the wall doesn't appear to have been moved in a while, and there's a small synthesizer keyboard. The music comes from a turntable on a wooden chest beneath the windows, hooked up to two small speakers, the cover to one of which has a gouge administered by something sharp. He says, "Right. Jasmine," demonstrating a memory more acute than she would have predicted.

"Where's Anna?" she asks.

"Anna has left."

"Why?"

"Well, Jasmine," he almost drawls, "you seem very pleasant but I'm not sure that's your business, is it?"

"Rather it is and rather it isn't. Your management has asked—"

"Yes, I just fired them," and he looks at a dusty telephone that shows no sign of having been disturbed. She can't be certain if he's high or exhausted; everything seems to take an effort. "Before you came. I need you to work for me now."

It's hard to tell whether he's thought of this on the spur of the moment or it's something he's been considering more than five minutes. "I shall pay you better than whatever they—"

"You fired them?" she says. "What for? And don't tell me it's not my business."

"They were . . . " He shakes his head and looks at the phone with dread. He says, "*People* . . . have been ringing me up . . . I don't know how they found me here . . . "

"The management?"

"Ringing me up . . . no, not the management, uh . . . need to put a stop to it. Need to stop with . . . " he waves his arm at the pentagrams on the floor and blinds, " . . . all this. It's . . . stirring up what should be left unstirred and now they're ringing . . . excuse me," and at the turntable he puts the stylus back at the beginning of the record he's been playing. The song begins again. He looks up from the chair. "What were we—"

"You fired—"

"Yes. Well, they really weren't handling my affairs properly, were they? I believe that they're stealing my money. It's happened before, you know. It's my fault, really . . . I signed the contract, knew I shouldn't . . . "

"That's why Anna left?"

"Anna . . . no, Anna and I . . . that's not why. This is *fantastic*," he says, leaning toward the record that's playing, "I'm thinking of covering this song," and now there's a spark of something in his speech, "it's from an old . . . what was his name . . . played Zorba the Greek, and Gauguin. Anthony . . . " He's wracking his brain. "God I hate it that I can't remember anything. Anyway it's from a movie with him and . . . Anna Magnani perhaps? Of course I can never do it like Nina Simone, I wouldn't bother trying. That's about as perfect a vocal as anyone is going to sing—no affectation, no posturing, not a false moment. Perhaps I'll do it like, you know . . . Neu!

or one of the German bands . . . are you familiar with the German bands?"

"No."

"Most Yanks aren't. Bloody stupid. Not you, of course, but then you're a homegirl, aren't you," he smiles.

"London."

"There you go . . . but that's why I need you, you see? There they are, all the reasons . . . for your very, very, very, *very* special combination of, of, of, of, of, of, of . . . *attributes* . . . "

"I'm certain I don't know what combination that might be," says Jasmine. "What happened with you and Anna has nothing to do with me, does it?"

He looks at her completely mystified. "Why would it have anything to do with you?" He thinks. "Didn't you and I just meet?" as though the possibility occurs to him, with some horror, that maybe they've known each other for years and he doesn't remember. "I mean . . . " slightly alarmed, " . . . didn't we?"

"Yesterday."

"That's what I thought. At the train station, wasn't it?"

"Yes."

He's relieved. "Yes." Then, "So what do you say? I'm leaving Los Angeles, of course."

"You are?"

"Oh yes. Didn't I say?"

"No."

"That was part of it with Anna."

"Where are you going?"

"I'm leaving this very, very vile place full of very, very vile people," he says. "Vile. Place. Full of. Very. Vile. People."

"Where are you going?"

"If I stay one more moment, I'll be very vile too. Perhaps," his voice falls to a hush, "I already am."

In the same hush he says, "I'm holding onto reality by a thread, really. Don't you know? And, and, and sometimes, sometimes I think I'm getting through, I think I'm getting things done, I think the work is happening . . . and then," he says, "then I realize, you know, *hours* have gone by, hours and hours and hours, and I've written, like, three or four or five bars of a melody and that's all. It's all I've done. It feels like I've written an entire song in minutes, when I've taken *days* to write the fragment of a *single verse*, and then I've written the fragment backwards and from the inside out and upside down. Do you know who I met here?"

"Are you going to answer my question?" she says.

"I *am* answering your question. Wait a minute. What question?"

"Where are you going?"

"Yes, that one. I *am* answering. Don't get tough with me, young lady," he says, half mocking, "I run things around here." He laughs. "Do you know who I met?" He picks the needle up from the record and begins playing it again. "Can't get enough of this bloody song," he mutters. "It was in a movie—perhaps not Nina's version, I'm not sure. Who was in that movie . . . ?"

"Who did you meet, then?" trying to keep him on any track at all.

"I said that, didn't I. About the movie. Sophia Loren. No, Anna Magnani."

"You met Anna Magnani?"

"No." Worried. "Did I?"

"Someone vile, you said."

"Not vile—*very* vile. Anthony *Quinn*. Mid-Fifties. No, not everyone here is very vile. Not every single last someone. Christopher Isherwood. Do you know who he is?"

"A writer?"

"My God! Another literate person in the music business, besides Jim and myself, that is."

"Can't say I know his work, mind."

"That's three literate people in the music business *and we're all in the same house*. An aeroplane crashes into this house and the literacy level of Los Angeles plummets . . . " He shakes his head, the math eludes him. " . . . plummets . . . three hundred percent. By the way, I see that look on your face. Don't discount Jim," he nods toward the living room from where Jasmine came, "when he's not being his iguanan self onstage, he's better read than the two of us put together. Well, not me."

"He was deep in the *Wall Street Journal* when I came in."

"There you are," he nods.

"Are you two . . . ?"

For a moment he's waiting for her to finish the sentence, then, "What? Oh. No! No, we're just trying to keep each other out of trouble. When we're not getting each other in trouble. And he's a huge talent. Huge influence on me, so if I can, uh, help . . . " He shrugs.

"I've never heard of him."

"Well," he shrugs again. "Jim is his proper name, of course."

"Are you going to tell me, then, where you're going? When you leave L.A.?"

"I *was* telling you. Christopher Isherwood used to live in Berlin. Back before the war. Wrote some very famous stories."

"Is he a Nazi too?"

He stops. "Of course he isn't a Nazi. 'Too'?" Jasmine doesn't say anything. "I'm not a Nazi," he says quietly. "Would it matter if I blamed it on the drugs?"

"No."

"No," he shakes his head, "quite correct. You're absolutely right. I made the choice to take the drugs, didn't I, so whatever bloody stupid things I do or say when I'm on them, well, then it's on me, isn't it."

"That's actually very sensible," she says.

"I'm . . . I'm . . . sabotaged by my impulse to be flamboyant about *everything*. But that whole sodding business about that so-called Nazi salute at Victoria Station," he argues fiercely, "was bollocks! On the life of my four-year-old son, I was *waving* to the crowd. Look at the fucking photo! Look at my bloody hand—it's no Nazi salute. A wave. Whatever other awful thing about me that you believe and that I no doubt deserve, you must believe at least that."

Impressed by the ferocity of his defense, she says, "I do."

"The whole Nazi business . . . " he says, trying to shoo it away like a fly, "I was just fascinated by . . . by . . . by the . . . romanticism of it—"

"*Romanticism?*"

"Of *course*. Nazism is *extraordinarily* romantic. It's King Arthur and all that . . . and what was King Arthur anyway but Jesus in armor, with his twelve knights? I understand how grotesque and destructive it finally all became . . . " Defeated, he sees the look on her face. "I know it's *evil*. I know *what happened*. Bloody hell," he continues quietly, "look, Jasmine. Can I call you Jasmine?"

"You know you can."

"I need to get out of this *steaming shit pile* of a city," he says with new intensity, "away from the coke, away from the pills. Away from the sirens, the fucking limos cruising the Strip . . . get to Berlin where I can clean up—"

"Think they don't have any drugs in Berlin, do you?"

"Yes, yes, I know—they have drugs bloody everywhere, don't they? But Berlin is . . . " He ties his robe around him more tightly and for the first time doesn't start over the record on the turntable. " . . . attached to the rest of the western world by a thread of track and highway, like the balloon on the end of a string, isolated, besieged. Haunted, insolent, bold. Divided down the middle—like *me*. Listen, Jasmine. I need you to fly . . . do you fly? . . . to Frankfurt and take the train to Berlin and find a place for us to live. For you and me and Jim, I mean. Somewhere not too far from the Hansa studios . . . do you know Hansa?"

"A German label, isn't it?" she says.

"They have their own studio at the south end of the Wall so we need something accessible. Of course I'll pick up your expenses and you'll have a month to track down something simple, in an interesting part of town but functional, anonymous, where one can go to a market and buy tea. Nothing extravagant, nothing rock-star. I mean that. I've never meant anything more seriously."

"Wait."

"Jim and I will be in France a bit, another studio north of Paris where we'll be laying some basic tracks . . . but we'll be coming—"

"Wait!"

"—by train and boat. What?"

She realizes she doesn't know what. "Nothing."

"Right, then. A new chapter! a new town, new career . . . "

"On one condition . . . "

"Oh yes, yes, I know," he says impatiently, waving it away, "listen," and in the brown light through the blinds he looks at her, "I can only guarantee that's not my intention and I shall never, never, never . . . " he waves again. "Just . . . I'll *never*, that's all. I'll never. Whatever. Who knows, right, luv? And Jim's a perfect gentleman, I might add, for a bloke who has the biggest cock in the history of rock and roll, and that includes Jimi."

"Should I even ask how you know this?"

"Luv, *everyone* knows this."

Within a single breathtaking hour she has in her possession a cashier's check for $15,000. Bundling up the books and records she can't bear to part with and sending them onto Berlin, Jasmine has the idea to give the rest to Kelly; but sitting in her car watching the house where she lived for three years, trying to summon up her courage, she hits the gas at first sight of the other woman. She listens for the tune of "Tezeta" coming from her womb, but hears nothing

She leaves like someone who's set fire to the building. Spends the night in the car before dropping it off with the Korean couple to whom she's sold it, then the last fifteen hours in the Lufthansa terminal waiting for her flight. When the plane stops over in London, she's mildly startled that her old city fails to beckon; from Frankfurt she takes the train through the long hundred-mile outdoor tunnel that runs from West Germany to Berlin. She takes a room at a small hotel off the Kurfürstendamm and retrieves her books and records.

She writes to him, *I've spent most of the past month familiarizing myself with a city that's desperate and alive, and finally yesterday located a residence that I hope both you and Jim find adequate. It's above a motor vehicle repair shop, very basic but comfortable enough, six or seven rooms with sky-blue walls and doors that open onto a small balcony overlooking a side alley. The floors are tile from before the War and there are carved high ceilings and a yard in front enclosed by an old iron gate. It's in the Schöneberg district on the Hauptstrasse, a short ride on the U-Bahn from Hansa Tonstudio 2, and mostly the people are working-class Turks which means . . . Turkish coffee! Christopher Isherwood lived in Schöneberg as well as Einstein, Marlene Dietrich, Billy Wilder, Klaus Kinski (cracked German actor I've not heard of but you probably have) and now someday someone shall write a letter to someone saying you lived here as well.*

Hello, luv.
Quick note to let you know that Jim and I are here in the Chateau Heroesville (sp?) north of Paris in Pantoise working. Delighted to receive your letter and look forward to joining up with you in Berlin in the next week or so or as soon as Jim disentangles himself from his dalliance with a beautiful asian who rather inconveniently is married to a French actor. I suppose he shall get a good song out of it if nothing else. The flat sounds suitable indeed and as I believe has been said we don't need or want anything luxurious. It is properly heated? is my only concern—the chateau where we record now is drafty and damp and I suppose I got more accustomed to all that detestable California sunshine than I realized, didn't I, even if I never actually went out in it when I was there, ha ha. Since Kill City and its streets strewn with winged corpses we've partaken of nothing harder than vino, being the best boys we know how to be. I look forward to Berlin and living as much like a normal person as I can get away with.

Cheers, D

Should she note in a letter the bullet holes in the Hansa recording studio near the Wall? Will this be thrilling or frightening or both? In the *International Herald Tribune* she reads that in five years the assassin of Robert Kennedy will be up for parole; she can't help regretting that he wasn't executed, she who might have assumed herself opposed to executions. It's not a matter of vengeance but rather some rightful order extracted from the anarchy of the world. Everything is personal.

When she goes to look for the clippings she's kept these years, beginning with the first she read in London about the trip to South Africa and the others afterward that made their folded way from one volume to another, they're nowhere to be found among any of her possessions. She's filled with reproach at their loss. She thinks of the aging clippings hidden forever in L.A. with Kelly, who never will know of them unless one happens to flutter from some book she randomly opens. This is the price, believes Jasmine, of such a cowardly flight, of leaving a woman like a man would.

On their arrival in Schöneberg, Jasmine realizes the two singers haven't entirely shed their bad habits so much as downscaled, trading drugs for garden-variety alcoholism. Methodically they carve up the calendar allowing for two days a week of prowling the clubs and bars and strip joints of Kreuzberg—the Exile, the SO36 overrun by German punks—then two days of calm and restitution at the flat, shaking off hangovers over coffee and books. The other three days are devoted to writing and recording at the studio within sight of the wall and its armed East German snipers, who are close enough to pick off one singer or the other and strike a singular blow against western decadence. For a while the two men and woman are tourists, driving in the Black Forest and visiting the Brücke museum, striking poses out of expressionist paintings and snapping photographs with a little polaroid camera picked up in a pawn shop. Sometimes the picture seems to vanish between the click of the shutter and the exposure of the negative; waving his hand, the flame-haired Old World wanderer given to believing such things says, "It's in the air. A ghost camera, taking pictures of the Old World disappearing."

"Yeah," cracks Jim, "or a camera that doesn't work."

The men sink into the anonymity they've craved in their ramble eastward. Turkish immigrants around them trudge westward, worlds passing at twilight, the visibility of each to the other dying at dusk. Session musicians come and go through the cavernous studio, a converted movie set from the silent era before the rise of the Reich where epic visions were filmed of sexy robots in Twenty-First Century Babels. The air fills with the chemical smell of old celluloid rotting in the vaults.

She's never seen musical instruments that look like these. It's as though they've materialized from the same silent science-fiction German movies whose rot the musicians breathe in and out as they play; the instruments appear more like time machines, or what she imagines a time machine might look like, transporting the traveler from the execution of a song back to its inception or forward to its completion—bending the music from the end or beginning back into the middle, and bending the music of years from now back to the music of years ago, to produce this music of the moment. It's as though Jasmine could climb into a song and ride it back ten years to the kitchen of an old Hollywood hotel, in time to prevent an assassination, or forward twenty years in time to prevent her own.

The first time that Jasmine sees the Professor, as everyone calls him, it's the middle of a stormy afternoon. She's arrived with recording contracts to be signed and finds him alone, hunched over one of the instruments in the barely lit studio; a tinny transistor plays a song from half a dozen years before— *and Ray Charles was shot down*—another musical age. He's lost in thought, staring at the studio floor covered with a couple dozen cards that might be from a tarot except without images or icons. Rather they're emblazoned with maxims and mini-manifestos that barely can be read in the room's shadows: EMBARRASS YOURSELF and THE SONG HAS SECRETS FROM THE SINGER and DO NOT BE BLIND TO . . . on one card and . . . YOUR OWN VISION on the next. Alone, staring at the floor trying to divine its instructions, when the transistor sings *I dreamed we played cards in the dark, and you lost and you lied*, the balding man in eyeliner laughs and glances over his shoulder at the radio

these dreams of you . . .

then looks up and smiles at Jasmine as though they've met many times. Over the days and weeks, sessions spill into other sessions, songs start out belonging to one man and end another's. More often the music is of a no-man's land like that which lies between the two western and eastern barricades that have come to constitute in the psyche of the world a single Wall.

It's a music of breakdowns and blackouts and "futuristic rhythm and blues"—the singer with the red hair calls it—about lovers in the Wall's shadow, and sons of the silent age and electric-blue rooms that no one leaves. "Fritz Lang's *Metropolis* starring James Brown!" the singer tells Jasmine excitedly one evening; she's actually come to find such grand pronouncements rather endearing. While she isn't sure she fancies the music or understands it, she senses it's not to be dismissed, though she's not inclined to let him know that. In the Schöneberg flat, the nearby table is stacked with art catalogs, jagged little polemics on aesthetic theory, modern novels. "You're really reading that, are you?" she says to him behind the thick paperback.

He shrugs, "I'm half Irish—me mum," and laying the book on his lap says, "Do you worry, luv, whether every note of an Ornette Coleman piece has meaning?"

"Maybe I do," she says, but she doesn't really listen to Ornette Coleman.

"Of course you don't. It's simple, really, a very simple tale—man sets out on a twenty-four-hour walk looking for home and, riding a wave of notes, finds the New World. It's a song we've all sung, haven't we? In this case it's Dublin but it could be Berlin or London or L.A."

Whatever his faults, a lack of graciousness isn't one, nor a lack of patience with anyone but himself, for whom he has none. "When Miles started doing funk-Stockhausen," he tells her, "did someone say suspiciously, Gone all musique concrète on us then, have you?"

"Probably someone did," she says, "or perhaps they just called it futuristic rhythm and blues."

"Look, the whole century has been about black and white fucking," and leaning in the doorway of his room she raises an eyebrow but he won't back down. "Absolutely! I'll bet," he says of the novel, "Molly Bloom really is a black girl and he just doesn't tell us. New York Jews like Gershwin, Kern, Arlen cumming southern Negro music while Duke Ellington ravishes Nineteenth Century Europeans like Debussy—rather the whole bloody point of it all, isn't it?"

"Is it?"

"But of course," he insists, "and I'm the new white Duke for the Old World in a new century, stealing the remains of black music and smashing it for good. Writing and singing it like a white limey, because what could survive *that*? And I should bloody well hope some Yank spade out there is doing the same to the remains of white european music. To everything there's a reaction. *Anticipate the reaction.*"

"That sounds like something from one of the Professor's cards."

"First rule of cultural warfare."

"Perhaps you should just be the You for a new century."

He waves this away like it's the least sensible thing any-one has said in a while. "Oh but I learned long ago I'm not who I think I am, I'm who the public thinks I am or I'm not anyone, am I? I steal *everything*, don't I? And someday, somebody shall steal *me*—put me in a movie or novel and," he cackles maniacally, "I'll be bloody indignant!" He says, "Tell me, luv, if I may ask. Where are your people from?"

"Ethiopia," she says.

"Truly? That's fantastic! Have you ever been?"

"I was two when my parents moved me and my brother to London. I went back for about a week, eight years ago."

"Fantastic, fantastic," he keeps muttering, "how perfect it is, then, that you're from there and now you're here."

"Perfect?"

"Abyssinia! The beginning of time, Ethiopia, and L.A. is the end of time, and this," Berlin at his fingertips, "is time in the crosshairs, where the latitudes intersect."

"On what map?"

"Not any map you *look at*, Jasmine," he says, "the map you hear. Come on, don't you like me by now? A little?"

"I've actually come to quite like you."

"There, you see? I'm so very, very glad to hear it," he says so wholeheartedly that she can't help being moved.

"You're not a Nazi," she points out.

"No. Thank you." He picks up the thick novel again. "I'll

never live that down and," he says quietly, "probably don't deserve to."

"Probably not."

"Well, no more headline chasing for me, for a while. I'm laying low. An Old World man who plunged into the heart of the New and it almost destroyed him." He tosses the paperback to her. "Try not worrying too much what the words mean. They're just notes. It's all really about the Old World discovering the New and waving goodbye to itself."

Has he forgotten that on the opening blank page of the paperback he's drawn a picture of her, one day as he sat in the recording studio gazing out the window at a couple by the Wall? He was a painter once, back before the music, before he concluded there was no future in painting. Or does he remember perfectly well and, very calculatedly, finds this an off-handed way of showing her? Whichever: Later when she opens the book she can see that the sketch on the inside is unmistakably her, in all her shades of brown but for the misplaced gray of her eyes.

She doesn't remember him drawing her, doesn't remember being in the recording studio when he did it. Was it absentminded on his part, his eyes happening to fall on her as his thoughts drifted; or if she wasn't in his presence, was it therefore more conscious? If she wasn't within sight, then she would have to have been on his mind. She has no particular interest in him that way and hasn't been aware that he has any in her; she has no interest in any of them—him or Jim or the Professor—and still hasn't on the night that it happens, she and the three of them. But she doesn't give the book back and in a few months when she leaves on the run she'll take it, with the sketch of her on the front page and carrying inside her belly the daughter named, by coincidence perhaps, since she never really reads the book, after the woman who voices the century's greatest yes.

B ut if there's truly truth in wine then she must wonder what really she feels on the night it happens, because there's so much wine that night, Jim having brought up from the club in Kreuzberg five bottles of a French vintage, trying hard as he is to stay away from the smack. And if there's not the wine then there's the marsh of the city in late summer, the body of Berlin swathed in ponds, the Havel and Spree rivers overflowing until by the fourth bottle the waters are splashing over the window sills of the upper flat above the Turkish garage.

By the fifth bottle Jasmine can perfectly see the submerged garage below, Turkish men and women and children floating among the automotive shrapnel. The sirens of distant Neuköln drone in the fog, yearning for the space age. About the time that Jasmine takes off her clothes and lies across one bed or another in one room or another of the flat, wrapping her naked body in a string of pale-blue beads until she's rendered herself Berlin and its ponds, made herself into the city, with the hinge where her thighs meet rendered the Wall mined with bombs, it's occurred to her that Jim somehow has hallucinogized the wine.

She's shocked at herself. She doesn't know herself at this moment, or what to make of the person she is right now; she's never done this before or anything remotely like it, even in her rock and roll life in L.A. and London where she was conspicuous for her sexual reserve. Istanbul hashish ground to a fine powder, she thinks, whispering, "Jim, Jim, you bastard," in the dark from one bed or the other in one room or the other, and someone whispers back, How's that, luv? or is it the Professor, whom she immediately knows in the intuition born of such wickedness is the most depraved of all. "That you?" she murmurs again but can't be certain to whom. As the song that snakes up the center of her to the back of her mouth shifts from the alien's croon to the iguana's deeper baritone, the touch must be the time traveler's, fingers spinning her red dial forward to the future—or perhaps she succumbs to her assumptions too easily, perhaps the Professor sings and the alien touches . . . until in the dark she's only confused. When it's over, swollen from their occupation and listening to the cascade of white waves inside her like the lapping of the Spree at the garage below, she muses dreamily *ah well they'll sort it all out down there, won't they?* and a few hours later, all tides receded, Schöneberg streets revealing barely a drop of the night's flood, she wanders the flat in blue morning light looking at each of the three men passed out on their beds in their rooms and wondering which of them made it across the Wall first, when she already knows quite certainly that she's pregnant with Molly.

It isn't only because the paternity is destined to be ever so unspecific. Jasmine would just as soon believe that among the three men, one is as much the father as the other. It isn't because any of them would reject her or paternity; rather it's because any or all might accept paternity that she leaves. This is something she prefers to do on her own.

She begins planning her getaway the afternoon that she and the two singers are driving down the Ku'damm and the crimson spaceman behind the wheel of the car spots out of the corner of his eye a stranger in the street getting in another car—*who*, will never exactly be clear. To an extent, Jasmine realizes, she's responsible: Flushed with some soup of hormones, bad dreams, unfounded premonitions and half-digested newspaper articles, she's convinced for a split moment that the stranger getting in the car is the assassin himself, the man behind the .22-caliber gun she read in the newspaper some months ago would be up for parole in five years. "It's him!" she cries, surprising herself.

"Yes!" agrees the spaceman next to her. "It is!"

What? She looks over. "It *is* him!" he says again, by which he means a dealer who sold him bad drugs or a businessman who cheated him in a contract or someone who slept with his wife (whom he isn't sleeping with anymore anyway)—none of them necessarily more or less likely than the man Jasmine has mistaken the stranger for; in fact the man in the street is a cabbie, getting in his taxi. Regardless, he's the object of no small ire, as becomes clear when calmly, with the tremendous focus and determination that the driver next to her brings to anything he wants to, he aims his car at the other and plows into it.

Jim cries out from the back. Of course there's an outburst from the surrounding throng on the busy boulevard and particularly from the cabbie, who leaps from his taxi and then, mid-protest, bolts, leaving the singer with the bright red hair to reverse the car, back up and then plow into the other again, and to keep doing it again and again. In the passenger seat in front, Jasmine grabs her belly so instinctively and protectively that had either man noticed, immediately he would have known; but the driver is only intent on demolishing the other car even as he demolishes his own, and his cohort in back is only intent on surviving the onslaught. "Stop!" is all she can keep saying.

The singer has brought with him back from L.A. a new-world madness to mix with the old-world's. "Don't tell me I'm not insane," he says to her the next blue morning, not unlike the one when she knew she was pregnant; she finds him standing in a window muttering.

"Right," she says.

"I know about insanity, don't I," he says matter-of-factly, "I have a brother who's insane, it runs in the family. My good fortune was I found a method for my madness," and he looks at her and says, "I'm going to be the first rock star assassinated."

"Brilliant," she sputters, "we're grabbing headlines again, are we?"

"It's not a romantic notion," he insists.

"Look here," she says, "I won't try to tell you about insanity if you don't try to tell me about assassinations. And just how disappointed will you be, mate," she adds scornfully, "if it doesn't happen?" But she feels the chill, and when she leaves forty-eight hours later, the only thing she takes that doesn't belong to her is the paperback with the portrait of her that he drew, some mysterious moment when she wasn't looking.

She means to have her daughter in London but gets as far as Paris and a flat in Montparnasse. A New Jersey punk poetess' record plays through the window of another apartment across the courtyard. No sooner has Molly slipped into welcoming hands than the midwife holds her up astonished at the hum from her little body; already the baby transmits on Molly frequency. For six months she has her mother's gray eyes, before they turn brown.

If no one can be sure where the frequency comes from, it makes sense anyway for Jasmine to try and return Molly to its source. Fifteen months after her daughter's birth, the little girl already walking adeptly, the mother spots a familiar redheaded rock star coming out of a hotel on the rue des Beaux Arts off St. Germain-des-Prés, and she pivots, sliding around the corner of rue Bonaparte just as he turns to do a double-take. Some mysterious music from some unknown place has gotten his attention. The next day from the window she spots him in the street below as though searching, and she lets loose the curtain from her fingers just as he looks up; she hurls a blanket over the child to smother her broadcast. The next morning the girl finds outside her door a small box.

Disregarding her mother's standing directive about answering doors to strange people and small boxes, the girl says, "Mum?" lifting the box's contents in her two small hands: the small camera from Berlin that catches images and strands them mid-air on their way to film.

When they move back to Berlin, taking a flat in Schöneberg not far from the one where Jasmine lived before, the small girl clicks ghost pictures from Checkpoint Charlie to the Brandenburg Gate. Sometimes the pictures themselves are ghosts, disappearing into the electric ether; sometimes the pictures are of ghosts, people who aren't there when she looks up from the camera. Sometimes the strangers in her pictures are ghosts of the past, sometimes they're ghosts of a future the girl may or may not know. Everywhere she goes, she trails visual octaves looking for a home; for years the only thing she prizes more is a paperback that her mother stole, with a drawing of her inside.

Not far from Checkpoint Charlie, near what used to be a recording studio and, before that, an old movie studio, a southern part of the Wall unravels into a stone labyrinth between east and west, provoking confusion on both sides. Lovers meet there and children play, and when Molly's mother takes her to it, the child hides in the maze of concrete, some of the passages sheltered by the debris of surrounding construction, others made blue tunnels by the sky above. Molly winds through the maze to the center and her mother always finds her, and only when Molly is older does she understand that Jasmine follows her music, left by the child like breadcrumbs.

Raised among Turks and Muslims, every now and then the girl goes to the local mosque where the constant humming from her is frowned upon. At the age of twelve she's there at the Wall's fall, taking pictures of people dancing along the edge, wine bottles in hand, her own small tune filling the pauses of Beethoven's Ode to Joy.

Like everyone who's grown up in Berlin, she feels the sense of liberation, as a line down the center of the century is erased and replaced by a hole. The fallen wall is the city's ghost limb, history an amputee that feels an appendage no longer there; but with the fall, something dark is unleashed along with the dream. Even the girl feels the shift in sentiment. When the army of skinheads that calls itself the Pale Flame marches down the Unter den Linden and screams at the mother watching from the sidewalk with her young teenage daughter—who already has the body of a woman—Molly is old enough to understand what foreboding is.

Is it the arc of the imagination bending back to history, or just coincidence the night that she seals her mother's fate? Molly enters a U-Bahn station near what used to be Checkpoint Charlie, not far from the Hansa recording studio, when she comes upon members of the Pale Flame beating a middle-aged man in the street. She darts into the shadows nearby, thanking the night for the color of her skin. Developed at sixteen years old and taught by her mother to keep herself covered and wary of male crowds, she's terrified, and only when the skinheads finish with the man in the street and leave him lying crumpled there does she run to him.

She hasn't seen a dead body before so she can't be certain about this one, but if this isn't dead then it ought to be what dead looks like. Kneeling by him, clutching all her papers and books, she barely can bring herself to whisper to him, afraid she'll make a sound, when to her horror she hears the song that's coming through her body grow louder, like someone has turned up her volume.

The body in the street stirs. She's so startled that she jumps back and flees, dropping by his side the old battered paperback with the drawing of her mother.

A few years ago, the first time she picked up the book, it wasn't her mother's picture she noticed. Molly just had turned twelve and it was the autumn the Wall fell and she still remembers, coming through the window of the flat where they lived, the music in the distance so celebratory and defiant that it drowned out her own; she picked up the paperback and there cascaded from its pages a folded newspaper clipping from more than two decades before. The girl stood in the middle of the flat scrutinizing the face of the man in the grainy newsprint photo when an astounded Jasmine said, "Where did you get that?"

The way she said it, the daughter thought she had done something wrong. "It was in the book," Molly said, frightened.

Jasmine had no idea how the clipping got there. She had looked for it everywhere before the book ever came into her vicinity or possession. Something strange happened in this moment that Molly discovered the clipping: When Jasmine reached for it, instinctively the twelve-year-old pulled it back. "Give it," Jasmine said quietly.

Molly looked again at the man in the photo. "He's very sad," she said to her mother.

"Yes," Jasmine said and turned toward the music coming through the window from the Wall. "He would have liked to be here now, to see this . . . and to hear it," and she smiled, "though he never knew much about music."

M olly said, "Is he my father?" and Jasmine's jaw dropped. "No," the mother answered, composing herself, "he's not." The girl clutched the clipping, looking at her mother quietly. "He's not," repeated Jasmine, "I would tell you." Molly handed over the clipping and the book, and her mother took them, opened the book almost absently, regarding the drawing of her on the inside front page.

Now, only after Molly has run into the mouth of the U-Bahn does she realize that she has dropped the book at the side of the man in the street aboveground. At first she dismisses any possibility of going back for it. The skinheads might return, the police might come or the beaten man might die in her arms or, rousing himself to consciousness, hurt her in some rush of adrenaline. No, she concludes, she can't go back. She has but to step onto the train and be swept to the sanctuary of Berlin's tunnels before the last five minutes overwhelm her like a wave.

B ut then she knows she must go back. The paperback she's dropped is one of life's markers, one of experience's receipts that may be destined to one day disappear; but not on this night, the sixteen-year-old decides, not in this way. Forget sentiment: Her mother's picture is in the book, which is to say that Molly has left behind identification; and before the doors close—the arc of the imagination bending back to the history it can't compete with—she steps from the train back onto the landing.

W hen she gets back to him, the man lying in the road shows no signs of having stirred further. No one else is in sight. There's no sound of approaching sirens, responding to a witness' call; the paperback is in such plain view that she can't believe she didn't see dropping it. She tiptoes to the body, looking around furtively, then snatches the book from the ground.

She opens it and her heart stops.

The page with her mother's drawing is gone. The serrated edge of where it's been ripped from the binding is as fresh as if it were flesh.

Again Molly drops the book in the street. Again she looks around, for some single white leaf blowing in the breeze along the street, and when she doesn't see it, again she runs.

How many times, Molly frets herself nearly into hysteria in the U-Bahn, has she thought of tearing that page from the book herself? After all, the rest is only a damned *book*, an over-stuffed frame for her mother's portrait; but exactly because it's such a frame, exactly because from the beginning it's provided the picture a context, she's never brought herself to remove the picture, and now it's too late.

When she finds the page—or rather when it finds her mother—it's exactly in the way that Molly never wanted to see it again, there affixed to the consequences of her mistake. It's two years later, during which that page might reasonably be assumed decimated by time and elements, decomposed at the bottom of some heap, forgotten in any case by Molly and written off to blind and mindless panic, when she returns to her Schöneberg flat one afternoon and, as soon as she sees the police, she knows.

She cries, "Mum!" and dashes through the phalanx, none of the police able to muster the force necessary to stop her. The girl who's now eighteen gets to the top of the stairs and sees through the doorway only her mother's legs sprawled on the floor; only then, in contrast to the body of the beaten man in the Berlin street two years before, can she really claim she knows what lifeless is. She never sees the rest. A German officer swoops in to stop her and when he turns her in his arms, she accidentally kicks the crumpled paper at her feet on the top step and sees the wadded pencil portrait, dropped there not so much as a calling card but because to the six thugs who read it like a map, it was as useless to them as their target.

For Jasmine, mercy lies in the first blow from the six young men with shaved heads coming through her door, knocking most of the life from her and making the other blows superfluous.

After that, her last moments slow down and take on an altitude. Shock and pain fall away from her. Life fades fast from what it is about the woman that her assailants most despise, which is not her black skin: It's those white woman's gray eyes to which they believe she has no right. If she had the time to be surprised, she might be surprised that she doesn't think of Bob at all. She doesn't think of the night of the three mad fathers. If she had even more time to consider this surprise, she would realize it's not a surprise in the least: She thinks of her daughter. She prays, in the moment that she has to utter a prayer, not for herself but that her daughter doesn't return too soon.

It's all Jasmine thinks about, because this is the radio signal sent from maternity's ethiopia: We think of our children. If you believe in no god then you accept that we're so programmed by nature to think of our children in our last moments; if you believe in a God then you know She/He/It wrote the program in the first place. Jasmine hopes in the last moments for a blast of divine foresight, another radio signal from the future that tells her that her daughter will be all right. She doesn't get this. Probably nobody gets this. Probably like countries, all people get is hope, and odds no better than even.

For Molly, what mercy there is in Jasmine's murder lies in that the girl has only one mother to destroy, as she now is convinced she's done. She despises the music that comes from her, that lured back the Pale Flame on that night she dropped the book with her mother's picture. She wants to turn herself off.

When she flees Berlin for Marseilles, she doesn't flee for herself or for her own safety let alone self-esteem. She has a body that men notice and that she sometimes trades on; she leaves behind, with the nights whose stories they tell, the *tezeta* of her commerce—cries through the latticed balcony doors. Men pay for the moans as much as the flesh. They pay for the music, the songs that rise up through them as if the men become tuning forks when they're inside her. The woman means to flee anything that she deserves, the good and bad equally, because her existence has been rendered so nihilistic that she doesn't deserve to deserve. So she doesn't flee her remorse, as though she might watch it from a departing train, as remorse stands there in the U-Bahn station watching her back and growing smaller. Later it will seem like there's no other place to which she could have gone but the wellspring of all chronicled memory, back to abyssinian purity, as though there's no guilt in such a place or at such a point.

A t the time that she takes it, the wandering journey from Marseilles to San Sebastian to Gibraltar to Algiers to Tripoli, she adamantly insists that in no way is it as though she's pulled there. The only thing she knows for sure when she finally arrives in Addis Ababa, a young woman at the dawn of what the western world calls the Twenty-First Century but for which Ethiopia exhausted numbers long ago, is that the last thing she deserves, the thing she deserves least of all, is to be a mother.

Am I a ghost? she wonders in her descent, following— into its labyrinth of tunnels and bridges, lined by high walls covered with moss—all the narrow, winding stone steps of her new abysmal city. Am I in an abyss of time, or one of space? Living on the outskirts of the eucalyptopolis nine years later, lying in bed she hears one night coming through the music of mosques and thunderstorms rolling in overhead a song she not only knows but was born of, and then a distant male voice in a familiar language that's not Amharic. Only after listening awhile does she acknowledge to herself that the transmission comes from her body. Not that it ever will really explain anything, she's picking up a radio broadcast from ten thousand miles away— . . . *for what happened last night . . . but then all the song says is that a change* will *come, not how fast, right? . . . and the really old-school one about the lovers at the Berlin Wall . . . who get to be heroes just for one day? That's for my four-year-old Ethiopian daughter, who I guess can't get enough of British extraterrestrials in dresses*—and months later in London, with Sheba asleep next to her in the dark, she still hears it, almost, or convinces herself she does, in the same way she's almost convinced herself she isn't dying.

In the dark between London and Paris, Parker doesn't like it when the train stops beneath the Channel. Reflexively he turns up his headphones, and his father in the seat across from him, who can make out the static of the robotic chooga-chooga from the music player around Parker's neck, says, "What are you listening to?"

S eeing his father's lips move, Parker pulls the headphones from his ears. "What?" the boy says.

"What are you listening to?" says Zan.

"Why?" says the boy.

"I was just wondering," Zan answers quietly. Parker remembers his dad taking him and his sister to that creepy underground bunker in London, and at the bottom the elevator doors opened to mannequins in cots; it was creepy, it creeped him out. It didn't matter that the bunker turned out not to be underground at all, it didn't matter if the whole thing was fake—it was creepy and now here on this train stopped in the dark, stuck under the flippin' ocean or wherever they are, Parker thinks it's like the bunker except worse. He looks around at the other passengers in the dim light and sees the dummies that he saw in the bunker. He sees one when he looks at his dad in the seat across from him; everyone on the train looks inanimate and stuffed, and Parker wants out and off. But he knows there's no getting out and off until the train moves and surfaces on the other side, wherever that is.

Zan feels his son slipping away. He's become aware of it since London, since Sheba disappeared, maybe since Viv disappeared, maybe before that. He says to Parker, "But when you like a certain song . . . "

"What?" Parker shouts again with great exasperation, not bothering to remove the headphones this time. His father's mouth keeps moving and finally the boy turns off the music player around his neck. "What . . . "

The father shrugs. " . . . because it's catchy or—" and Parker snaps, "A lot of annoying songs are catchy." At this point, Zan thinks, I should understand that music is about teen tribalism. At his son's age, musical taste is an act of revolution. Zan doesn't particularly like music that's political; the song he played the morning after the election—*but then all the song says is that a change* will *come, not how fast, right?*—only is political because it plummets into the personal and emerges as politics on the other side of confession. Yet Zan learned long ago from his teacher at the university who once was Trotsky's bodyguard and Billie Holiday's lover that music which isn't at least politically aware has nothing to say about anything, and that political people who are unmoved by music—whether it be rock and roll or Broadway tunes—aren't to be trusted.

In any case music isn't something over which a healthy twelve-year-old bonds with his father. Between a twelve-year-old and his father, music is the line in the sand. Out of those politics is born taste. Taste gets better but, Zan hopes, not perfect. When your taste is perfect, it's not yours.

When Parker was four, the age that Sheba is now but before she was born, his father drove him to preschool one morning and they came to a place on the canyon boulevard where a truck had spilled oil that slicked the asphalt. Their car spun out and another car spun into them colliding, and when the spinning was over and everyone stopped, Zan turned from behind the wheel to the four-year-old in back and said, "Are you all right?" Yes, the boy nodded in his stoic fashion. If he nodded yes, whether he was really all right or not, or whether he even knew he was all right, then in his own four-year-old mind he took some small measure of control of the chaos that just had unfolded.

Arriving in Paris on the Eurostar after its unscheduled pause in the Chunnel, leaving the Gare du Nord and crossing the rue Dunkerque on their way to the Gare de l'Est, Parker sees the taxicab heading toward him not at all in that slow-motion way that everyone says things like this happen. There's nothing slow-motion about it; it all happens faster than the boy can compute before his father grabs him hard by the hand, so hard his hand crunches, and yanks him from the cab's path. His father says, "Are you all right?" and Parker nods as stoically as if he were four; but he's not all right. It's not just that his hand throbs. It's not even just the spectacle of the cab that nearly hit him flying into the limousine before it, then throwing the gear into reverse, then shifting into drive and slamming into the limo again.

Everyone on the sidewalks watches the cab reversing and crashing into the limo over and over. Dimly through the back window, the cab's passenger grabs her head when she flies into the seat in front of her. At the age of twelve, Parker feels his first grown-up cognition of the fact that sometimes there is no exerting control. Sometimes everything loses control and there's nothing to be done about it, and things have been out of control for a while now—since before the Chunnel or London, maybe before Sheba.

Though he doesn't understand the details, Parker knows about the house. He knows about the money. He remembers one afternoon, back in the canyon, the panic in his father's voice when he hustled the kids into the car to drive down to the bank because Zan just had gone online to discover no money in their account, so he needed to make a deposit before checks started bouncing. Now his mother is missing, his little sister is missing, and though of course Sheba drives him crazy he can't help being upset that she's disappeared, as upset in his adolescent way as his father, and it's annoying, to be upset about Sheba. It just would be better if Sheba weren't missing because then things wouldn't be quite so out of control. Everything got harder in all their lives when Sheba came, the boy thinks—why wasn't I enough, why wasn't it enough for my mother and father to have *me*? Why was I so *not* enough that they had to go halfway around the world to bring Sheba to their house? and it will be half a lifetime before he understands it's never been that he wasn't enough, it's that his parents' love for him was so great as to set loose within them a terror more than they could bear.

F lippin' little jerkwad. He remembers back in London, the nanny accusing him of losing his sister on purpose in the maze, and his blood boils. Now Sheba's gone and his mom is gone and he's far from home, everything out of control, and there it all is before him now in the scene of this cab crashing into the same limo over and over. As people watch, the cab's passenger finally throws open her back door on the other side and flees—and the boy and his father have walked another quarter block down the rue Dunkerque when something occurs to Parker and he stops to look back, to look for her among the crowd in the twilight before his father pulls him on, as though they have any hope in hell of catching the next train tonight.

Zan and Viv each have a different dynamic with Parker. Zan is steady, calming. Viv and Parker clash, especially over how he treats Sheba; not so long ago the mother posted a sign in the house that read PARKER BE NICE TO YOUR SISTER OR FEEL MY WRATH. But the two also have an intimacy that father and son don't. The boy will confide in his mother what he won't in his father: Let *them* have the Talk, Zan has thought more than once. Zan is ballast, Viv is sail. They've both noticed that Parker is at his best when the parents have had an argument concerning some point of child-rearing; Parker has enough friends whose parents are split that when his own parents fight, it's a shot fired over the bow of the family, chastening him into doing whatever he can to set right the ship of domesticity.

There's never been a doubt in Zan's mind that when Sheba first became part of the family, it was hardest of all on Parker. In the two years since Sheba's arrival, Parker has turned more volatile, explosive. This has coincided with the onset of adolescence, a time when every affront listed on the ledger of his still brief life takes on a scope worthy of tribunals in The Hague. It bugs the twelve-year-old as much as it pleases him that, among his friends, his parents are considered the cool ones—the mom who's turquoise and the dad who plays music on the radio; and now Parker's salutations, cordialities and exchanges are spoken in the language of estrangement. Though the boy has been calling his mother and father "Viv" and "Zan" since he was Sheba's age, the implicit remove of a first-name basis, which between children and their parents is tantamount to last-name basis, becomes all the more meaningful.

Testosterone abides. Lately there have been eruptions of violence. Years of sensitive parenting early on, strict supervision over what the boy watched or was exposed to in movies or on television, aimed at cultivating the next Dalai Lama, vanished in a flash of hormones around his eighth birthday. Soon the house was a paramilitary compound, fully stocked with any kind of weapon of any ballistic—air pellets, paint balls, small BBs—that wasn't actual bullets. "Shall I shoot it?" Zan heard Parker say one afternoon back in the family room of their house, and when the father turned to look, there on the wall was a small rat.

Immediately enflamed, Zan said, "Yes," and Parker pulled the trigger. With a squeak, the rodent fell. Half an hour later, Zan was in the office upstairs when Parker came in, tentative, as close to weepy as his age allowed anymore. "What's the matter?" said Zan. Softly Parker said, "I feel bad about it. It was a little one. It made a noise when I hit it." After a moment Zan said, "I told you to shoot it, it's not your fault. Listen, I can't say I'm sorry about killing the rats. But it's right that you have feelings about it." They went downstairs and Zan looked for the body of the mouse behind the sofa where it fell; it wasn't there and, for his son's sake, Zan was relieved. "You didn't kill it," he told Parker, "it would be here if you did. Must have winged it."

"Good," said Parker.

Flickers of conscience aside, lately the boy puts his fist through the thin walls of his room. No wonder, thinks Zan, his hand hurts all the time. "You have a right to get angry," Viv rails at their son, "but you don't have the right to destroy the walls!" though Zan wonders if Parker knows about the foreclosure and finds a certain justice in taking out his anger on the house. Zan and Viv buy for Parker a punching bag in the form of a man whom the boy names Alejandro.

More alarming have been Parker's plots to escape. After one blow-up, Zan caught him trying to go through the two-story window: "You care more about Sheba than you do me!" the boy yelled at his father. "You're better off without me!" and though Zan realized some of this was drama engendered by too much reality TV and internet posturing, Parker shook with a fury that wasn't faked. One time he actually left. Forty minutes later he was back, but not soon enough to undo the trauma; and since then, every time Zan hears the slam of a door or finds a window agape, he wonders if his son has gone. Of course Zan and Viv don't feel remotely ready for any of it. Zan still is recovering from his son casually using the word "orgasm" in conversation with his buddies in the back of the car on the way home from school.

He's twelve. It's part of his job description as a twelve-year-old to believe the modern age began the day he was born. To the extent that it was about anything to Parker, the recent election wasn't about history, it wasn't about politics, it was about one candidate being cool and the other one not; if there was a single kid in Parker's school who was for the other guy, he or she kept quiet about it. Parker is the mindless embodiment of the oldest liberal cliché: Some of his best friends *are* black, particularly Thomas, the son of a black mother from the Bahamas and a white German body-builder who scandalized Parker's school by showing up at a Halloween festival as an SS officer. Turning stereotypes on their heads, in the election the black born-again Christian mother voted for the white conservative and the white German with SS fantasies voted for the black liberal. "No more old men," Thomas' father scowled. Like any kid who instinctively understands he's a resident of the future and already has his young eye on his true home in time, Parker is bored by the past, so it means nothing to Parker now that the city where they arrive the next evening, after spending a night in Paris and taking the long eleven-hour train, again and again has been at the crux of the past century.

B ut Zoo Station, where once Zan came into Berlin fourteen years before, right after the fall of the Wall, has given up to the new Hauptbahnhof its gateway to the rest of the world. As their train approaches over water—the surrounding lakes overrunning their shores in the rain to form a moat—the sight of the new trainport, emblazoned on the outside with neon stars, and the windowless future-city of globes, with its panoramas of graffiti and passages in the sky mirroring the hundreds built underground half a modern era go, perk Parker up for a moment.

In the Hauptbahnhof, Zan stares at the U-Bahn map in mute and utter confusion. He never understood the city the first time he was here; it had a hole in the middle, and Zan has learned from Los Angeles that it takes a lifetime to navigate such cities. He leads Parker to several hotels off the Kurfürstendamm, with its dark clotted shadows of the trees that line it and the display windows of the shops that shine like gold boxes. At every front desk Zan asks if by some chance someone with Viv's name or description is checked in, and then asks for a room, always concluding to his son, "We're not staying here." One hotel, he explains to Parker, "has no WiFi." Another "has no room-service."

246 · STEVE ERICKSON

At midnight, when they check into an inn at the southern end of the Wall where an old recording studio used to be, Parker looks at the room and then his father in disbelief. It's bare, cold, damp; there drifts through the window languages unlike any the boy has heard. The tiny television has something Parker has never seen: antennae, which makes it look like a monstrous bug. "Here?" Parker howls in disbelief. "*They* don't have WiFi! *They* don't have room service!"

Zan returns his son's livid gaze in crestfallen silence.

"This is horrible," says Parker. "The other hotels at least spoke English."

Zan is tired of every single decision being about money. He doesn't flatter any sense of his own victimization by believing they're exactly poor; Zan understands that a crummy hotel isn't a serious definition of poverty. Poverty, he knows, is not only having no money or resources but no hope; and though he has no idea what hope they might reasonably entertain at this point, he hasn't yet given up assuming that it exists or someday will. "Parker," he answers his son quietly, "we couldn't afford the other places. I'm sorry."

To Parker, the endless survey and rejection of hotels this evening—it wasn't really endless, only four or five, but seemed endless to the boy—wasn't unlike watching a cab crash into the same limo over and over. It's an old part of town where they are now, and the dreariness he feels is compounded by the sight not so far away of the Potsdamer Platz at its most ultra-modern; once the no-man's land of the Wall before monied victors of the Cold War like Sony and Mercedes moved in, it hovers in their room's window taunting them.

Parker feels the future snatched back from him again. He feels like someone who's been sentenced to a penal colony on another world, or like the astronaut he sees in science-fiction movies always floating in space, with that single fragile line the only thing that connects him to home, or something with the name of home—the line you know is bound to break.

The "bathroom," the boy is mortified to observe, isn't separate but part of the same single room where the beds are. "You can sleep in the tub," Zan tries to joke about the large white porcelain bowl that is the room's most prominent furniture. Parker glares at him. He refuses to take a bath. When he goes to the bathroom he insists on turning out the room's light, sitting on the toilet and finally managing to pee by pretending his father doesn't exist.

The next day, the two go to the eastern side of the Brandenburg Gate, out on the Unter den Linden. To Parker, the massive boulevard is as wide as a river—and suddenly the idiocy of the entire journey becomes so evident that even a twelve-year-old can see it, maybe especially a twelve-year-old. The man and boy stand on the edge of the boulevard gazing across.

Zan says, "Come on," and the two traipse from one corner

of the Gate's shadow to the other. Zan tries to calculate angles from which the photo posted by Viv online was taken. "But is this the way it looked in the picture," Zan keeps muttering to no conceivable response from his son, "maybe over there?" and then they relocate themselves to another place.

This goes on for two hours. Afterward, with Parker in tow, Zan checks all the hotels in the area. They walk from one to the other, fumbling through English requests and German responses. Trying to ask himself why Viv would be in Berlin and what she would be doing here, Zan leads the boy to the Ethiopian embassy not far from the Gate, a relatively modest if distinguished two-story white house on Boothstrasse. From there they take the U-Bahn back to the Hauptbahnhof where they check the surrounding hotels. As darkness falls on a futile day, Parker concludes ruefully, My father is a moron.

I'm a moron, Zan groans to himself, stealing a glance at his son's face. Beyond the inexorable compulsion to respond to the SOS of his wife's online photo, the man accepts what he's put off knowing until this moment, that nothing about the decision to come here has made sense—as though Viv walks the city waiting for her family to show up.

What do we do now? he wonders. Leave post-its on the Gate's pillars? *Viv, come home?* Though the father barely can remember the ways in which twelve-year-old boys feel lonely, he remembers enough, and knows what the loneliness grows up into; and though he can't be sure at which end on the scale of profundity is most profound the feeling of being lost and at loose ends—when you're young, and closer to the beginning? or when you're old and closer to the end—he knows the feelings are kin enough that no amount of resilience, seasoned or not, overcomes it. He's wracked by the unstable existence to which his son has been delivered, when the guilt isn't dislodged by how he's abandoned his daughter back in London, in her little life of abandonments.

On the U-Bahn back to their neighborhood, sitting side by side, Parker stares out the window. "I want you to write down my cell number," Zan says. Not turning from the window, after a moment Parker says, "Why?"

The father pulls from the boy's coat pocket a blue marker. "Does this write?"

Parker takes off the top and slashes the marker down the back of his father's hand, leaving a hostile blue streak. "It writes," he snarls.

The father looks at his hand and the evidence of the boy's assault. "O.K. So take down this number."

Parker says, "I don't have anything to write it on."

"Write it on the palm of your hand," says Zan, holding up his own hand.

"My hand still hurts. From when you crushed it," Parker says.

The father takes a deep breath. "A taxi was about to run into you. Is it really going to hurt your hand to write on it?"

"Yes."

"Write on your other hand."

"Then I have to use the hand that hurts to write. Besides I'm right-handed," though he has to stop and think, as he always does, which hand is right and which is left.

"I'll write it."

Parker says, "We don't need to."

Zan says, "Just in case."

"In case what?"

"I don't know. In case . . . something . . . "

"What?"

"Something happens."

"What's going to happen?"

"We get separated or something."

"Why would we get separated?" the boy's voice rises.

"We won't get separated," the father assures him.

"Then I don't need to write it," Parker declares and turns back to the window.

Back in their neighborhood, they duck into a café called the CyberHansa. Zan doles out the euros, buying his son a roll and a coffee drink. "We can get online here?" he asks the woman behind the counter, but Parker already has pulled the laptop from his father's bag and logged on. "Can you find the page with Mom's posting?" says the father, trying to nurture a conspiratorial bond with the boy.

Parker is having none of it. "Of course," he snaps.

The father watches his son, giving him the full rein of his twelve-year-old attitude at its most merciless. After a moment Parker pulls back from the laptop as if studying it, his brows arched. "What?" says Zan.

"It's gone."

Z an says, "Gone?"

"Mom's photo," says Parker.

"What do you mean gone?"

"I mean it's gone."

It's taking a moment for Zan to fully absorb what his son is saying. "No, wait. Gone?"

"Zan," Parker says evenly, "it's gone."

"What does that mean?"

"It means what gone means. It means it's not there."

B efuddled, Zan says, "But it was there."

"Yeah," Parker says. He adds, looking closer, "The weird thing is my comment is still . . . " He shrugs.

Zan has moved from his side of the table to Parker's. He looks at the laptop. "What comment?"

"You told me to post a comment? To send Mom a message." Parker points at the screen: *Were r u.* "Were are you?" Zan reads back. "What does that mean, Were are you?"

"*Where* are you," corrects Parker.

"There's an h in where. Then what happened to Mom's photo?"

"Don't know."

"What do you mean you don't know?"

"Zan," the boy shouts, "what do you mean what do I mean?"

T he two return to the room in sullen silence. The boy climbs into the exposed bathtub and sits there, glaring. He's being dramatic but that doesn't mean he doesn't genuinely feel dramatic. "But is that unusual," Zan gamely tries to resume the conversation, "for the photo to have been there and now it's not?"

"I don't know," the boy says—still glaring at nothing—in a way that means, I don't care.

Zan is beside himself. "But why," he flails for some sense of it, "did you say, Where are you?"

"Why wouldn't I say that?" Parker finally turns to him.

"I don't know," the father shrugs. "Why not, We're coming to get you, or . . . "

"First of all," the boy leaps from the bathtub, "you didn't tell me what to say. If you wanted me to say that, why didn't you tell me? Second, when you told me, I didn't know we were coming to get her. I didn't know we were going to take this über, über, *über*-stupid trip to this stupid place!"

"Don't shout."

"I hate this! I hate this place! How are we supposed to find Mom?"

"We both saw the photo, right?" Zan says, and he's not being rhetorical. *I mean, we didn't imagine it, did we?*

Parker begins to cry furiously, like back in the canyon when he punches holes in the house. Sure enough, he pulls back to put his hand through the wall of their room and Zan says, "Your hand," meaning the one the boy hurt in Paris.

It stops Parker long enough that he kicks the wall instead, burying his foot halfway in the plaster.

"Jesus, Parker!" his father shouts. Looking over his shoulder for a landlord to come through the door, Zan says, "You can't do this here! We don't live here! This place isn't ours."

"Nothing is ours!" the boy cries. "I hate everything! I hate you and I hate Mom and I hate Sheba!"

The father turns to the door and turns the latch so no one can come in. It takes only a moment for him to do it but it's long enough so that when he faces back to the room he finds it empty, the second-story window open, in its black square the visual echo, outlined in electric blue, of his son having gone through it.

Zan must shake himself loose from his shock. He dashes to the window to find that Parker has dropped a meter or so to an overhang and now slides the rest of the way, sore hand or no, down a drainpipe. "Parker," Zan half-whispers and then, full-throated, "Parker!" as the boy falls into the street and sprints into a foggy Berlin night that falls into nothing.

Zan nearly tumbles down the stairs of the inn in pursuit. He staggers out into the street and takes off in the direction that Parker ran.

Running and stopping to listen for the boy's footsteps, hearing nothing he runs further, but in no time comes to doubt where he is and the direction he's chosen. "Parker!" he calls, and a light comes on in a window but he doesn't care; he continues calling the boy's name. After ten minutes he realizes he's not only lost his son but himself in an anonymous part of the city with once industrial intentions, the wasteland's only interruption being the U-Bahn station east of him.

The father peers at the U-Bahn, wondering if the boy ran there. But Parker doesn't like the dark closed places. Zan moans, "Parker, please come back," not loud enough for anyone to hear but God, and in the dark he turns where he stands, constantly spinning as if to create a vortex that might catch the boy in its sway. Over and over as he spins, Zan says the boy's name, an incantation to conjure him.

At a loss, he begins to stumble back the way he came when someone hits him in the head.

There's another blow from the other direction and Zan knows there must be at least two of them, whoever they are, maybe three or four, and he falls to the street.

On his way to passing out, memory floating away like a balloon that Viv got for Sheba once while shopping, which the girl let go just for the sensation of watching it vanish, Zan feels hands in his pockets emptying them before he closes his eyes. He whispers his son's name and has a moment to regret it, hoping his assailants don't hear.

Zan often points out to Viv that sometimes she thinks about telling him something and, once she thinks it, believes she's done it. Not long before they left Los

Angeles for London, she answered tearfully that maybe sometimes he just doesn't remember her telling him.

Now lying in the street he has this thought that not only is
she right and his memory fails ominously, but that in fact the
reverse of what he told her is true—that what he thinks he tells
her in fact he's never said, that in fact what he thinks he's told
everyone he's never said at all to anyone. That for months he's
imagined himself saying things that he never did: All those
times, all those people from Viv to J. Willkie Brown who
observed how recently he's turned into a chatterbox, were only
voices in his head made manifest in hallucinations. Really?
Me? On the radio?

S uddenly it seems absurd. Suddenly Zan is convinced,
lying there in the street, that like the character in his new
and utterly misbegotten novel, he's been whiplashed to
some other place in time except it's another present rather than
the past; he's been swept up and deposited in a warp of voices
saying things that haven't been said but only considered—
political rants, personal observations, plans and promises still-
born, playlists of songs and those who never sing them—and
that in fact nothing about his life is real anymore if it ever was,
he has no son, he has no daughter or wife or house.

S ome months ago, shortly before the election, Zan under-
went a routine medical procedure, and lying on the table
he was fascinated by the part of his brain that resisted the
anesthetic even though he chose to have it and in fact would be

terrified of not having it. Then, lying on the table feeling his mind resisting, he worried that—like someone who can't sleep because he lies in bed worrying about not being able to sleep—he might not be able to go under and would remain conscious during the procedure. Not to mention the enormous conceit of believing that his will was stronger than anesthesia, Zan was caught between clinging to awareness and desiring its surrender. His last fleeting thought before the anesthesia took over was to wonder why the patient is asked to count backward from one hundred when he never gets past ninety-seven. Wouldn't starting at ten do? Or five?

Back in the canyon, the canyon that he's not even sure anymore he's ever lived in, Zan would drive through pockets of sunlight that he recognized as the same sunlight from forty years before when he was eighteen years old. Driving into this light he would have the feeling that he seems to have more and more as he gets older—of the past seeping into the present and marked by the quality of a particular light when he turns a bend of the road. Light is constant, he thinks, it has no past or future but always is present, so it's always the same light; and entering these grottos of the same light that was there so many years ago, he remembers everything that happened and who it all happened with, stalactites of light and most of all the songs, every fissure with a melody all its own.

But now in the Berlin street his unconscious mind understands that none of this about the light is true. His mind understands that light dies like everything else; it's not the same light at all. It's a new light from the sun or maybe a star that already has died sometime during the thousands of years that its light was en route. He understands that what's constant isn't light but shadow, that it's the shadows which are the same regardless of what light casts them. Songs are more transient than light because, unlike light that bleaches the earth or sears the flesh, a song never leaves a trace except with whatever listener can or will attest to it. The listener becomes not just a collaborator with the singer, he becomes the keeper of the song, seizing possession of it from the singer; the listener knows hearing the song more than the singer can claim singing it. If light is a ghost picture that will disappear, time is a child's game of telephone, humming at the beginning of the line a melody transformed by a series of listeners to an altogether other melody at the end—and then who's to say it wasn't that final melody all along?

Nonetheless, in such moments of light and song, past and present coincide. The deepest cell of memory's catacomb is more accessible to Zan than the most shallow; he remembers more vividly the quality of light at a given moment forty years ago than the name of someone he met yesterday. Zan has become frightened by his memory's daily, even hourly insurrections. He's become as terrified by the prospect of dementia as he is by all the other prospects that terrify him—more, of course, because in memory lies the self's archeological remains. Almost idly, Zan has considered some plan by which someone euthanizes him before he allows madness to consume him. But when you have children, you don't enjoy the luxury of any melodrama other than the one you're actually living through.

In retrospect it's inevitable that when X's *Bloom in FutureLA* is published in early 1921, no one notices. No one comments on the passages of revolutionary stream of consciousness, no one cares about the mindbending erudition or how the book proposes to sum up western civilization in a twenty-four-hour stroll.

Rather the Irish plagiarist's version a year later, set in Dublin, receives all the attention, just as it did before history and the imagination circled back on themselves in the form of Zan's protagonist. X's subsequent novels go unnoticed as well, even as he's bitterly certain that, if anything, he's improved on the rough drafts of pretenders. Finally, with X's rendition of a Southern novel about a man who goes crazy not knowing whether he's white or black, the *New York Times* offers a conjecture, part manifesto and part exposé.

The headline of the review reads AUTHOR PLAGIA-RIZES THE FUTURE. The piece continues: " . . . as if larceny of the future is any less dubious than larceny of the past, Mr. [this being the *New York Times*] X—who doesn't have the courage of his own name, never mind his imagination—is that most derivative of novelists, plundering concepts and ideas advanced with more skill and maturity in years to come by other authors better suited to them. The sad lesson of Mr. X's career is that while genius can be faked, authenticity cannot, so let us leave this slipshod and overwrought body of work on the ash heap of tomorrow where it belongs . . . "

Of course what the reader of Zan's novel knows, and what even X himself may suspect, is that this review is written by the novel's author, though whether in some collaboration with the zeitgeist even Zan can't be certain. Over the course of the next two decades X wanders west. He flees the East Coast's centers of higher and refined thought until he makes a home amid the West Coast's various ignominies of artifice and audacity, where shamelessness has so little shame it doesn't bother calling itself something else. In the late Forties after the War, his literary life a distant shambles, he finds himself working in a small radio station off Hollywood Boulevard, of which the only attraction is the library of 78s by Ellington, Hodges, Holiday, Vaughan, Hawkins, Powell, Young, Webster, and Parker, who's not to be confused with a twelve-year-old boy named after him fifty years later, and whose father calls him now from the dark Berlin pavement. Fate blesses X by letting him live long enough to again see the Sixties, after already having seen them once at the age of eighteen. Fate curses X by making him, in the year 1968, ninety-one years old.

It was a time of compounded half-lives, when history shed its cocoon every three months and out emerged a new history, and if you were alive then—Zan never has dared tell his children because they would find it so insufferable and he could hardly blame them—you knew it was special even at the moment you were living it. To be sure they were silly times, trite before they would seem to have been true enough long enough for anything to be trite. They were indulgent and childish when not utterly confused, imposing their own conformity especially among those who fashioned themselves nonconformists. Zan can't watch a video of the era, even if it's only the scratchy little mental video of his memory, without wincing a little. Years afterward, the Sixties became a preposterous and unreasonable burden to everyone who followed.

B ut everything glistened beyond chemical inducement, the stars in lawns and the dark gawking windows of the sea, the wondrous clockwork of the banal and the shimmer of every color as though the world was washed down in the early hours of each morning by a rain collected in the clouds of every dream the night before. The time existed in some impossible eclipse of the moon by the sun, the two having changed places, the luminance in closer proximity than the lunacy until, at some point that no one noticed until it was too late, the two changed back. Stupid though it all was with a narcissism mistaken for innocence, it also was an epoch stoned on the waft of possibility. Years later Zan knew that if he could find a wind tunnel blowing him back, he would throw himself into its mouth without hesitation and never stop riding the gale.

For years following the publication of his last novel, Zan had nightmares about Ronnie Jack Flowers. It wasn't that he supposed Flowers might retaliate in some way; rather Zan remains tormented by what he believes is the single greatest lapse of his life, at the very least born out of so much naïveté as to have caused destruction. Some, including friends of Zan, found what he wrote about Flowers so reckless, so thoughtlessly cavalier, that they couldn't help wondering if he did it on purpose. They couldn't fathom any other reason for doing it; people were furious with him, and what Zan couldn't stand was that Flowers thought he did it on purpose too—and why wouldn't he think so? Then Zan began to wonder if he *did* do it on purpose; and if it wasn't racism, then was it an unconscious blow against the opportunism of Flowers' convictions? Zan went from bookstore to bookstore buying up copies of the novel to get it out of circulation.

Over time Zan made some fragile peace with the episode. He tried to convince himself that although one is responsible for what he does, he can't be responsible for every injustice and unfairness with which the culture responds; and for his part Flowers picked up the bits of his life, worked for a while with a civil rights group in L.A.—so Zan could tell himself that the man was forced by what Zan wrote to stop living a lie, forced to do with his life what he ought to be doing. But this is crap and Zan knows it. It was the other man's choice how to live his life, even if it meant becoming a rightwinger and a phony one at that; and Zan's betrayal, if betrayal doesn't necessarily call for malice, exists on its own terms.

In the Twenty-First Century "the arc of the story changes," is how Zan concludes his address on the novel in London two weeks ago, which is another lifetime to the man lying in the street. Behind Zan's lectern is the blow-up of the television image of the president, branded with the word ANTICHRIST. "Maybe this has been going on awhile," says Zan, "but now the arc of the imagination bends back to history, because it can't compete with history." A black Hawaiian with a swahili name? It's the sort of history that puts novelists out of business. The arc of revision bends back to the original, except now the original has been revised to the point it's become a negative of itself. In its umpteenth rewrite, the story is still—as some back in Zan's country would have it—that of a baby born in secret, smuggled to a land where he'll become king of its people, except now it's not a new testament but a demonic scheme, now it's a sign from God not of a beginning but an end, and now the protagonist no longer is the pale glowing image into which the original story transformed him from his hebraic reality over two thousand years of rewrites, but the reverse.

What was white is black. The arc of the story has gone so far, who's to say that the revision hasn't become the original? Who's to say that Saint Mark himself didn't get conked on the head and mugged in the streets of Alexandria, and then wake up and steal his story from a newer future-version dropped at his side? Who's to say that in another past he didn't get knocked unconscious and wake to find, left there beside him by some mysterious stranger, the version of the story that he copied, after turning the black antichrist into a golden hero? Maybe our version of the story, from this time, is the real one, and the other from two thousand years ago is the clone.

He's the mix-tape president of a mix-tape country, full of songs that it seemed everyone heard and loved and sang in common when he was elected. Now no one hears that song anymore, only all the other songs on the tape that they ignored. He's a partisan. He's a pushover. He's a radical; he's a sell-out. He's rigid, he's vacillating; he's naïve, he's expedient; he's ubiquitous, he's remote. In Zan's lifetime never has a president been heard so differently by so many, but what everyone now holds in common is what they *don't* hear anymore, which was his music that once so mesmerized them and now seems to have gone silent.

Has it really gone silent or is its power simply exhausted, the same song but sung to a different and more desperate wind that casts the words and music on ears that have grown deaf to it? For months the new president was the only thing that made Zan happy: *He made me believe in the country of my dreams*, but is everyone therefore complicit in the Great Wake-Up from that dream, as accountable for what they chose to hear as for what was sung? If in fact it isn't really the song that's changed but the listener, then is it not only no longer the same song after all but never was? Can it be one song one moment but then, listened to another way, another song, though the same melody and lyric and singer? Was there a secret country that all along hated the song, waiting for the other country that Zan loves to become deaf to it and lose its love for it and faith in it?

How can you believe in a god, J. Willkie Brown asks Zan at the pub outside the university following the lecture, and Zan answers, swallowing the last of his second vodka, "Because I don't believe it's all molecules. Because I don't believe the conscience translates into a chemical equation. Because men and women run into a hundred-and-ten-story building to save perfect strangers, overcoming every instinct of self-preservation, when the hundred-and-ten-story building right next to it has just collapsed, which means people act not only in the face of nature and self-preservation but outright rationality. Because there are dimensions of nobility that can't be diagrammed on a blackboard in a class. Because men wrack their brains trying to think of ways to turn their fellow human beings into lampshades, which means there are dimensions of barbarity that also can't be diagrammed on the same blackboard. Because I believe such unquantifiables abound beyond dispute, along with evidence that human behavior is animated by spirit. Because I think the existence of the soul proves the existence of God, not the other way around."

I'm a traitor. Better to admit we're traitors of the country of the banged gavel, the salem stench, the hate that hates in God's name, so we might be patriots of the other country of the eternal pursuit, memory's mystic chord, our nature's better angels, and the promise that no God can help loving even when we break it. By its nature, my version of the country is blasphemous. By its nature, it allows for doubt, the possibility that my God is wrong and yours is right. The other country, where I commit treason, denies doubt, views it as a cancer on the congregation.

The one thing that Zan knows for sure is that, should the song of his country finally fade and be silent, it will never quite be possible again to believe in it. This is the problem, he reasons, with presidents who can't be as big as the reasons they embody. A body can only hold reasons so big. Should the silencing of the song come to pass, not only will Zan be complicit in the loss of his own faith, he will be complicit for having had faith in the first place. But without such faith, the country—this country in particular—is nothing.

Without such faith, I'm nothing. This is the occupational hazard of being of my country, the way one's identity becomes bound up with a landscape that manifests in its soil and psychitecture an idea, with a people still fighting over who they are because when nothing else is held in common but the idea then if the idea isn't held in common there's nothing left except the mystical name of the place that evokes something different for each person but which each person allows himself or herself to believe is the same thing evoked for every other person.

At the campaign rally forty-one years ago, pulled to safety from the frenzied crowd that threatens to catch him in its undertow, the eighteen-year-old Zan feels in his ear the breath of the young black woman who rescues him and whispers something he can't hear; but lying in the street now, he almost does.

Lying in the street now, Zan confronts the breakdown he's been trying to avoid since London. He's stunned by how much this moment feels like a bookend. Finally overwhelmed by despair, that grief of the soul, he cries, My God, where's my boy? Where's my little girl? Where's my wife, where's my house? Where's my art, where's my country? How did I lose it all? At this moment he's convinced it's all been a dream: "I know I did something wrong," he sobs out loud, "but I don't know what." What lapse of perspective undid him? What ambition failed him? What did he take for granted? What did he value too much or too little? What thing was undone that should have been done, or what was done that shouldn't have been? To what dream did he commit himself that was folly? How is it that he was so old when he was so young, and how has he now been reduced to something so childish even as he's so old?

When he hears himself whisper his son's name again, he opens his eyes with no idea how long he's been out. His head pounds and the rest of him throbs. He tries to rise and almost makes it up onto one leg but collapses. He lies in the street another minute looking at the fog above. "Parker?"

He turns to look at the sidewalk and in the dark sees a girl younger than Sheba standing there watching him, being pulled away by a mother who assumes he's a derelict in a stupor.

He makes himself roll over and again gets up on his hands and knees. His face is dried and caked into a mess of tears and blood, and as he reaches up to wipe his eyes clear, he sees the blue streak that Parker made there earlier tonight when he slashed Zan's hand with the marker.

Of course Zan doesn't have his cell anymore, his muggers having taken it. Horror wells up in him at the thought that Parker might call and its new owners might answer, but then he remembers with relief that, in defiance, Parker refused to write down the number. The man wipes his eyes again and gets on his feet, holding his hand up to a streetlight and looking hard at it; and the simple streak of blue confirms for Zan the reality of having a son who made that mark.

When he wipes his hand against his face, the streak smears like a real mark would, unless he's hallucinating that as well. But Zan decides that he won't allow himself to believe this; he decides that whatever faith he has left, he'll summon for the sake of believing in the mark on his hand and thereby his life.

He gets back to the inn and totters up the stairs inside. At the door of the room he's looking for his key and, not finding it, wonders whether it was taken with his phone. As it occurs to him that maybe he rushed from the room without the key and should check whether the door is locked, it opens from the other side.

The boy stares at his father. "What happened?" he says in the smallest voice his father has heard from him since the time the car crashed in an oil slick on the canyon boulevard. Zan grabs his son and pulls him close; Parker crumples into his father's chest. "What happened," he murmurs again in his father's shirt.

"I'm O.K.," Zan says, "please, please don't leave again."

"I won't. I'm sorry. Are you O.K.?"

"I am." He might have a cracked rib. "Looks worse than it is."

"I'm sorry," Parker says again.

"No," the father whispers, "I made a mistake. Mom wouldn't have wanted us to leave Sheba." He says, "We have to go back and find her."

"O.K."

Somewhere three young Germans tally up the night's bounty, enormously disgruntled. The cell phone they took from the foreigner is the only thing of any value and its charge is nearly dead, and of course stolen cells are good for an hour or two at most before they get reported and turned off. One of the three men is staring at the cell when it rings. He hits the receive button and holds the cell to his ear.

"Zan," comes a woman's voice. The three look at each other. "Zan, it's me." Now disgusted with how poorly the night has gone, the man curses into the cell and hurls it through the air, the words "Zan? It's Viv, where are you?" forming an arc in the night before the phone smashes against the stone stubble of what used to be the Wall.

But what, Viv asks herself five days ago, would a room at the beginning of time sound like?

Looking back over her shoulder from where they've come, Viv says to her driver, "No, this isn't right," when he takes her deep into the heart of Addis Ababa, leading her by foot down the winding stone steps into the labyrinth of tunnels and bridges lined by the high walls covered with moss. Figures in white gauze dart from the shadows in a collision of pedestrian alleys, still smelling of the mustard gas with which Mussolini massacred a million Ethiopians seventy years ago. There bubbles up out of the earth three thousand radiant millennia; overhead, a sirocco blows in from the moon.

What would a room at the beginning of time sound like? she wonders back at the hotel later that night—or is it morning? sometime, night or morning, after returning from the center of the capital's ancient quarter where the driver took her, when Viv looks at a western calendar rather than an Ethiopian one and realizes the date is a week later than she thought. Could I have lost track of time that much? she asks, standing on her hotel balcony, looking at a photograph in her hand as though it has an answer, when all it has is the face of a young woman who is dead.

In the labyrinth, when she says to the driver, "No, this isn't right," he turns and answers, Please. I can take you back to the car if you wish, he says, but if I do, you'll never find what you're looking for.

At the center of the quarter, in white rock that's part wall and part ground, is an entrance at an angle that's part door and part hole, and as it begins to rain, Viv steps down and in, ducking slightly though she's only a little over five feet tall. She passes through a cloud bled of light into a room or cavern just a bit less dark, as her eyes adjust to the stub of a single burning candle on the other side where she sees the young journalist whom she hired to find Sheba's mother. He rises from where he's sitting on the rock.

He says, "Hello, Viv," and extends his hand. She says, "Are you hiding?" but he seems sanguine, almost good-natured about it. "Yes," he says, "for a while." "How long?"

"I don't know. I'm not sure. Maybe it will not be so bad, maybe I will be able to leave the city at night."

Upset, Viv says, "I'm sorry that I got you in this much trouble."

"But you do not make the trouble," the journalist assures her, "others make it. You asked a question that you have a right to answer."

"My daughter someday will want to know who her mother is."

"Of course," he answers.

"She'll hate me if I haven't tried to find out." She begins to cry and stops herself.

"Everyone who loves your daughter understands this."

Viv says, "I'm not so sure."

"I have news," he says. "In a way it's bad news and in another way . . . "

"What's the bad news?"

"The bad news is that the woman we have been trying to find is dead." He takes from his back pocket the photograph and hands it to her. "But the other news is that she almost certainly is not your daughter's mother. So it means that your daughter's mother may still be alive. It also means that there is no answer to your question at the moment, and that now it is a harder question than ever to answer."

Viv looks at the photo as well as she can make it out in the dark of the room and the light of the small candle. "How did she die?" Viv says. The woman is young though hardly a girl; in the dark of the cavern she doesn't look like Sheba, nor will she on the hotel balcony the next morning when Viv looks at the photo again in the light of day.

"That's not certain but it's not important," the journalist answers, "she is not the woman you look for."

"How do you know?"

"It's better that I don't answer this," the journalist explains sympathetically, "it may even be better for your daughter, if she were to return to Ethiopia someday."

"I'm sure someday she'll want to come back."

Music is what a room at the beginning of time sounds like—and when Viv steps into this place, do the days pass in a matter of moments? When she slips the dictates of western months, succumbing to a calendar drawn to the rhythms of a different moon, is she bound as well to slip old temporal moorings that measure, as much as anything that people have learned, what people have forgotten?

It's a music of subterranean harmonics, half voice and half caw, and comes from some human source like Sheba's music does, except it's not coming from the journalist *and certainly it's not coming from me*, thinks Viv, *I never could carry a tune* and there's no one else to be seen. It comes from the room itself, the woman and the journalist at the very axis of the transmission as though they're standing in one of the chambers of Sheba's radio-heart, from a time before she was born.

Minutes later, or is it hours or days? rising from the white rock at the city's center Viv brushes her head against a sagging sky the color of mauve. The blue eucalyptuses against the Entoto Hills have turned to glass, and in the sagging mauve sky a flock of flamingos bursts into flames. It reminds her of the time back home when the canyons were on fire, the inferno roaring toward the house; all around them the family could see the hazy hot red flare that circled the night. Viv and Zan packed up Parker and Sheba in the car along with the personal effects and valuables. It was shortly after Sheba came to Los Angeles—definitely it was *after*—and, two years old in her booster seat in the back, sucking her thumb, the girl wondered in her infant fashion how her life had come to this, on the other side of a world on fire. Viv remembers a talk that she and her husband once had: If ever there was a decision to be made for either mother or father to save each other or the children, they would save the children. It was the easiest thing they ever agreed on.

The firmament went up in flames that night and now rising from the white rock, at the center of one of the highest cities in the world, Viv reaches up and draws a blue line in the ash sky. She looks at the blue dust on her finger then looks up and knows with certainty that the woman in the photograph that she holds in her hand is buried there behind the sky's soot. When Viv reaches up again and scoops out of the heavens a hole, the music roars up out of the hole in the white earth behind her and through the blue puncture she's made, like air sucked out of a rocket in space.

No, Sheba's father says the next day when Viv goes back to the family to show them the photograph. The aunt won't look at it; the grandmother is near blind with cataracts. Sheba's father takes the photo, and as Viv hands it over and the father's hand stops briefly midair before taking it, she makes no effort to hide the intensity with which she studies his reaction. He doesn't look straight at the photo but peers down as though his lids might hide whatever Viv can see in his eyes. After several seconds, maybe as many as five or seven or eight, he says, utterly impassive, "No."

But, she thinks, the eight or seven or five seconds are endless; he takes so long to answer. And now she wishes that she pressed the journalist to explain how he knows what he thinks he knows, so that she can put Sheba's father's no in a context of pain or fear or the same rejection by which he so long rejected fatherhood. "No," he says for the third time, either to make it final or to protest one time too many.

Viv's last night in the hotel she is too distraught to sleep. Outside her window a storm blows into Addis, and lying on her bed in the dark she feels the room tremble around her, the floor tremble beneath her; as the wind picks up though the balcony doors, she thinks the rumble of the room is from the storm but then realizes that the thunder coming up through the bed is percussive and mesmeric, and it's music. Full of wrath and sorrow at everything, Viv hurls the sheets away from her, gets up. Beneath her brief lowcut nightie she pulls on some jeans and shoes and throws a wrap around her shoulders and heads downstairs to the lobby.

The storm is picking up when she reaches the ballroom of the hotel. Enough of the eucalyptic wind from outside finds its way through some hidden breach to rustle the room's potted fronds and small dingy chandeliers turned down low; Viv buys a glass of tej, the moonshine honeywine once made by Sheba's grandmother. She drinks it down, buys another.

He took too long to say no. He said it too many times. To clear a space in the middle of the large ballroom, its round tables have been pushed to the walls with such abandon the wind might have blown them there, and the room churns with five or six hundred otherworldly-looking Ethiopians with their african skin and european features dancing to half a dozen musicians on a bandstand at the room's far end. Viv buys another glass of tej: *Who is she?* the woman in the photo, *and if she's dead and has nothing to do with Sheba then why show me the photo at all?* and, watching the dance, immediately she knows she'll never know.

Unlike in the West where the dance begins in the feet and moves up the body, here in the city of the abyss the dance begins in the shoulders, the part of the body made for bearing a weight, shoulders shimmying as though to shake away the burden of human time before the dance moves down to the clasped hands that lurch forward in a frenzy to cast something off, down to the legs galloping to catch up with whatever gauntlet the hands have thrown.

To Viv the music isn't african in any sense with which she's familiar but a bizarre blend of funk, swing, big band, cabaret, manzuma, armenian soul. It's a rhythm and blues from the future that's spiraled round the sphere of time to come back up through its birth canal. Beginning seventy years ago under the rule of Mussolini and sung down through the communist Derg, the songs have become a code: "Wax and gold," the Ethiopians call it, when the golden messages of liberation and revolution are hidden inside the wax of the outer lyric and melody; and through the century the songs have been passed bearing the secret songs inside. In the swept ballroom of the Addis hotel tonight the band begins to play "Tezeta" and dancers break off in circles, partners claiming the center in order to dance each other into submission. As the small wrap slips from her bare shoulders, the white woman with paling blue hair finds herself vortexed into one of the circles with a young Ethiopian woman who smiles at her; ululations rise from every throat around them. Eighteen hours from now, under the English Channel thirty-six hundred miles away, Zan will think to himself how music plummets into the personal and emerges as politics on the other side of confession.

At the airport early the next morning, Viv finds there's not enough credit on her card to get back to London. Her cell hasn't worked since she got to Addis and the battery is dead, and if she returns to the hotel and stays another night to email Zan, it's money that could go toward getting her back. She's not certain what Zan would be able to do anyway. Zan would be the first to acknowledge that it's in such situations when he becomes most flabbergasted that Viv is coolest.

Beginning to feel the hangover of the long sleepless night, she finds thinking that much harder. She decides to try and use the credit card to buy a less expensive ticket to some place in Western Europe from where she'll find a way to England. Her best prospect appears to be Berlin, more out of the way than she would like, and she's about to book a seat when, at the last moment, a flight to Paris becomes available.

After the seven hour flight to Orly by way of Khartoum, Viv takes a bus to Paris' outskirts and then the metro further into the city, making the mistake of getting off at Châtelet. From there she could transfer to a direct line to where she wants to go but doesn't know this; pulling her bag into the street, she keeps hailing cabs until she finds one—in the thick of rush hour as dusk falls on the city—whose driver seems to understand that she needs to get to whatever station will put her on the express rail to England.

Once in the taxi, however, she's not so sure the cabbie understands at all. The only thing clear is he's drunk and agitated; she can smell the Côtes du Rhone like she's sitting in a cask of it. "Train station!" she keeps trying to explain, "anglais!" but then realizes it must sound like she's commanding him to speak English when what she means is England. He

276 · STEVE ERICKSON

lets loose a torrent of French and something else, Turkish or Eastern European she supposes, and then—with deliberation and intent, she's certain—he drives his cab straight into the limousine before him, nearly hitting what looks in the twilight and blur of the event to be a young boy about Parker's age, pulled from danger at the last moment.

Viv hurtles forward in the back of the cab, hitting her head hard on either the ceiling or the seat in front. To her astonishment, the collision hasn't sobered the driver but sent him further into a rage. He backs up the cab and floors the accelerator, careening again into the limo in front, and then does it again.

He keeps doing this until finally she grabs her purse, throws open her door, leaves behind her luggage and lurches from the vehicle. She half expects to leap into the path of oncoming traffic; the repeated crashes, however, have brought everything around her to a stop. She hits the ground, stumbles, picks herself up and keeps running, into the large glass building before her, and the only thing that could almost astound her as much as what she's just been through is to discover that in fact she's where she wants to be, in the Gare du Nord, from which the Eurostar departs for London.

She doesn't have enough money for the train, and on sheer adrenaline from what happened in the rue Dunkerque outside, she almost slips past the ticket booth before one of the officials stops her.

Depressed and rattled, she can't bring herself to sleep in the station. She wanders several blocks east, to the cheapest no-star hotel that she can find on the rue d'Alsace.

P aying for one night upfront, she spends the next day at the Gare du Nord casing the crowd like a thief, sizing up its ebbs and flows, points of vulnerability. She thinks, I've become the vagabond rebel of my youth, who hopped trains on a whim. She spends a second night in the hotel, slips out in the morning without paying, spends the second day at the station; hungry to the edge of nausea, she rations out to herself juice and a single baguette. Having left her bag with her clothes in the cab that she fled two days before, she breaks down and buys a hairbrush and clean underwear.

From Addis to Khartoum to Orly to the Gare du Nord, she's viewed every telephone—the broken ones on the walls, those on the other sides of windows, those that people gaze at in their palms as they walk along never looking up—with an unbearable longing, believing her family only a flurry of digits away. When she finds a public phone that works, she stares in dismay at the foreign instructions, terrified she'll waste what money she has on a call that won't go through. For as long as she can remember, she's had a recurring nightmare in which she rushes from dead phone to dead phone trying to make a call; and now she's in that nightmare. A couple of times she asks someone if she can borrow a phone and they just push past, glaring at her temerity if they understand at all.

I must seem like a panhandler, another homeless beggar, she thinks, and then realizes that in fact at this moment that's exactly what she is. In the Gare du Nord she feels herself under the surveillance of patrolling police as though she's wandered over from Pigalle to ply her trade. Her hair has grown out but still has streaks of a pale blue that faded back in that room at the center of Addis Ababa.

In the light of the sun coming through the station's skylight, Viv eats the rest of her baguette, drinks the rest of her juice and watches a single butterfly flutter out of the morning mist and steam off the railway tracks to the glass above. The butterfly has wandered into the station through an open door, or where the trains come and go, to spend the rest of its brief life amid the furor of people and machines in passage—and as Viv watches, she wants to shield it in armor. She wants to envelop it in one of the metal frames with which she surrounded her stainless-glass recreations back home, to honor and protect what's all the more beautiful for its precariousness; but she can't do that anymore. Someone took from her, carelessly, a singular and beautiful vision, in order to steal not only her past but her future.

No, she thinks. She's lost her armor but not her future or her vision. Looking at the train to London on the other side of the station, there it is, right there, the future just beyond the ticket gate; it begins in mere moments. All aboard.

Viv ascends to the level from which the Eurostar departs. Milling with the crowd that files toward the train, she presses past the officials taking tickets; when she hears an authoritative declamation of French directed at the back of her head, she picks up her step, and when she hears another she moves at something only slightly less conspicuous than a mad dash, darting in and out of other passengers, knocking some out of the way. She steps onto one of the sleek cars and makes her way up the train, slipping in and out of doors, dodging the attention of whoever's behind her; she disappears into a bathroom and locks it. Staring in the mirror, struggling to hold herself together, Viv waits for a pounding on the door.

The Belgian conductor doesn't catch up with her until beyond Brussels, after more than an hour of the woman flitting into bathrooms and working her way through the train—at which point she finally acquiesces all composure. In an explosion of sobs she tries to explain to the conductor and British security official what happened in the taxicab in Paris, her long trek from Africa, the distance from her family and the dead cell phone and the incommunicado status of her life, never mind a dark foyer in the Garden of Eden where time drains out of the floor like water from a shower. For a panicked moment, she thinks she's lost her passport.

Before she got back together with Zan and became pregnant with Parker, Viv lived by herself in the industrial loft section of downtown L.A., in a mammoth stone bunker from the balcony of which she could watch the trains roll in and out of Union Station between her and the sunset. The night she split up with Zan, as he was fleeing to Berlin—it was during the following two months that she had her affair with then Hollywood-based J. Willkie Brown—she watched from the landing the Southwest Chief pull out of the station and, grabbing nothing but her toothbrush, she jumped in her car and raced the train to Pasadena, arriving in time to hop on. She didn't have a ticket then either. "Where are you going?" the conductor asked in Pasadena, and she answered, "The sunrise," which turned out to be Flagstaff, she and the rest of the train's staff drinking enough tequila to make her wonder ever after just how sober train travel is.

Now the Belgian conductor on the Eurostar who otherwise seems so sternly disapproving reappears twenty minutes later with a sandwich and plastic cup of red wine, for which Viv thanks him gratefully. Eating the sandwich, she pulls from her purse the photograph of the young woman that she was given in Addis and looks at it. She reproaches herself now for not having pressed harder for answers from the journalist, for not having pressed harder for answers from the grandmother and aunt and father. Zan believes in the integrity of secrets, that some things aren't meant to be known; by this, thinks Viv, he really means mysteries. Is there a difference between a secret and a mystery? A secret sounds dishonest, like something withheld, as opposed to a mystery, where something is unknowable.

But God keeps more secrets than anyone. Is it a conceit, then, for a human being to presume that a mystery is a secret, or is it an aspiration to a larger wisdom? Viv can't answer this. She just knows that now there are things about Sheba and her mother and her past that will be secrets forever, and that the acceptance of this, however unsatisfactory, is a fitful grace.

In the seat of the train where she's been consigned for the duration of the ride, trying to reclaim a sense of calm, she has a sudden burst of disorientation and becomes convinced for a split moment that the train in fact is barreling south, back toward Africa. For a while she contemplates the contradiction of someone with wanderlust having no sense of direction.

That wanderlust she inherited from her father, the son and grandson of locomotionists who never could stay put, packing up five children and moving them all to Africa when Viv was twelve. As Zan would point out, Viv has a hard time staying put too. Thirty-six hours after any trip she becomes possessed of whatever is the newest strain of cabin fever, or maybe she invents one. Is Sheba's adoption somehow an expression of that? she wonders as the window of the train exchanges the black of the european night for the black of the tunnel beneath the Channel. Is a restlessness of the body a restlessness of the heart? Like futuristic rhythm and blues, has Viv spiraled round the sphere of her own life to come back up through its birth canal and find waiting for her a small daughter of the abyss?

I'm a flawed human being! Viv moans to herself for the thousandth time in her life. The voice in her head is a running monologue of personal failings. She's heard that a family is only as happy as the mother, and she knows that the girl she brought into all their lives is trailed by the betrayals of one mother after another; this is Sheba's special burden that no one else can understand. Not so long ago, back in the canyon, Viv asked Zan one day, "Where's the joy in our lives?" and Zan looked at her like she spoke some language as lost as the time back in that room in Addis. At this point Zan will settle for freedom from the fear to which he wakes every morning. But Viv will not, and neither will her wanderlust.

At St. Pancras a little before midnight, Viv is escorted by the conductor and security official to a back room in the offices of the Eurostar. In the room is a desk with a telephone and several chairs. The walls are bare.

Viv asks to use the telephone and is told to be seated. She waits half an hour before the security official returns to the room with someone she takes to be a policeman and another official affiliated with the railways company, who sits behind the desk and takes over the conversation. "Of course," she says to Viv, "you know it's a serious matter to breach the gate as you did in Paris and not have a ticket."

"I didn't have the money," says Viv.

"Yes, well," the official sighs, "that rather goes without saying, doesn't it? But that's not an excuse, is it?"

Viv realizes it's good she's exhausted. Otherwise this is the sort of situation where she typically, to use her word, effervesces, and she senses that now effervescence is the wrong strategy; she still has signs of turquoise hair, effervescence enough. "Why have you come to London, then, Mrs. Nordhoc?" says the official.

"My husband and children are here," says Viv. "My husband has business."

"What sort of business?"

"He's giving a lecture. Or . . . " Viv thinks. " . . . he may already have given it by now."

"Do you know where he's lecturing?"

"The university."

"Yes," says the official, with a greater sigh than before, "we have a number of universities in London. It's a big city."

"I know." Viv says, "I don't remember which one."

"Where is your family staying?"

"In a hotel." When the woman across the desk says nothing, Viv tries to effervesce after all, laughing wearily, "There are a lot of hotels, aren't there? Like universities."

"I don't suppose you know which hotel."

"I . . . " Where she sits, Viv sways a bit from the exhaustion. "Can I call him?"

After a moment the official says, "All right," pointing to the telephone. "If it's a number from back home then you need to dial zero one." This confuses Viv, and in her fatigue she finds herself punching the wrong numbers. The other official from the train dials for her and hands her the phone.

It rings several times and her heart leaps when there's an answer. "Zan!" she says, but no one says anything. "Zan, it's me," and then there's a distant, abrupt expletive in a foreign language. "Zan," she says again, "it's Viv, where are you?" before the line goes dead. "That wasn't him," she says to the officials.

"I dialed correctly," says the official who dialed the phone.

"It wasn't him." She thinks she's going to cry again and says, "Can I make one more call? It's local—I think it's local. I'm pretty sure. I don't have the number but maybe it's listed." A minute later she says on the phone, "James? Sorry to wake you so late. It's Viv. I'm in London."

An hour later, J. Willkie Brown shows up at St. Pancras and pays for Viv's train ticket. "I don't actually know," he says in the taxi on the way to St. John's Wood, "what hotel Alexander is at . . . I mean," he hesitates, "I had the bill taken care of through the university because, well, he's seemed in some distress. Very worried about you, of course."

"I've completely lost track of time," says Viv.

"The school will have a record. We'll find out first thing in the morning."

It's strange to see James again. Viv says, "Thanks for bailing me out. I tried calling Zan but . . . "

"He was leaving messages," James says, "that were . . . a bit frantic. Needed to talk urgently but never said what about, and we kept missing each other. The last was three, four days ago . . . so I figured whatever it was got resolved. Had his hands full, of course, with the children, until the nanny showed up."

In the back of the taxicab, London swirling by her, Viv nods, and it's a minute or so before she thinks to herself, The nanny?

At James' townhouse, Viv barely sleeps on the sofa he's made into a bed for her. "No bag?" he says while fluffing cushions, and when she explains about the insane cab in Paris, he gives her one of his clean undershirts to wear; now in the dark she stumbles from the sofa to the window and stares out at the city, wondering where her husband and children are. Before the window, she closes her eyes as if trying to pick up a signal. She's up early the next morning, and when James emerges from the back room fully dressed, he sees the look on her face. "School office opens in thirty minutes," he assures her gently. "I'll ring them in twenty."

H e says, "Looks like you had a restless night."

"Yes," she says.

"Tea?"

"Please."

"How have you been? Aside from everything."

"Great," Viv answers somewhere in the upper register of hope, "aside from everything."

"Really?"

"No."

"That did sound," he says, "rather like the usual upbeat Viv answer." She watches him shuffle around the kitchen. "One of your more endearing qualities, I should add," bending over with apparent difficulty to light the stove.

"Nothing," she replies, "that winning the lottery wouldn't solve."

"Let's try to arrange that then, shall we?"

"Zan suspects I coerced you into this lecture thing, or whatever it was." She adds, "Not that you can be coerced."

"By you?" says James. "Of course I can. You know that. You're quite notorious in the art world these days, I hear."

She folds her arms. "I guess. Not something I like talking about."

"But you should feel vindicated," he insists. "It's accepted by virtually everyone that the bastard ripped you off."

"I don't want to be a chapter in someone else's story."

"We're all chapters in someone else's story. You should feel vindicated."

W hen she asks, "What about you?" she has no idea it's a real question until, curiously, he shrugs, "How's that?" before rushing into the rest. "Work goes all

right, I suppose—new piece about the impact of torture at
Guantanamo on the Muslim . . . well, never mind. Alexander
and I got into a bit of a row about it."

"Zan in a row?"

"Nothing explosive."

"Why *did* you invite him?" she asks. "I mean the lecture, or
. . . whatever it—"

"Oh," James throws open his arms.

"Oh?"

"When one's timer has been set, your perspective becomes
fixed, doesn't it? To whatever moment it's going off."

"James?"

"From that moment, everything looks different." He shrugs
again, this time less curious than ominous. "I, uh . . . have some
health issues."

"My God. Are you all right?"

"Not a matter of making amends, mind," he continues,
"there are no amends to be made, are there? With you or
Alexander." She watches him; he sips his tea, won't look back
at her. "Did you find the girl's mother?"

"Complete dead-end," she answers after a moment. She
takes her purse from the table and opens it. "No one will tell
me how she died, and in all likelihood she isn't Sheba's mother
anyway." She says, "I never should have gone."

"But you had to go," says James.

"Zan didn't want me to."

"But he understood. Ronnie Joe Somebody."

"Not the same thing." She finds the photo in her purse and
gazes at it as she did on the train last night.

"A moral compulsion, though, wasn't it? To take responsibility, even for the thing you're not really responsible for.
Another endearing Viv quality."

"My moral compulsion got me a photograph"—she hands
it to him—"of the wrong, dead woman."

James does a double-take. Viv's not sure she's ever seen James do a double-take. "But this woman," he says, "is very much alive," which isn't as true as he thinks.

L ess than an hour later, in the back of another taxi on the way to Zan's hotel, Viv says for the fourth or fifth time, "Are you sure?" and James answers, "Well, I suppose I can't be absolutely positive, but let's say I'm more sure about it than about most things."

Viv says, "I always thought you were sure about everything."

"Exactly." He says, "What no one knows is who she is. All manner of confusion there. Alexander thought I arranged it, I thought he arranged it, and when he asked her, she said you arranged it."

W hen they reach the hotel, the woman behind the front desk looks at Viv and asks to speak to James in private. "James," Viv says a moment later, "what's going on?"

Brow furrowed, James answers, "Alexander and your son checked out of the hotel four days ago."

"Zan and Parker? What about Sheba?"

"Apparently," James gestures toward the front desk and seems to choose his words as carefully as possible, "the girl went missing."

Viv staggers a bit. "My *daughter*, James," she says, flashing anger, "you keep saying 'the girl.' My daughter."

"Sorry."

She hardly can get out the words. "What do you mean missing?"

"With the nanny. Alexander was quite distraught, of course—she, uh," indicating the front desk again, "this lady knows his books . . . well, anyway, he left instructions before he and the boy . . . your son . . . "

Viv sinks into a chair. Looking back and forth from Viv to James, the woman behind the front desk says, "Your husband and son left their bags here, with a number. Then when the woman and little girl came back, I tried calling but no one answered."

There's a pause and Viv and James turn to her. "Came back?" says James.

"The little girl and nanny."

"Sheba came back?" says Viv, rising.

"Oh yes," answers the woman. "They're upstairs right now."

The woman calls to Viv, halfway up the flight of steps, "Third floor. I couldn't put them in the same room, it was taken, so they're down the hall—thirty-seven, nicer, actually . . . " and Viv already hears her daughter's music. "I called for a doctor an hour ago," the woman turns to James. "Since they checked in, she hasn't seemed at all well. The African lady."

Upstairs beyond the door marked thirty-seven, in the morning shadows slowly bleached of night by the sun through the window, the little girl with the thumb in her mouth who never has understood western time retreats to the middle of the room, watching Molly unconscious on a bed in a small alcove in the room's far wall. Sheba thinks to herself, She sleeps, or she's sick—did I make her sick? and in her heart the girl finds herself back in Ethiopia, two years old again and on the precipice of abandonment again like when her mother—her other mother, with the blue-green hair— first came to get her. Since they have been here in this room—bewildered by western time, Sheba has no idea how long—the girl has stood at the woman's side stroking her wet brow, wondering where her father and brother are, having almost come to believe they wouldn't abandon her. Back in Ethiopia, at a moment when she nearly had a family, she remembers that her name was something else though she can't quite remember: *Zan?* no that's her father's name, if he's still her father. She returns to the bed and is stroking the arm of the young woman, who at this moment is a color more volcanic than brown, when the door of the room opens behind her.

Sheba looks at Viv and wordlessly crosses the room to her, puts a small arm around her for a moment as Viv pulls her closer whispering her name. Then the child pulls Viv by the hand over to the bedside. Staring at the woman who clearly is delirious, Viv can't know that once this woman transmitted music of her own, because it's gone completely quiet: "My God," she hears James behind her, "how long do you suppose she's been like this?"

"She needs a doctor right away," says Viv.

"The woman downstairs said she called for one this morning."

"It's her," says Viv, "isn't it?"

"Yes."

"Isn't it? Doesn't she look like . . . the woman in the photo?" by which Viv means almost dead.

"Yes."

Viv turns to him. "Do you have it?"

"Sorry?"

"The photo?"

Reaching inside his coat, then to the other inside pocket, James murmurs, "It's here somewhere," checking the outer pockets, then patting his pants pockets. Then he checks the coat again. "After all, it didn't just disappear."

The doctor says, "Forgive me for being blunt," but he doesn't seem to Viv the sort of doctor who needs forgiveness in order to be blunt. "I can relocate her to a hospice," he says, "but don't know that there's much point, is there?"

"I don't know," Viv says, *you tell me.* Sheba hasn't moved from her place by the woman's bed, she hasn't stopped stroking the woman's arm. The girl is the calmest Viv has seen her; it's terrifying. Viv looks at Molly visibly bobbing on her sea of delirium and says, "What's wrong with her?"

"She's slipping away," the doctor snaps, then, looking at the little girl, softens. "She's slipping away," he says again.

"But what's she dying of?"

"She's dying of *dying.* It may have been coming on a long time, but there's no way to know that," and he adds, "Have you made arrangements for her daughter?"

Viv says, "I'm her mother."

"How's that?" says the doctor.

Viv starts to repeat herself but stops.

James says, "Shall I stay, then?"

"No," says Viv. "Can I call if I need anything?"

"Of course."

"Thank you." He's half closed the door behind him when she says, "James."

He turns and peers at her through the doorway.

"We never . . . " she says. "We didn't really talk about you."

"Another conversation," he says, sounding falsely chipper because James never is truly chipper, one of the things that he and Zan always have had in common. "For another time."

"Let's make sure to have it."

"Right," he says, but both know they won't, before it's too late.

Afternoon passes and night falls. From outside, rising from the crescent circle of Cartwright Gardens are the sounds of people returning from work, students from school, diners in nearby restaurants. From the pub halfway down the block comes a roar of approval; someone has scored a goal or try. In the park across the street a couple argue, more and more audibly; the guy is losing. If time is a child's game of telephone, now at the end of the line a simple melody hummed in someone's ear long ago is a din beyond human pitch, the ashen silence that blots out every song, when light isn't the norm of things but an aberration in the black. Trying to pull

Sheba to her, Viv feels this calamitous silence pass over, the room enveloped by that momentous passage to which every life bears witness at some time and stands vigil, before it finally is itself borne witness to, and the subject of the vigil of others.

Z an, where did you go? Viv asks, staring out from a window several windows down from where Zan asked something like the same question of her. Where did you take my son? How did the determination to uncover and understand the bonds of this family lead to such a smashing of it? Is life a plate on which we've spooned so much that all it could do is crack?

Gently she tries to pull Sheba from the woman in the bed but the girl won't have it. Sheba clutches Molly's arm the way she used to clutch Viv's in her sleep, runs her fingers along the profile of the dying woman's face as she did Viv's those first nights that Viv came to get her more than two years ago in Addis Ababa, "Tezeta" curling through the window. When the girl falls asleep on her feet and crumples to her knees, still she won't be dislodged from her place.

A m I a ghost, wonders Molly in her delirium? She tosses and turns on the bed in a blur of reverie. If so, how long have I been one? Is it since Ethiopia? Is it since Berlin and my mother? When did the music turn so low? The stroke of a small girl's hand is the only thing that tethers her to another world and keeps her from slipping away for good into this one.

In Hyde Park, Molly holds the girl's hand as they watch Zan and Parker cross Kensington Road and make their way to the Ethiopian embassy. Ninety seconds after the father and son have disappeared around the farthest corner of Prince's Gate, Molly leads the girl from the knolls of the park between Carriage Row and the Serpentine, in the direction of Earl's Court where Molly has been staying, exactly the opposite way from where Zan and Parker will go looking for them an hour after visiting the Ethiopian ambassador.

At Earl's Court the woman and girl catch the Circle Line to Westminster, where they transfer to the Jubilee Line that takes them to Waterloo. Ascending from the underground onto the main level of Waterloo Station, they board the train for Hampton Court, the same train they rode before.

By the time the woman and girl disembark at Hampton Court, the warm morning has become an unseasonably warm afternoon, unlike the last time they came to the palace when black billowing clouds rolled across the sky.

It's an hour and a half since Molly told Zan that they would meet. The woman and girl follow the same red brick bridge to the palace and beyond.

Am I a ghost? wonders the woman on the edge of the three-hundred-year-old maze. It seems like the two stand there all afternoon before she pushes Sheba toward the maze's entrance. "Remember?" she says to the girl, who turns to her. Did I become a ghost, Molly thinks, when I stole the motherhood I never was worthy of? "I'll come find you," and Sheba walks toward the entrance with no discernible trepidation, and disappears.

Molly remembers when she was a girl living in Berlin a few years before the Wall fell and her mother took her to the southern part of the divide not far from Checkpoint Charlie, near what used to be a recording studio and, before that, an old movie studio. There, as though a prophecy of what was to come, the Wall unraveled into a stone labyrinth between east and west, and within the maze Molly hid from her mother, running down concrete blue passages canopied by sky and the dark tunnels sheltered by the debris of surrounding construction. Winding her way to the center of the maze, she waited and her mother always found her, the mother's ear for the music of her daughter as unfailing as Molly assumes a true mother's always will be.

If I'm a ghost, can I pass through the maze's shrubbed walls to the center? Already be there waiting when Sheba gets there? So the girl will know she's never lost and that Molly will never lose her? The woman knows her own music has faded. She can hear her decrease in volume, she hears herself turned down. When she hears music from the maze, when she hears the girl's music wind its way back to her, she knows there's no mistaking it for the echoes of her own.

She follows the music in. She goes right to the girl at the center; Sheba looks up at her. Since Molly came, she hasn't sucked her thumb until now. "I'll never lose you again," Molly says.

They hide in the hedges when the palace closes. Has anyone ever hidden overnight in the maze? She swallows the child in her arms so as to keep her music quiet— *Jasmine, I saw you peeping*—and then when night falls she unfolds herself to let the child out, and a tune smokes skyward. They lie in the center, the girl in the crook of the woman's arms, and watch it drift to a star.

Unable to dislodge Sheba from her place next to Molly, Viv falls asleep with her on the floor, the outside noises of the neighborhood flickering like embers beyond the window. It's early in the morning—Viv isn't sure of the time— when she lurches awake to the sound of the door, and there against the light of the outer hall are two silhouettes that need no light other than the one in her heart.

Staring at each other, Viv and Zan have so many of the same questions—where were you? why did you go? are you all right?—and share so few answers except one— never mind; never leave again—that all the questions cancel each other out. Her son puts his arms around her in a way that he hasn't since he was Sheba's age and says, "We thought you were in Berlin."

"Berlin?" she says.

Zan shrugs helplessly, "I . . . " and she touches the marks on his face where he was beaten and throws her arms around him. They hold each other, one or the other reaching over to turn off the light in the hallway outside the door, one or the other quietly kicking the door closed until they're back in the dark. On the floor by Molly, Sheba sleeps.

She is two again, as when her other mother with the blue-green hair first came to get her in Ethiopia, and now as then the child is too shackled by loneliness to speak, the child who never has felt loved first and foremost, loved beyond and before anyone else, the child who must compete with other children for love and be always convinced she has lost, who somehow can imagine a blind parental love unconditioned even as she doesn't yet believe she has known it. Like someone once said of God, if you can imagine such a love then it must exist.

At the center of the maze, when the little girl feels a single tear leak from her eye, she turns in the woman's arms so no one can see it and so it soaks nothing but the ground beneath them. The girl is too little to know how profound it is to feel nowhere to belong; maybe no one at any age understands feeling grief for what can't be remembered. But though she barely remembers anymore the world she came from, half of her brief lifetime ago, she knows she never wanted to leave it, that she left part of herself there, so her grief is a secret from herself and until she learns the word for this secret then it's not a grieving that heals anything.

T hen who are you? Molly says to the girl in her arms, and are we really here? Are you who I think you might be, or just who I always hoped you to be but never were? Is my own mother here with us now? Do I hear her wandering the green passages just the turn of a corner away, or does she hear you, mistaking your music for mine? I never called you by a name except once—but is it yours? and do you need one? Or is it just I who need for you to have one?

D oes one need to travel a birth passage, womb to uterus, to be a daughter, if already you're the descendant of an unforgiving century? Tell me now, if you know, because now I must leave by the other passage at the other end, that emerges to a place that it's not yet time for you to go.

A few minutes later Viv must pull Sheba away from the bed, however adamant the girl is otherwise. "Come on," she says quietly, "come," but Sheba slips from Viv's grip; Zan gently takes the girl's other hand and tries to draw her away as well. The girl resists and when she begins to cry—always the loudest little person Zan has known, more volume per capita than any single body he's ever heard, like a boombox in a confessional—no sound comes from her, Radio Ethiopia gone silent, just the twisting of her little face. If Viv and Zan are to have with Sheba at least one more act of parenthood, this must be it: "She's not there anymore," Viv whispers to the girl, trying to think of a way to say it, "she's here, she's around us," looking around them in the dark, "but not *there*," indicating the body; and Sheba, supernaturally cognizant beyond what the span of such a short life allows, wonders how many mothers she has to lose, into how many mothers' bodies she has to press her own, into how many families she has to storm her way in order to make a home. "She's not there but she's here," says Viv, "let her go," and—though she doesn't say it out loud—be my daughter again.

She's nobody's daughter for a while. She doesn't talk to any of the family. She doesn't defy Viv and Zan or argue with Parker; the nights after the coroner comes and takes Molly away, the girl lies on the floor by Molly's bed with her back to everyone. All her demands to be part of the family have gone silent; she makes no music. She can't quite precisely be called inconsolable because she's so deep in herself that she gives no evidence of anything to be consoled. Neither Viv nor Zan can get her to come to bed with them; crumpled half asleep on the floor next to where Molly died, she is not moved by any coaxing. I'm a professional, she murmurs. She sleeps there until the father picks her up and carries her to the other bed, but when they wake in the morning she's back in her place on the floor and doesn't give it up until the night before they're to fly back to Los Angeles, when Parker calls to her softly, "Hey, buttmunch, come here," and only then she picks herself up and scrambles under the blankets beside her brother.

Their last hours in London, the family continues in the hush of what's happened, no one speaking, all domestic blasts defused, too little oxygen among them for any volume. When the kids are out of earshot, Zan tells Viv, "The bank took the house today," and at first she doesn't say anything. "It's posted on the loan website."

Finally she nods. "Today? You mean right now?"

"Well," he shrugs, "today or yesterday. Nine hours between here and L.A., or eight hours—I'm not sure." After a few seconds he says, "So we don't have a home any more."

"Well," Viv answers, "we don't have a *house.*"

One or the other of them, or both, wonder whether to go back at all. But whatever the practical possibilities of staying in London, neither takes the idea seriously enough to broach it.

Zan tries to remember if he ever really thought they would save the house. "I think I thought," he says to Viv at Heathrow, at the gate waiting for their flight, "or hoped . . . not that there would be some executive decree or anything but just that . . . the atmosphere, the *mood* in the country, would so change that it made a difference. Now that seems really stupid."

"No, it doesn't," she tries to assure him. "Really."

"He used to be a writer once," says Zan.

"Who?"

"The president. That should have tipped us off right there."

There have been presidents who have written, he thinks, but that's not the same as being a writer. That's talent when what Zan means is temperament. This is a president who's devoted much of his life and energy into figuring out who he is, an occupational hazard of someone with the temperament of a writer but surely not a good thing in a politician. Isn't a politician who cares about who he really is doomed? Isn't a politician who believes that his identity is his own rather than the public's destined for rejection? Failed writers should be something other than presidents. Radio broadcasters, maybe. At least the ones who play music instead of talk.

The president is in trouble, Zan realizes, watching the news in the airport lobby. He thinks he's who he thinks he is; he doesn't understand that, in political terms, he's who the public thinks he is or he's no one. This was the great test, whether there was a song the country could sing in common. Instead, more than ever it's a country of many songs all of them noisy, without a single melody that anyone cares about carrying. The country is a babel of not just melodies that no one shares but memory; and as Babel fractured language into thousands, the country is the sum total of a memory fractured into millions, not one of them a memory of the country as it actually has ever existed.

One night in Indianapolis forty-one years ago, the rest of the country detonated by the assassination of a black Georgian preacher in Memphis, Jasmine lies on the floor of the hotel room, and on the bed beside her the man who wants to be president against all his own best interests says, Who knows how the country finally will ask for forgiveness, or how that forgiveness might be given? Who knows what historic moment can represent that? The pain that can't forget must find a way to rain forgiveness on the heart until, against our will, there grows from it the wisdom and grace of God. So tonight we pray for the fallen man and we pray for his family; but let's say a prayer as well for the country we love.

It's a country that does things in lurches, but when the high altitude of the great leap—of either faith or imagination, assuming one exists without the other—has given way to the next morning's bends, the country peers around and wonders where it landed. Be that as it may, Zan can't relinquish his memory of the melody, can't bring himself to be unhaunted by it. There's no other song he believes in more or nearly as much. By the din of circumstance or the roar of other voices or some combination of them, in the void no one else sings anything else as true or worth singing. Zan's country always has belonged to the rest of the world's imagination more than its own, and sitting here in an airport three thousand miles away, he still hears the song around him, from London to the ruins of the Berlin barricade once built in a futile attempt to keep the song out.

In the midst of Heathrow's insane customs-free bazaar, Zan leaves Viv and the children at the gate a few minutes and retreats to the men's room to make a phone call back to Los Angeles. "Loan number?" comes the voice on the other end of the line that Zan recognizes. "Three zero six one three nine five one nine eight," Zan says. He's known it by heart a long time.

"Address?" the woman says.

"1861 Relik Road."

"Are you receiving mail at that address?"

"Yes."

"Are you living in the residence?"

302 · STEVE ERICKSON

"We've been out of the country for a while, but it is our residence."

"The record shows that the deed on the property has reverted to the investors who financed the original loan and that the property now is the subject of a formal trustee sale."

"I understand. I'm calling because my family and I are returning to L.A. today and I want to arrange access scuzbag to the property."

For a moment there's silence on the other end and then the voice says, "I'm sorry, sir. Did you say you want to arrange access to the property?"

"Yes, please," says Zan. "As I indicated, we've been out of the country for sometime now and we're returning today, and if at all possible there are personal possessions inside the house evilbitch that we need to retrieve."

There's another silence on the other end and Zan imagines the woman staring at her phone, maybe trying to switch the signal on the device to a different and better reception. Finally she says, "I need to ask you to repeat that."

"I said we're coming back to L.A. today and I need to get into the house if I can, to get some of our personal affects."

She says, "I don't think that's what you said."

"I'm sorry?"

"That's not what you said," the other voice says. "Not the first time."

"Uh, well, exactly in those words, maybe not."

"You said something else."

"Maybe in different words," he agrees.

S he says, "No, you said something else. Not just in different words. There were other words."

"Just now?" he says.

"A moment ago."

"The 'maybe in different words' part?"

"No. Before that. Sir," she resumes heatedly, "you'll need to notify the foreclosure department to make those arrangements."

"Which arrangements?"

"Arrangements to get in the property. I can transfer you to that department, if you would like."

"You don't happen to know whore of babylon if the locks on the house have been changed, do you?" Zan says.

"What?"

"You don't know if the locks on the house have been changed yet?"

She says, "You said something else."

"Actually, I . . . did I? I think this time it was in those words. Hey, listen," he says, "I'm not sure what you think I said, but this call is from London so I should just phone again tomorrow, maybe, once we're back? In the meantime I want to thank you and your fine institution for all the help and understanding you've given us over these many difficult months."

He thinks the line has gone dead or he's lost the connection when she answers quietly, "Yes, sir. You're welcome, sir."

O n the flight, Viv sleeps and Parker plays a video game on a small screen in the seat in front of him. Watching him, Zan wonders, How long it will be before I know what my son feels about everything that's happened? How long will it be before *he* knows? Will we talk about it before I die? *He and his sister are going to lose me before they should have to* and Zan feels worse about them than himself. Sheba refuses to take any Benadryl and Zan doesn't force the issue; the girl says nothing, doesn't make a sound. Sometimes she watches the small TV but mostly stares out the window.

F rom LAX, Zan calls the Añejo in the canyon and the family waits for Roberto to pick them up in his truck. The next morning Zan returns alone in Roberto's truck to the house.

A sign reading BANK OWNED hangs in front and the yard is overgrown. Viv's car that was in the driveway has been towed. Zan's is parked in the lower part of the backyard; the older woman who lives next door tells him she claimed the car was hers so the bank wouldn't take it. "I appreciate it," Zan tells her. "Fuck them," says the old woman. Down the steep drive, Zan tries to affect the stroll of the not too mortally humiliated.

T he lock on the front door has been changed. Zan goes around to the back and gets down on the ground and pokes his head through what used to be Piranha's door. The house smells. He pulls out his head and grabs the dog door with both hands and rips it free from the larger door. Positioned on the ground again, on his back he can reach just far enough inside to turn the lock of the door, hoping it's not bolted. Once more he withdraws and, catching his breath, opens the back door and walks in.

None of the Nordhocs' possessions inside the house have been moved. What would they do, Zan wonders, pile it all out on the street? When he walks from the kitchen to the dining room, he sees something dart out of the corner of his eye; he hears scampering around him. He can talk himself into some sense of satisfaction about the rats taking over the house but still he's glad none of the family is here to see it. Emotion wells up in him but, he thinks, I'm not going to shed one fucking tear over this fucking house.

He spends the day loading as much as he can into Roberto's truck and then his own car. Literature and volumes of history, music, family memorabilia, Viv's art and photographs, copies of Zan's four novels, files that include accounts, life insurance policies, past tax records, the kids' birth certificates and social security numbers. He grabs blankets and a small table and the rocking chair from the family room. He remembers the night that the fire in the canyon swept close enough, and Zan and Viv prepared to evacuate, loading up the car—so they've already prioritized things. In their minds, they've been on the verge of escaping for years.

He returns Roberto's truck to the Añejo. "I don't know if I can unpack it tonight," Zan whispers. The men stand outside in back of the bar, next to the small shed from which Zan broadcasts his radio show. "We can do it tomorrow," says Roberto. "I'll help."

"Thanks."

"I would have helped you move it all out."

"I didn't want anyone else to see the house."

Roberto says, "We've missed your music."

"I made playlists in my head," says Zan, "in London. But I don't think you want to hear them."

Exhausted, Zan drives his car to the old railroad bridge down the road where the rest of the family waits for him. In the gentle autumn night, with the blankets from the house, Viv makes a place to sleep. "Roberto sent shrimp enchiladas from the bar," Zan says, laying out the food. "Rice and refried beans."

Parker says, "I like black beans."

"I can't keep up with you," Zan says, "I thought you liked refried beans. Your taste changes all the time."

Viv calls, "Sheba, come eat," but the girl doesn't answer so everyone else eats. Zan remembers that the supposedly haunted railroad bridge used to freak out Parker and he suppresses the impulse to talk about devil rites and Indian ghosts, which ordinarily Parker would find entertaining. It would be like talking about tsunamis while driving Pacific Coast Highway. "Are you going to be all right here?" he says to the boy.

"What do you mean?" Parker says. "Why wouldn't I be?"

"No reason."

"Isn't this bridge supposed to be haunted?"

"By the ghosts of Indians. It's O.K., they're on our side."

"How do you know?"

"I promise you, they are."

"How long are we staying?" the boy says.

"Not long. We'll work out something soon, I promise."

"You promise, you promise," a bit scornfully. "Once you promised about the house, too."

"I know I did," Zan quietly replies. "And I did everything I could to keep the house and keep that promise. It doesn't mean I won't find a way to keep the next one."

Parker nods. "O.K., Dad."

V iv says, "If the creek were up, we could sleep to the sound of it beneath us."

"Isn't that the creek?" says Zan, listening.

"I hear it too," says Parker, "it's not the creek. It sounds like a radio far away," and all of them turn toward the end of the old bridge and gaze up at the apex of its frame where the four-year-old girl is perched, staring out at the mouth of the canyon and whatever should roll in from the ocean.

Z an walks over and looks up into the rafters. "Sheba," he says, "come down. You could fall. There's food," indicating the enchiladas. The girl glances at him, then back toward the sea, then climbs down the ladder.

As she sits eating her enchilada, Viv says to her, with what she hopes is just the right degree of bluntness so as to arouse a response, "Would you rather be called something other than Sheba?"

"What?" the girl says.

"Would you rather be called someth—"

"But *what*."

"Whatever feels like it's your name."

The girl thinks. "Isn't Sheba my name?"

Viv says, "Yes. But you can always change your mind later."

"I can?"

"Yes."

"Maybe later."

"O.K."

"When I grow up to be who I am."

"All right."

Dusk falls and what's left of the light leaks from the day. Zan wedges a flashlight between the bridge's rafters and turns it on, splashing it against the ceiling of the old railroad car. Both kids are asleep where Viv made a bed, but after half an hour Sheba rises and walks over and for the first time since London slips into her mother's arms there in the rocking chair—where years ago Viv breast-fed her son—that Zan borrowed but she has taken back.

As Viv rocks in the chair to her daughter's new music, Sheba curls in her mother's arms as she used to with the guard at the orphanage back in Addis Ababa, when as a two-year-old she rose in the night and ran through the yard in the rain to his post at the gate. Asleep, the girl dreams of the leviathan wave that roars through the mouth of the canyon but, reaching the railroad bridgehouse and lifting it from its moorings like a boat, becomes a gentle tide sailing her family to somewhere better.

Though to the outer waking world Sheba's dream is only a few seconds, in her sleep she understands it's a long voyage. Poised at the ship's bow, transmitting a distant song, she sails in search of the word that will name her, a word for those who've never belonged anywhere and who make their own belonging in the same way that people used to name themselves after where they belonged, the same word as that for the grief that goes on grieving for what's not remembered but can't be forgotten. As the girl and her brother and mother and father step from the boat onto shore, the word isn't paradise or heaven or utopia or promisedland but rather a name as damaged as it is spellbinding to everyone who's heard it since the first time anyone spoke it, then tarnished it, then hijacked it, then exploited it, then betrayed and debased and then emptied it, loving the sound of it while despising everything it means that can't be denied anyway because it's imprinted on the modern gene which is to say that even as the girl pursues it, it's already found her, passed on by her adopted father in whose ear it was whispered one afternoon when, from a crowd desperate to hear the secret of it, he was pulled by a young woman of the Old World and the beginning of time, and now it binds daughter and father though neither knows it, she carries it in her fierce core, armed to defend it with that blade of a finger she draws across her throat, and the word is america.

ABOUT THE AUTHOR

Steve Erickson is the author of eight previous novels as well as two nonfiction books about politics and popular culture that have been published in ten languages around the world. Currently he's the editor of the national literary journal *Black Clock*, published by the California Institute of the Arts where he teaches, and he also writes about film for *Los Angeles* magazine, for which he's been nominated for the National Magazine Award. He has received the American Academy of Arts and Letters award in literature and a fellowship from the John Simon Guggenheim Foundation.